SAFETY MEASURES

MAEVE HAZEL

MEDGIDIA, 2023

First Edition

ISBN 978-973-0-39178-7

Edited by: Alli Morgan, Salma & K

Cover designed by: Emily Wittig

Proofreading: Salma (@salmaslibrary_)

Formatting: Hailey Dickert

playlist

Imagine Dragons – *Bad Liar*
Olivia Rodrigo - *Vampire*
The Weeknd - *Die For You*
Billie Eilish - *What Was I Made For?*
Harry Styles - *As It Was*
Sabrina Carpenter – *Nonsense*
The Kid LAROI – *Love Again*
Jaeger – *Love So Good*
Niall Horan – *Heaven*
Taylor Swift – *Lavender Haze*
Isabel LaRosa – *i'm yours*
Charlie Puth – *Light Switch*
Rival, Dyson – *Home To Me*
Elley Duhé – *Middle Of The Night*

Trigger Warnings

...fore reading 'Safety Measures' please make sure the ...ics below won't affect you in any way.

...eavy:
  Alcoholism
  Addiction
  Open door, consensual sex
  Death of parents
  Emotional abuse
  Abandonment

...oderate:
  Mention of Cancer
  Violence

Dicktionary

Here's a little guide for my smut lovers who want to find the spicy scenes quicker, but also for those who prefer to avoid them.

Get your self-care toys ready.

To those who hurt in silence and cry on their own shoulders. Even if you don't have anyone, know you're not alone.

PROLOGUE
BLAISE

Fifteen Years Old

"Are you sure, Moon?" he asks, hiding a lock of hair behind my ear with a tender and smooth swipe of his fingers, almost as if the strand obscures his view of my face.

He wouldn't be asking me this if he knew how often I've imagined this exact moment happening. Even though we promised that what we were about to do now is nothing more than taking off the pressure of a first kiss from our shoulders. But it's impossible to label it that way after going to sleep with him in my mind and waking up, only to find him still there.

There's a reason why he's not aware of what I feel— if I tell him, he'd back away, and that's the last thing I want.

1

I bite back the consuming shiver running down my spine, and my gaze drops to his lips. The tip of my finger traces their shape in a circular motion, his sharp breath feeling warm on my skin.

How I am ever going to get enough of this is beyond me.

"Yes," I whisper, leaning closer.

A drop of a flame spills on the gas of my emotions, setting my courage on fire and giving me the push I need. I straddle his lap like this isn't my first time doing it.

Fun fact?

It is.

His stare captures my throat in a tight grip. Our breaths come out wobbly, and I don't know why it's so hard to think. Or how I can feel his eyes on me but not see them.

Ares tilts his head back, with no words or protests that indicate he doesn't want us to continue. He props his elbows on the roof, his back to my window, and I can't help but notice how he moves so cautiously, fearing the slightest motion will fracture our moment open.

I swallow.

Just go for it.

Even if my legs tremble with the heavy weight on my shoulders, I lower myself on him. The intense contest between our eyes continues. Maybe he can see through mine that I'm not a kid anymore. That I've grown up.

I'd give a lung to release the shaky breath fighting to escape my throat, but doing that will only show how inexperienced I am, and that's not what boys like. Boys like when girls take the first step, radiating confidence with a touch of pure domination—I eavesdropped on one of Ares's conversations with a guy at school about how he finds it insanely hot when "chicks" do that.

So I keep my breathing steady as I battle feelings too stubborn to stay locked up inside.

"Touch me." It's an attempt at acting confident, but it comes out more like a question. "I mean, I know it's your first kiss too, but don't just stand there—"

Whatever I want to say fades into nothingness. He sits up and grabs my waist, fingers digging into my skin while one palm travels until it reaches my braid and tugs on it.

Ares pulls out his handsome smirk before his hand goes back to my hip and squeezes it tightly.

"Okay, now's the part where you're supposed to kiss me," I tell him, straightening my back.

I'm not sure if I can handle the smell of him or the soft paths his fingers leave behind without getting tomato cheeks.

He chuckles, shaking his head. "You just can't keep your mouth shut, can you?"

His warm palm covers my cheek, and I lean into his hold at the same time he comes closer.

My body pulses with anticipation while I hold my breath. I'm one step away from closing my eyes when I realize he's not making any move to kiss me. Not even when our lips touch.

I've gotten us this far, but I don't want to be the one initiating the kiss. As childish as it is, I stepped on my pride first, and it's his turn to do it.

He takes his time brushing my skin in slow strokes, twitching his jaw, biting back his smile at my obviously ending patience, and I close my eyes with a deep inhale, allowing myself to enjoy his presence before I reveal just how desperate I am.

Is he trying to make the wait insupportable until I give up and beg for what I want?

These days, it's harder to understand what boys want rather than understand girls. And in the time I struggled to put myself into his place, I came to a realization I'm not a big fan of: maybe I'm not his type.

Over the years, I've seen Ares with a few girls, and none of them were blonde. Brunettes or girls with red hair are the only ones walking under his arm in the school's hallway.

It's not until I open my eyes again, ready to do it without a second thought, that his lips slam onto mine. The realization of it quickly sets in.

Ares's lips are on mine.

Ares Hart is kissing me.

His tongue devours mine, singing the sweetest song I've ever tasted. I bury my hands into his hair, earning a sound from him that has me clenching my thighs together. He breaks away slightly, staring at me with hooded eyes. He lowers himself fully onto the rooftop of the house, then lifts my butt and places it on his stomach.

For a second, I'm worried he won't kiss me again. That this is where our first and last kiss ends.

But then he speaks again.

"Come here," he murmurs, dragging me by my neck to him.

At the sound of his rough voice, butterflies swim in my tummy in a happy dance I got familiar with after spending the majority of my time in his presence.

I follow his grip and kiss him, the moment lasting much longer this time. The most embarrassing sounds slip past my lips, and because he seems to like it, I don't try to hold them in next time.

My dreams were far away from the actual experience. His palms weren't as rough when they studied my body as if I was the most interesting subject, his lips weren't as eager to have mine tangled between them, and I wasn't as overwhelmed with the same heat as I am now.

There's no doubt I could set both of our houses on fire with nothing but a flick of my fingers.

Because my mind is too preoccupied to handle the

intense feelings threatening to overflow, my body slides down on his, needing to get closer to him. It eventually gets what it wants, and I end up on his lap, sensing just how much he wants me.

As much as I'm satisfied with the thought at first, the moment he turns into a rock under me, I know the buzz of happiness in my chest is about to disappear at any second. Still, I remain hopeful and try to move upward to remove myself from his crotch.

He gently pushes me away.

"I—"

He lifts me off of him, then puts me down and stands to his feet. Fingers ram through his messy hair, and even through the darkness of the night, I know he can't look me in the eye.

My lips are glued together all the time he spends trying to sort out his thoughts. What can I possibly say anyway?

Instead of talking, I observe how conflicted he is with himself. I don't like the idea of him fighting his own mind to find out if what we did was wrong or not. Because I know him, I know he's doubting this. Us.

"I'm gonna go." He points his finger behind him toward the window of his room.

Don't go, I want to say.

He stares at me with squinted eyes, waiting for the words to come. I do nothing but open my mouth and close it repeatedly, my throat blocking any sound from traveling all the way to his ears.

Ares scratches the back of his head, whirling on his toes before jumping from my roof to his. My heart breaks at the sight, and I get up to my feet, content on stopping him from walking any further. Yet when he turns around to throw me one last look, I freeze in my place with unspoken words sitting on my tongue.

He's gone.

I stare into the dark that once held the shape of him, nodding at his ghost as tears break free.

All this time, I thought he didn't like me because I was a child. Now I know it's him who is the kid.

Why wouldn't he stay to talk about it? To tell me what has gone wrong? Or what's bothering him?

It would've been better to face the harsh truth of his rejection than watch him run away from a thing we both want.

A shadow appears behind the curtains of his window, and I suck in a deep breath, waiting for him to come back here. He stays in the safety of his room like a coward, roaming fingers through his hair, and I stay here, on my roof, watching him through blurry eyes.

If he doesn't walk outside, I'll never let him kiss me again. Please come.

Lights flick off, along with the proof of his presence.

No, let me rectify—I'll never let anyone kiss me again.

CHAPTER ONE

BLAISE

Just as I'm about to drift off to sleep, my phone buzzes on the nightstand.

No one texts me after midnight besides *him*. He's a little over six feet tall and has eyes blacker than your darkest dreams. Curly, messy hair covers his forehead, and tattoos decorate his skin. A perfect comparison to the ocean. Quiet, calm, and peaceful. Until he isn't.

I sigh before peeling my eyes open and grabbing the phone that shines brightly against my face in the dimly lit room. It takes a moment for my eyes to adjust to the sudden light as I check the message.

ARES

Good night, Moon?

A smile stretches on my lips. This question has to be the most constant thing in my life. For the last fifteen years, it's been his way of making sure I'm okay—a small gesture that I'd feel empty without.

Even when we were too young to have phones of our own, he saved money and bought two cheap ones. Since then, Ares has kept his promise to text me every night before bed.

On the nights that were the hardest to get through, he'd sneak over to read me *Goodnight Moon*—a silly book for kids, but the reason for my nickname and all late evenings together. He'd read it over and over again until I fell asleep, just like my dad used to do before everything changed.

I rub my eyes, trying to clear my vision before typing a reply.

ME

Yeah. Good night xx

Usually, he either says good night back or doesn't reply at all, but this time, his response comes quickly.

ARES

You going to sleep?

My eyes squint in the darkness, trying to make sense of Ares's words. He normally has no problem being straightforward. While his question catches me off guard, I know not to look too much into it.

ME

Yeah. Had a long day at work.

We both work at Westnook, a bookstore and coffee shop, but Ares is also a book editor in his spare time. The owner of the store, Rhodes, is close in age to us and more like a friend than a boss.

Most of the time, Ares and I have different schedules, but during busy times, we all try to cover as many shifts as we can to help out. It's a team effort.

ARES

Cool. Night.

ME

Why? Everything okay?

Three bubbles jump on my screen.

ARES

It's fine. Go to sleep.

ME

Tell me.

ARES

Go to sleep. It's nothing important.

I let out a long breath.

Ares has been in my life since I was born. It might seem like an exaggeration, but it's not. The two of us and his younger brother, August, have always been a family. And I know him well enough to know something's wrong. He said it's nothing important.

It's definitely important.

Ares and I bicker and tease each other. To everyone else, it might seem like he hates my guts, but that couldn't be further from the truth.

ME

Rooftop?

I stand up at the knock on the window and walk the two steps toward it, then open it and carefully climb onto the narrow ledge that leads to the rooftop. The roof stretches across the porch below, and it's a shared area between our houses, a space that has become our meeting place since we were little.

Ares is already there, lounging on his usual spot near the edge. He's dressed in a tee and a pair of gray sweats, legs stretched out in front of him, leaning on his elbows. My gaze wanders over his muscular arms covered in tattoos. Even though I can't make out the details in the dark, I don't need to. They're all etched in my memory.

The three crows on his bicep. The Greek god below his collarbone. The tiny one between his fingers—my personal favorite—that reads "CONTROL" in all caps.

The single word that does his temperament justice.

Seeing his skin painted so beautifully always made me wonder how the ink would look on mine. Someday, I'll get a tattoo just to see how it feels to have it on my body.

I plop down next to him, and we sit in silence,

watching the sky covered in a million shimmering points of light.

"Wanna talk about it?" I ask loudly enough for him to hear as my gaze stays pinned to the stars.

He tsks.

I don't push him to talk. If he wants to open up, he will. There's no point in insisting.

Even though I don't want to interrupt the silence I know he wants to have with me, I'm a talker by nature. I'm going to explode if I don't speak.

Stealing a glance his way, I tuck a few stray hairs behind my ear and take a deep breath before turning my body toward him. He cocks his brow at me, knowing something's coming.

"Are you still editing Sylva's book?" I grin, clasping my hands together.

He looks unimpressed, almost like he saw this coming, and it's no wonder he did. I always nag him about it.

It's not my fault he happens to be the editor of my favorite author. I have a bookshelf dedicated to her books—special editions and all—and I need to be updated on everything she writes.

What other source could be as good as Ares?

"Depends." He barely nods, squinting his eyes at me.

"So you are," I state. "How is it so far?"

Ares remains stoic. "Good."

"Come onnnnn," I plead. "She never writes just 'good.' That would be an insult. Give me more details." My smile stretches even more.

He watches me for a few seconds while I try to maintain my smile and patience steadily. "Good and interesting."

Even though it's a rational and logical thing, it sucks Ares cares so much about confidentiality. He could still be like *oh, I'll accidentally send this entire manuscript to Blaise,* and no one would know.

I groan, bumping my forehead on his shoulder. "You are no fun. What's the use for you to be an editor if not to share the juiciest pieces of information with me?"

His lips twitch into a smile. "Right."

Fortunately for him, I decide to drop it for now and enjoy this moment.

Crickets chirping fills the silence, joining the harmony of our breaths. I look over at Ares with the moon shining over him and can't help but feel a sense of peace and calm.

The same way it's always been around him.

My feet carry me down the stairs as the scent of coffee brewing fills the air—Nanna's way of letting me know she's awake.

I started my day early, ready to tackle some writing for the novel I started over a year ago. The ending is so close I can almost taste it, but it's also become the reason why I have a hard time finishing it. My obsession to perfect things has taken over, slowing my process to the point that all I do is write, edit, and delete. I try to spend as much time as I can with Nanna when I'm not at work, so I do all my writing before she gets up in the morning.

When I get downstairs, she's at the kitchen table, dressed in the usual nightgown with her white hair sitting perfectly above her shoulders. If there's one thing she loves more than cooking, it's taking care of her appearance, including styling her hair first thing in the morning. I guess it's rubbed off on me too because mine's usually braided or styled in some way.

Next to her, a few ingredients lie on the table as she gets up to pour the coffee into a mug. A smile appears on her lips as soon as I start talking.

"Are we having waffles or pancakes for breakfast?" I ask, knowing it's one of them. I give her a side hug and kiss her forehead, then take the mug she's handing to me.

"Take a guess." Nanna smiles at me, then heads over

to the cabinet where we keep our waffle maker. I can't stop the enormous grin stretching on my face.

After taking a sip of my morning caffeine and letting out a pleased moan, I place the mug on the counter.

"Let me." I smack her hand playfully away when she tries to open the bottom cabinet.

She sighs, annoyed, but I throw her a look not to argue. Her back isn't in the best condition, so I try to help as much as I can. I take out everything we need and put it on the counter.

"Need a hand?" I wiggle my eyebrows, excited to make waffles with her. We've been doing this since I was too little to even hold a fork in my hand properly.

Nanna shakes her head, laughing. "You're just like your mother."

I smile at that. "How so?"

"Kind." She grabs the bowl I set out and cracks two eggs in it. "Smart." I add the sugar. "Carefree. She always had a constant smile on her face." We pour in the milk as I picture an older version of myself. "She used to coddle me as much as you do."

I take the bowl from her and add the oil. I mix it, watching how her eyes sparkle when she speaks about her daughter.

"Sometimes, I forget you're not her." She pauses and smiles at me, placing a comforting palm on my shoulder. "You laugh the way she used to. You have the same contagious energy and the same fire in your heart."

Warmth spreads over my chest, and a blurry blanket covers my eyes. I blink the tears away and wipe my nose after sniffing. When she senses me getting emotional—as I always do—she changes the subject.

"How's your writing going?"

I shrug. "Could be better."

She nods, her thumb moving a few hairs behind my ear. "Have you tried taking a break?"

"No," I admit, not liking her suggestion.

"And why is that?" Nanna cocks a brow.

I avoid her gaze but tell her anyway. Her eyes are like a magnet to my thoughts. And I like that. It gives me the chance to open up and have another opinion besides my own. "It'd feel like betraying them."

My love for writing started off as a way to cope with the loss of my parents. It's the last string binding me to them, and I have no intention of cutting it.

"Oh, honey." Her warm palms spread on my cheeks, and I give her a sad smile as she caresses my face in slow strokes. "I'm sure your parents are so proud of you. They are right here"—she places a finger on my chest—"no matter if you decide to take a break or not. They're here."

"Thank you," I whisper, grateful for having her. I hug her tightly, keeping her close to me.

"A break might do you good," she says when we step out of the embrace.

I nod. "I'll think about it."

Nanna pats my cheek and kisses it. I immediately sink into her touch.

"Why don't you put the batter in the waffle maker for us?" She goes to wash her hands in the sink. "I'll sit down for a minute."

"Sure," I say hesitantly.

I force the question that's sitting on the tip of my tongue away. I watch her disappear into the living room as I plug the waffle maker in and pour some of the batter in. After the first two are done, I grab a plate and put them on it.

"Do you want honey or syrup on yours, Nanna?" I shout.

She grunts something, and I frown, not under-standing what she said. I take a step out of the kitchen and repeat the question in the hallway. After a couple of seconds in silence, I realize she won't reply at all.

Shaking my head, I put our plates aside and head to the living room. She most likely got caught up in her soap opera. Again.

I walk in and open my mouth to argue with her about it, but I'm knocked down and frozen in place, not really comprehending what I'm seeing at first.

Blonde-white strands that were perfectly placed just minutes ago now hang messily around her face, covering it partially. Her tiny body is close to falling, and the severity of the situation makes every cell in my body rush with adrenaline as I run the two steps toward her.

Leaning down, I brush the hair away from her face as muffled and slurred words escape her lips. Her eyes look lost and vacant. One flutters uncontrollably while the other remains completely still, paralyzed.

I took a first-aid class for work and came to learn plenty of things about strokes. I never thought I'd actually have to use them.

Taking a deep breath, I force myself to calm down, knowing there's no time to lose. I check her pulse and make sure she's breathing properly.

My fingers tremble as I take the phone out of my back pocket and frantically dial 911. Loud ringing seems to echo in my ear for an eternity before I finally hear a voice on the other end.

"911, what's your emergency?"

CHAPTER TWO

ARES

As soon as I reach the end of the hallway, I spot Blaise and August in the lobby. Round eyes slowly rise to meet mine, a spark glistening in them when I hurry my pace.

My chest heaves after running all the way from Westnook to the hospital. When August called me, I barely hung up before dashing out of the bookstore, addressing four words to Rhodes: "I'm not coming back."

I might not have known the intensity of the situation at that point, but seeing the worry traveling across Blaise's features, I know beyond a shadow of a doubt I was right. I'm not leaving her side.

Blaise swallows the moment I approach them, dropping her gaze to the ground and stealing from me the view of her eyes. They are the only ones that could make me understand the emotion coiling through her.

The tip of my finger sneaks under her chin, lifting it until wide-set pupils dilate on me. "How is she?"

A barely noticeable smile stretches on Blaise's lips. "Stable."

I nod at the great news, relief coursing through me.

We've known Catherine since we were little, and knowing how severe strokes can be, my mind wandered to the worst. I think it's because we've always seen Catherine as this short, fragile woman, when in reality, she's tougher than half of the men in this world.

"Thanks to the sea buckthorn, I'm telling you." August pops in, and I acknowledge him for the first time since I got here.

Blaise laughs, and I take sight of him, letting the corner of my mouth pull into a smile at the idea.

Catherine is convinced that sea buckthorn will keep us young and healthy. She's been making us drink it at dinner since we were kids and thinks we're all on board because we're doing our best to make her believe we're *actually* drinking it. The taste is fucking disgusting, so we all pour it into the sink when she's not looking.

The thought of her stomaching that truly scares me. But who knows? Maybe she just doesn't have taste buds.

"Yeah." Blaise wipes the smile off her face with a thumb. "I'm just glad I was there." She hugs herself, moving her weight from one leg to another.

I know she's thinking about what could've

happened if she weren't there, and I decide to not let her give it too much thought.

"Did a doctor come up to you yet?" I ask.

She fidgets on her feet, then looks like she just came back from whatever movie her mind was playing.

Blaise bobs her head. "She said they have to keep an eye on her for a few days, and if everything's under control, they'll let her go. The bad part is that it might be hard for her to speak and move for a while."

August bumps his elbow into her side, plastering the usual smile that never misses the opportunity to stretch on his lips. "You have nothing to worry about. Life only gives you what you can carry."

"Right." She forces a smile, and I know it'll easily fall back down. "I'll just go to the bathroom real quick, and then we can go to the waiting area."

Blaise takes a step back, then walks into the bathroom next to us at the same time August lets out a sigh.

He threads a hand through his curly, short hair, glancing toward where she was standing mere seconds ago. "I was only trying to make her feel better."

"Well, it's fucking shitty to be in her position, so let her consume her feelings a bit before throwing in positive quotes," I say, leaning my shoulder on the wall behind me.

He snorts. "*Positive quotes?* Where did that come from?"

I shrug. "Sounded like a 2012 tweet to me."

August shakes his head, laughing. He takes the place next to me, stealing a smile from my lips when he grins like the idiot he is. We both look at the door, waiting for her to come back.

Knowing Blaise, she'll cry in the bathroom, put on a mask she won't be able to hold for long, and then come out like nothing happened.

It takes every ounce of control to not go after her.

She needs a moment to collect herself, and I don't want to be the one to take it away.

A few minutes pass, and when the clock ticks the last second of my patience, I straighten my back, deciding to check on her.

As I walk away from my brother, the bathroom door swings open, revealing Blaise's small figure. The proximity between us takes her by surprise, and she crashes into my chest with a *oof*. My hands automatically find shelter on the sides of her waist.

Blaise squeezes her eyes a few times, looking like she's trying to regain her vision. She wakens in my hands, arms circling my neck while I steady us both.

"Whoa, whoa. You okay?" August joins us as soon as he notices the shift in Blaise's state, concern etched in his features.

"Yeah." She tries to raise the head that just fell onto my chest but fails. "I think I'm a bit dizzy," Blaise murmurs the words, and I look up at August.

"Can you bring her some water?"

He walks away before I even get the chance to finish the sentence.

My attention moves back to Blaise. I take a rebellious strand of hair and lock it behind her ear. "Have you eaten anything today?"

What a stupid question. Of course she didn't.

She shifts in my embrace and somehow manages to stand on her own, removing her hand from me. I still don't let go, sure that if I set her free of my touch, she'll break into a puddle at my legs. Blaise balances in place and looks up at me, some of the color returning to her face.

"I was making breakfast when Nanna..." She taps her forehead, gesturing with her other hand. "You know."

My jaw ticks, and before I can say anything else, August returns and hands her the bottle. As she drinks the water, her features release tension gradually. My back unties thousands of knots, and I realize how tense I was myself.

When it comes to Blaise, worry comes naturally to me. We've known each other since we were kids, and since the day she was born, I've felt a desperate need to take care of her. And that feeling has never eased to this day.

Blaise gulps down the liquid in one long swallow, exhaling a relieved breath once she clears the bottom.

"We should get up to the waiting room so she can sit down," August suggests, and I nod.

"Come on." I nudge my chin in front of us, then place an arm around her shoulders.

"I'm okay," she lies.

"The fuck you are," I counter.

"Just like you were 'okay' after you ate that calamari at your graduation?" August asks, raising his brow.

Blaise snorts, apparently amused at the memory. Well, we aren't.

We almost shit our pants when we saw her face transforming into a red balloon. She kept claiming everything was fine, but if it weren't for us dragging her ass to the hospital, things could've gone worse. It was her first time trying calamari, hence why she didn't know she was allergic.

It's safe to say we never let her eat any type of seafood again.

"*That* was different." Blaise points her finger at us before we start walking.

CHAPTER THREE

BLAISE

I've been trying to fall asleep for an hour now, but the pounding in my temples is stronger than my body's need for rest. So I just keep my eyes closed in the hope that sleep will find me.

One. Two. Three. Four. Five. Six...

"I know you're awake." His voice touches my ear with a soft brush of his breath.

A shiver runs down my spine. "I didn't say otherwise."

Something weighs on my legs, and curiosity wins. I peek through one eye and lock in a smile when I see a chocolate cupcake with ice cream on top—my favorite.

Picking my head up off his shoulder, I cast a brief look at Ares. He's reading on his Kindle, but I feel the heat of his stare as I take the pastry between my hands.

"Mmm," I murmur after taking a bite, almost spitting out the dessert when I finally see his face.

A laugh shocks through me, and I don't know if it's because of the lack of sleep, but I can't find myself to stop.

"What?" Ares asks, giving me a better view of the chocolate smudged around his mouth.

Each time I try to explain my reaction, I only burst into another round of laughter. It worsens when August walks up from his seat, brows furrowed in confusion.

I plaster a palm over my mouth to prevent the food from spilling and keep it there until my cackle fades. Eventually, I manage to swallow the contents and pull it together.

"You just have a little..." I extend my hand and swipe the corner of his lips. It does nothing to help clear some of the insane amount he has smeared on.

I don't even know how he turned into this eight-year-old boy who doesn't know how to eat properly.

He stares at my thumb, raising an eyebrow. "And here I was, trying to be a gentleman and not laugh at the disaster on your face."

Before I can say anything else, he scoops icing off my face with his finger and brings it to his mouth, which is curving into a playful smile.

Ares's eyes gleam with something indecipherable but powerful enough to make me feel like layers of my skin are shedding under his gaze.

My thighs brush along each other as I straighten my back and fidget in my seat. "You must not know what you look like." I chuckle, sure that I can't be worse than him.

He shrugs, then turns back to his Kindle, acting like nothing happened.

"You're not going to wipe it off?"

Ares shakes his head. "Nah."

I give August a look, who's finally on the same planet with us and eating the croissant Ares got him.

"You literally look like you took a shit out of the wrong hole," August pops in, taking a bite from his food.

Ares is serious for a moment, but then his shoulders start to shake, and we start laughing in unison. The three of us share the moment until it passes, our thoughts roaming back to Nanna and how this isn't fair to her.

We shouldn't be having a great time when Nanna is unconscious in her hospital room, fighting every second. A sense of guilt travels between us, sobering the carefree feeling to reality.

August unlocks his phone, and Ares takes paper towels out of his jeans pockets, handing one to me. Once we're sober, he gets back to his reading device.

I lean over, trying to get a glimpse. He tilts the Kindle toward himself, blocking my view before turning it off, and I take the chance to steal the device from him.

He doesn't even bother to take it back from me. Ares simply slumps into his seat, cocking a brow in challenge. I unlock it and start reading out loud.

"I slip two fingers inside her…" My words fade as I stop mid-sentence.

What are the chances I read exactly that sentence?

A smirk finds its way on his face as I hand the Kindle back to him. I knew he was a book editor, but I had no idea he was into smut. I always thought he read historical bullshit or anything close to that.

"Is that an instruction manual or something? I'm hurt you didn't think to ask me for advice." August's lips twitch from how hard he's trying to hold his laughter, a hand lying on his chest.

"It's romance," Ares says, unamused. "And don't act like you have any other experience besides your right hand."

August raises his brows. "Really? Because you know so much about my sex life."

"You're eighteen." He narrows his eyes at August. "I really don't want to hear about what you consider a *sex life*."

"At least I have one." August winks at Ares, smirking.

Ares shoots him a look. "Fuck off."

Looking down at my phone, I notice the visiting hours should start in almost two hours. I have enough time to get back home and get everything Nanna might need while she's here. *And I can clear my head while I'm at it.*

"I'm going to run and grab some things from the house for Nanna," I announce, getting to my feet as I stuff my palms into my pockets.

Ares squints his eyes at me, putting his Kindle to the side. On the other seat, August shakes his head, clearly not a fan of the idea.

"I'll take you." Ares stands up, towering over me. He plays with his car keys, ready to go.

I shake my head, knowing that some time alone would do me good. "Actually, I'd like to be alone for a bit." I nod to myself and twist the hem of my shirt with my finger.

Ares looks down at me with those dark eyes of his, leaving no space for arguing. The silence between us stretches on and the weight of his gaze becomes almost unbearable. I try to hold his stare, but eventually, my eyes flicker away from his, unable to handle the intensity.

His brow lifts slightly, his voice soft. "You sure?"

"Yeah. I'll be back in time for visiting hours," I say.

Avoiding eye contact, I extend my hand toward August, whose concerned eyes are fixed on me, a mix of curiosity and suspicion etched into his features. I pray that neither of them asks any more questions because I can still feel Ares's eyes burning into my skin.

Fortunately, August gives in and simply hands me the keys. "It's parked near the emergency room."

Without any other word addressed, I turn around and take the elevator before leaving the building. The soft touch of summer surrounds me as emotions build inside, threatening to overflow at any second.

The time I spend searching for my car makes keeping the tears inside a challenge. I blink repeatedly in an attempt to fight them away, but it does nothing to ease the blurred vision.

Finally, I spot it and speed-walk the remaining distance to it. Before I can open the door, a large hand gently grips my shoulder, and I close my eyes, swallowing a sigh of exhaustion.

Great time for someone to want to talk to me.

I turn around to find Ares, who watches as a rebellious tear slides down my cheek. He clamps his mouth shut, the muscles in his jaw tightening.

It's a struggle to figure out what exactly it is about his expression that cracks me wide open, spilling my feelings into a puddle right at his feet. Tears sting my eyes, and I look away.

"Come here," he murmurs, softly tugging me toward him .

My gaze flicks back to him. I bite my lip, hesitating, but it doesn't last long because my body decides on its own and falls into his arms, playing the perfect role of a traitor.

His strong embrace covers me like a shield, and my forehead drops on his chest. For the first time in years, I allow myself to tell his heart the story of mine.

The last time I was in his arms feels like an eternity ago. He's not one to hug people, but when we were little, I was always clingy enough to force him into it.

I inhale his masculine scent, my sobs quieting at the familiar smell of rosewood.

God, I've missed this. So much.

It's only now that I realize his hand is in my hair, stroking it slowly and gently. I close my eyes, enjoying the sweet sensation of his fingers caressing me.

"I'll drive you home, Moon." He says it low, firmly, like he's giving me no room to argue with him about it.

Shaking my head against him, I step out of his embrace and ignore the instant loss of his warmth. I wipe the tears off my cheeks and straighten my back.

"No, no. I'm fine." I plaster on what I hope is a convincing smile.

He tilts his head, and his eyes say, *Come on, Blaise. Who do you think you're fooling?*

"I *am*." I fight back against his unspoken words.

"Let's go." He starts walking toward the car, but I grab him by his elbow.

"Please," I beg him, my shoulders dropping.

His beautiful eyes search my face a thousand times, checking for any signs that may show I'm not okay. He looks away, sweeping a curl from his forehead. "Alright."

He nods, and before a smile of victory breaks free on my face, he continues, "But text me when you get home."

"Will do." I rise on my tiptoes, kiss his cheek, and get in my car before he changes his mind.

I start it and drive off, my heart pounding as I see Ares in the rearview mirror, standing where I left him, fingertips grazing where my lips touched moments ago.

CHAPTER FOUR

BLAISE

After pulling in front of my house, I kill the engine and get out, eager to get rid of the suffocating space in the car. With a deep breath of refreshing air, I send Ares a text as promised.

An awkward cough rings in my ears, and I look up at the front porch next door, where an unpleasant surprise is waiting.

Please tell me I'm hallucinating.

Because I don't know any other way to remove myself from this situation, I blink repeatedly, hoping she'll disappear so I can continue my day.

"Blaise." Her motherly eyes beam at me, and I realize that magic trick works in movies only.

My head shakes, the movement like an automatic response to her presence.

"Please, go." My voice breaks, and my mind is

already overflowing with too much to have enough power to say anything else.

There's no way I can even put up a fight with her right now. Today has drained me, and it's not even over. I can't physically and mentally do anything else. I can't scream at her or act like she owes me anything, and I can't be happy to see her either.

Because I'm not.

She may have given birth to August and Ares, but she was also like my mother in some ways, especially after my parents died. Or at least, I thought she was.

But as I stand here looking at her, I feel nothing but anger. She was supposed to be someone I could trust, someone who loved and protected me, and yet she wasn't any of that.

I'm not sure if I'll ever be able to forgive her and repair the relationship that once meant so much to me.

"I can't." She shakes her head from side to side, the corner of her mouth quivering. "I have to see them." She walks to me and stops next to my car, caressing my hand.

"Please," I beg, my voice cracking. "Not today."

"I'm better, Blaise. Look at me." Tamara steps back enough so I can see her whole body.

She does look good, better than the last time we saw her months ago. She's beautiful as always and doesn't look her age—how she's been every time she came back.

"I need you to leave." I do my best to speak gently,

but by the way her face drops, you'd think I just slapped her.

"They are *my* kids, and I have every right to see them. I'm two months sober." Her tone turns harsh as she points a finger at me.

Like *I'm* the one who pushed them away.

With Tamara, you never know what's true and what's not. Either way, two months isn't enough. Her numerous attempts to stay after a couple of weeks sober is proof that it never has been.

"That's good, Tam." I fake a smile. "Listen," I begin, doing my best to not look at her face that's so good at manipulating, "your timing isn't the best. My grandma is in the hospital and—"

"Catherine? Is she okay?" Tamara grabs me by my elbows, her eyes widening beneath her furrowed brows.

She has a soft spot for Nanna, just like everyone does. Nanna treated her better than any of us ever did, showing her mercy and love with every chance she had.

Too bad she never deserved her kindness.

"Oh, I'm so sorry, Jellybean," Tamara whispers, and my heart shatters at hearing that nickname. "I'm not going to leave this time," she promises.

I wipe my cheeks of the tears that stubbornly wash over them and try to put the situation with Nanna aside. A sigh falls past my lips as I hug myself. "We both know this isn't the first time you've said this."

"I know, but I mean it this time. I'm two months

sober."

"Not a first either." I shake my head. "Do yourself a favor and go to rehab, Tam. And stick to it this time." I step away, but her voice keeps me in place.

She shrugs, catching a tear that slipped under her eye. "Can't."

Before I can stop myself and the curiosity inside me, I take the conversation further. "Why?" I ask, narrowing my eyes at her.

Her head hangs low when she replies. "I can't afford it."

Of course she can't.

That's no surprise. She's never come back home prepared to give her boys a *good* life. No matter if that was the promise she was screaming about every time she left. Tamara's all talk.

I hate myself for even considering using the resources I have to help her. I know I'm not doing the right thing, but I can't stop myself.

"Do you really want to get better?" I look her directly in the eyes.

She gives me a smile that somehow passes as sincere. "Yes, Blaise. I want that."

My mind wanders to how she was back then—the way her hugs used to feel, how her laughter used to sound, and how she could bring a smile to anyone's face —and I know I'll regret not trying. At one point in my life, she was a rock to me, and I can't help but think about the universe deciding it's time to be the same for her.

I guess the only silver lining of losing your parents at seven years old is having the funds to use when shit hits the fan. Nanna and I agreed to use them only in case of emergencies, and to me, her medical bills and health are far more than that.

And since I'm already taking money out, why not give Tamara her last chance to fix things?

"Do you have a phone?" I ask, and she looks up at me, nodding her head.

Tamara hesitantly takes it out and hands it to me. I quickly save her number in my contacts, deciding against giving her mine. It's for the best if she doesn't have my number yet.

"Once Nanna gets better, I'll text you to meet me." I exhale a sharp breath. "And you won't come back here. You have to wait for my message." I try to sound dominant, to make sure she understands the importance of what I'm saying. I don't want Ares or August to see her lurking around the house. "Understood?" I raise my brows at her.

Tamara takes her phone back from my grip, squinting her eyes. She slowly nods. "I swear." She lifts her hands in the air in surrender. "But can I at least ask why? I want to see them, Blaise."

I straighten my back. "Because I'm taking you to rehab."

CHAPTER FIVE

ARES

It's the second day since Catherine's been out of the ICU and the three hundredth time I tell Blaise to rest before she passes out from exhaustion. She's sitting in the same chair she's been in for hours, stroking Catherine's cheek in a lovable brush of her fingers.

I lean my shoulder on the doorframe and watch how Blaise's head falls to the side, but it quickly raises, and she resumes her previous position. Blaise lowers herself to the little space left between Catherine and the edge of the bed, gripping her hand tight to her chest as she lets out a sigh.

My feet carry me the two steps to the small hospital bed, and I place a hand on Blaise's back, not willing to put up with her stubbornness anymore. She needs to rest.

She looks up at me, brows furrowed, eyes struggling

to stay open. Dark circles blacken the skin under her eyes, and the red on her cheeks has faded, only two blonde strands of hair giving them some color.

"Mmm?" she murmurs, resting her head against my chest, not fighting the sleep anymore. My stomach tightens at the contact, but I don't move.

"Let me take you home so you can rest for a couple of hours," I say, hoping she'll agree. She can't continue like this.

Blaise shakes her head. "No."

"I'll stay with Catherine. You need to rest." I try to gently take her by the arms, but she removes my grip.

"I won't leave her side, Ares," she says in a frustrated tone, and it's clear she has made up her mind. I know I have no chance to convince her to go home.

So damn stubborn.

Drawing in a deep breath, I get out of the room and return a few moments later with everything I need tucked between my hands.

If she's not going to go home, then she's going to rest here.

I put a hand on her shoulder, and she groans, probably thinking I'm here to bug her. "I already told you I'm not going anywhere."

"Just sit up for a second," I tell her, and to my surprise, she listens—reluctantly, but she does.

She sets Catherine's hand free and steps aside.

Tired eyes follow every move of mine. I place the pillows and the blankets down, rotate the chair, then bring the other one in front of it. I take one of the blankets and spread it over both of them, then put a pillow on the backrest close to her grandmother. It's as close as it can get to a bed.

I gesture for her to sit down.

A grateful smile plays on her lips as she makes herself comfortable. I tuck her into the cover I have left, and she grips my elbow before I can turn around.

"Thank you," she whispers, sleep lowering her eyelids. She makes a pleased sound, sneaking a hand from under the blanket and placing a palm over Catherine's.

Thanking me feels like what I did was out of obligation, when in reality, there's nothing I wouldn't do for her.

Blaise has to be one of the most stubborn people I know. She'd do anything for the ones she loves, enough to forget she has to take care of herself too.

I back away, ready to occupy my spot on the doorframe. But it's already taken.

"Hi." Selah talks in a low tone, gaze locked on her friend behind me. "How are they doing?" she asks, taking two steps forward.

"Catherine is stable, sleeping a lot. Blaise is drained," I admit, stuffing two hands in my pockets.

She nods, biting the inside of her cheek.

"How's your brother?" I ask, knowing he's been in the same hospital for a while.

Selah hugs herself. "Cancer's really kicking his ass." She steps aside and goes further into the room, not one to give more information about sensitive subjects than necessary.

The red-haired girl lowers her knees, stroking Blaise's hair. Her eyes slowly open, smiling along with her lips.

"Hi there," Selah says, getting some hairs out of Blaise's face.

"I'll get you a chair," I offer and make my way out.

Knowing she has a good friend like Selah by her side makes leaving much easier. They both could really use each other right now.

"I think that's all," August says as we close the trunk, ready to take Catherine back home.

I look around, trying to remember if we forgot anything. "Where's Blaise's coffee?" I ask, knowing I told him to buy one for her on our way out of the hospital.

"Her car." He points with his thumb at the Kia Rio behind him.

At the exit of the hospital, I spot Catherine in a

wheelchair and a nurse behind her. Blaise smiles down at her grandmother, caressing her hand—the same way she has for the last six days.

Catherine can walk on her own again, but doctors suggested bed rest as much as possible. Safe to say she fucking hates it.

The look on her face says it all.

I open the back door to my vehicle since Catherine will ride home with me and help her get inside. Catherine makes herself comfortable, only the unaffected part of her lips raising into a smile.

After making sure there's nothing else she can help us with, the nurse walks back inside the hospital.

Blaise's shoulders drop, and knowing I can't really do anything to help her makes me feel useless as fuck.

"She's going to do better at home, Moon," I say, giving her arm a squeeze.

"I know," she murmurs, tucking stray hairs behind her ear. "Head straight home. No stops, okay?"

"Come on, let's head to the store," August pops in, and before Blaise gets in her car, she throws me a look to make sure I understand.

I don't.

The food in the hospital was shit. The least I can do is to give Catherine a proper meal since the doctors told us she can eat, but I still have to keep an eye on her..

We part ways, and the moment I reach for the car handle, my phone buzzes in my pocket. I pull it out to find a message from an author who was supposed to receive feedback from me this morning.

When I woke up today, I only knew I had to bring Catherine home from the hospital. Other than that, I forgot about any other tasks.

Fuck, I guess I remember now.

The manuscript is already done. I just completely forgot to send it back with everything going on in my mind.

I quickly type a text to let the author know I'll have it sent by early afternoon.

Being a part-time editor has its perks—like being able to work from anywhere as long as I have my laptop —but I didn't even consider bringing it with me.

After stuffing my phone back into my jeans, I get inside the car and bring the engine to life. In the rearview mirror, Catherine's reflection is absently staring out the window.

We drive home after stopping to get some food from Chick-fil-A, and I turn the radio on for Catherine, thinking some music will do her good. I start humming a song, and she quickly follows while eating her sandwich.

Once I park the car, I kill the engine and get out of my seat.

As gently as the first time, I get Catherine out. She mutters something under her breath that sounds like it's definitely not a "thank you" for my help. I laugh at the way her face scrunches with displeasure, and I squeeze her in my arms for reassurance while we walk toward the porch.

"You always took care of me and August. Now it's my turn to take care of you," I say, meaning it.

Catherine stops in place, her tiny hand tugging me to do the same, and I look back at her to make sure everything's okay. When I meet her gaze, her blue eyes are glossy with tears.

Fuck, I can't stand seeing her cry.

My shoulders slump as I wipe a tear off with my thumb before kissing her forehead.

"It's not a bad thing. You need to rest," I say gently. "Let's get you inside."

CHAPTER SIX

BLAISE

It feels good to finally be back home, to have the boys around for dinner, to have our lives back, and to simply sit here together with food on the table and smiles on our faces. And as much as I'd like to enjoy this moment, I can't help but think how lucky I was to have them by my side the whole time.

Ares and August made sure I had everything I needed, treating me like their own sibling—though I don't know if Ares would fit in that category—and what did I do? Hide the fact that Tamara's back.

The entire time I spent in the hospital, I tried to figure out if I should tell them or not. *Why wouldn't I?* was my first thought.

Truth is, it'd make a lot more sense to make sure she actually wants to get better before saying anything. Because it's all for nothing if the only reason she agreed to go to rehab was because it's the first chance she's had in years. She should be going for herself. Not for the boys. Not for anyone. It should be *her* who yearns for a change.

To keep this from the boys, though, is something I can't do forever. I know I have to tell them right after I drop Tamara off at the rehab and ensure she won't leave as soon as things get hard.

My gaze wanders to Nanna, who's slapping August's hand away along with his help. She's still weak, her hands still shaking, yet she refuses any form of assistance. Not even if it's meant to get her eating.

A knee bumps into mine, and my gaze snaps to Ares. His brows are furrowed, eyes pinned on the fork I stopped midway to my mouth. I didn't realize my thoughts were so loud to stop me from eating.

Both Nanna and August look at me.

I laugh it away, eating the lasagna. Their eyes are still glued to me, so I swallow the food, plaster on a cute smile, and look at Nanna.

"Do you like it?" I ask her as I take another bite, ignoring the brush of Ares's knee.

She smiles at me, a corner of her lips lifting as her right hand trembles in a thumbs-up.

"Learned from the best," I say, raising the fork in the air like a toast.

"But *didn't* beat the best," August jokes, winking at Nanna.

No matter how many times she tries to teach me how to make it, it's never the same mouth-watering taste. It's good, sure, but not like hers.

She rolls her eyes, her sassiness on full display even in her condition. The next time she tries to eat, her hand trembles hard enough to spill some of the food on her shirt. August slowly drags her hand down and grabs a napkin. He sobers her but stops in the middle of the task, noticing Nanna's grimace.

"Don't give me that look." He takes the fork, grabbing another bite from her plate. "I'm just helping."

Nanna mutters something but lets him.

Ares and I share a look, then chuckle when we see the expression on Nanna's face. Soon after, August joins us. Nanna shakes her head, but the right side of her lips stretches into a smile.

At one point, she refuses to eat anymore and relaxes on her chair. I know she doesn't like this at all, so I decide it'd be better to spare her from the pitifulness we're showing her without meaning to.

I clear my throat and stand up, the table now empty of food. "Want to go to your room?" I ask her, and she nods.

August rises on his feet. "I'll take her."

I shake my head. "You guys should go rest. We got this." I smile at them, placing the plates in the sink.

"I—" August tries again, but Ares pats him on the back as he sits up from his chair.

He pushes August toward the hallway and turns to me when his brother walks to the door. "Are you alright?"

My throat tightens under his gaze. He almost watches me like he already knows the answer and waits for me to confirm it. I lean my hip on the counter, hugging my chest and giving him a smile before talking.

"Why wouldn't I be? Nanna's back. Everything is fine. Amazing, really." I smile, biting my tongue.

He squints his eyes at me. "Alright," he says and whirls on his feet. "I'll act like I believe it for now."

Ares leaves, and my shoulders drop in relief before I can stop them. When I look at Nanna, her face is as suspicious as Ares's.

I sigh. "Come on." I gently grab her by the elbows, getting her on her legs. "Let's get you to bed."

We slowly make our way through the living room, and even though I know she'd like to stay there and watch TV, she needs good rest. For some reason, she has always preferred to sleep there instead of her bed. I'll never understand why. A couch would definitely not be a good place to sleep. She knows it. I know it.

We walk upstairs, and I help tuck her into bed, then kiss her forehead. "I love you a thousand lives," I whisper before stepping out of the room.

After switching off all the lights in the house, I go to my room, ready for a much-needed shower. I stretch my neck and tilt it to the sides a few times, taking away some of the tension there.

I enter my room and don't waste any time as I grab everything I need, then head to the bathroom.

As soon as I'm under the warm water cascading down my body, I take a deep breath and enjoy the sensation. Only when I feel my muscles relax do I turn off the water and step out of the shower, reaching for a towel to dry myself off.

I drag a white cropped shirt over my head and pink panties up my legs, then walk back into my room. I close the door after me, and my heart almost rips out of my chest, grows legs, runs to the window, and jumps when I see Ares lounging on my bed.

"How about knocking next time, huh?" I say, trying to catch my breath.

His eyes travel from the tip of my toes, the panties I have on, my naked stomach, the valley of my breasts, to my neck, which constricts under his gaze. It feels like a tough grip, a snake that circles around my throat, his hold gradually tightening.

"No." He says it so simply, but it sends shivers down my spine and sets free a shaky exhale I didn't even know I was restraining. He slowly looks up at me, the corner of his lips tugging upward into a smirk. "I think I'd rather not."

He seems to enjoy himself, so I turn around to give

him a reason to shut up—and a moment to regain my breath—flashing him with my butt.

"Fair enough," I say, then make a show of swaying my hips as I walk to the laundry basket and stuff the clothes I wore today in there.

My knees straighten, and I lean forward to grab a pair of socks from the lowest drawer. Not because I need them, but because it's the only reason I can find to bend over. Next, I take a pair of boxers and thread them in the side of my panties as I make myself busy. All the time, Ares's gaze follows me.

I brush my hair and look through my clothes even though I don't need anything. When I want to take an empty bottle of water from my desk, a strong grasp catches my arm.

The boxers disappear from where I put them. Ares's hand stretches the pair in front of my eyes, and he gets closer to me, his lips almost touching my ear. I hold my breath, waiting for him to speak as soft drips of perspiration dance on my neck.

"Put. These. On."

I slowly turn in his embrace, finding the courage to cock a brow in challenge.

He's silent for a moment. Waiting for me to oblige.

Out of nowhere, he sets me free and grabs me by the waist, and somehow, I land on the edge of the bed. He drops to his knees. My breath quickens.

"What are you doing?" I question when he parts my legs open.

Ares looks up at me, eyes hooded.

Why is it suddenly so hot in here?

He grips the boxers tighter, silently asking me to follow through. My insides clench, and I try to drag myself further from him. He doesn't let me. Not until I do as he says. With every protest of my mind, my body obeys and lets him guide my legs.

"What does it look like?" He grabs my soles and hooks them in the material. "Putting these on myself since you're so stubborn."

His finger brushes my skin in a soft, painful trace. I swallow, then sit up so he can drag them all the way up. My hands look for support on his shoulders.

I can't help but hold my breath when he gets to my hips, pausing there for a second. He looks at me as he pulls the boxers up and releases them, careful to slap the waistband against my skin.

I bite back a gasp.

"Better," he says, throwing himself on the bed.

Before joining him, I close my eyes and take a deep breath. It doesn't help with the fluttering in my stomach or the things going on below my waist. I turn around on my tiptoes and notice what's lying on his chest.

My gaze darts from him to the object. "I can't believe you still have it," I say, not able to contain the surprise in my voice.

He smiles as I take the book between my fingers and flip through the pages.

It's been so long since I last saw this.

"Come on." He pats the empty space next to him. I quickly get under the covers, knowing what will come.

Ares sits fully dressed on top of the blanket.

He takes the childhood book and opens it to the first page. Before starting, he looks down at me but says nothing. I know this is his way of saying, *I know something's wrong with you.*

He begins to read. I don't know for how long I watch him or the way his lips move when he talks. All I know is that he says the last line when I'm close to slipping away.

"Good night, Moon," he whispers, signaling the story ended.

I don't want it to end. "One more time, please," I mutter as I lose the battle with sleep.

CHAPTER SEVEN

BLAISE

My eyes catch sight of her small frame and the way she's constantly biting her lips before I reach the parking lot. She scans her surroundings, probably wondering if I've changed my mind.

Well, I haven't.

Her attention is drawn to me, as if she's felt my presence—the same way she used to when I was as *tiny as a jellybean.*

I hate that nickname so much right now.

And I miss it at the same time.

Because when you love someone who's changed over time, you can't undo the strong feelings you once had. Not if they hurt you, not if they turn into a completely different person.

That's the thing with Tamara. No matter what she

does, I can't help but think about who she used to be and the chance of her coming back home.

Since my parents never had that option, it comes naturally to me to do everything in my power to make sure Tamara gets to use her chance.

I remove myself from the depths of my mind the moment Tamara climbs in with a smile on her face.

"Hi," she says hesitantly after buckling the seatbelt.

It's inhuman to stay nonchalant under the eyes that once looked at me with so much love—the kind of love only a mother can offer—mostly because Tamara isn't innately a bad person. I don't think anyone can be fully good or bad. We all have our strengths and flaws. The best we can do is try to balance them.

I clear my throat, realizing my gaze has lingered for too long. "Hi."

My hand shifts the gear in reverse, and we get out of the parking lot with no other words addressed.

A lump makes its way through my throat, along with the hole forming in the pit of my stomach—a warning. "Sentimental" has always been a word that has done a great job of describing me, but it sucks when I get this overwhelmed around *her*.

I've come to the conclusion that Tamara doesn't deserve my emotions, but being this close to her changes things.

"Is this... rehabilitation institution far from here?"

she asks, pulling me from my thoughts as I drive onto the highway.

I glance out of the window. "Yes and no."

She laughs.

Don't laugh, don't smile, don't speak.

Sure, I was the one who chose to do this in the first place, but she doesn't have to make my time trying not to wake old feelings harder.

"What's that supposed to mean?" She tilts her head to the side, watching me.

I don't want to look at her because I know she shifted in her seat to get a better view of me. My chicken ass prefers to ignore it.

The only thing I need to do is to drop her there and drive back home, and then I don't have to worry about the proximity between us anymore. That should be easy.

Feeling her eyes on me, I bite the inside of my cheek. "It's one hour away."

"Oh." I can see from the corner of my eyes how she lowers her head on the headrest, a sigh falling past her lips.

"That way, you'll think twice before leaving."

She nods, avoiding my gaze.

"I'm telling the boys." I'm not doing anything wrong, after all. I'm helping her get better. To be honest, I don't even know why I'm saying this to her.

"Don't tell them." She brings her hands forward.

"I'll pay you back as soon as I'm out and get a job, but please don't tell them."

Don't tell them?

Does she even know what she's asking me to do? To hide something from them would require never seeing them again. I *can't* lie to their faces.

I shake my head. "No. I—"

"Please, Jellybean. When you guys see me next time, I want to be good."

Tamara senses me holding back, so she continues with what I know is only meant to manipulate me. "I want my children to be proud of me. I want *you* to be proud of me." Her palm rubs my shoulder in a comforting motion.

Despite the blurry sheet covering my eyes, I won't shed a single tear for her. I have to keep reminding myself this is all a game to her, a lottery, and if she gets lucky, she wins.

If only she wouldn't sound so sincere.

I blink away the tears and focus on the road before talking. "I want you to make us proud, too, Tam. But asking me to keep this a secret is too much."

Of course I want to help give her life sense again, but I won't put the trust of the most important people in danger so she can shoot her shot. And Tamara always misses her shot.

Nevertheless, I already decided to tell them the truth as soon as I get home.

"Please," she begs, then removes her hand from me. "If you want me to get better, I need you to do this for me. I want to show them I changed."

She doesn't understand.

My jaw twitches as I strain my teeth. "I can't hide it for that long."

She hesitates. "How long?" I can hear the loud swallow passing through her throat from here.

I've been anticipating this question, but since it might make her second-guess her choice to go, I kept hoping she wouldn't ask. It's justifiable why she asked, considering she'll be the one spending her time there.

The longest Tamara's been sober is probably five months. She'll sometimes stay sober for weeks, sometimes for three months, but she always relapse.

That's exactly why she needs to stay longer than that.

"Six months."

She sucks in a breath, the silence surrounding us.

The first month is already paid for, and I know there might be a chance for her to refuse to go to rehab now. If there's anything she's good at besides manipulating, it's running away. And I'm afraid there's nothing I can do if she decides to.

"Okay."

My head snaps towards her. "What?"

She smiles back at me, and I focus on the road. "I'll do it as long as you keep this between us."

Can't she see how much she's asking me to do?

Those boys read me like an open book. Goddamn it, *I'm* an open book. You don't even need to read it because I'll read it out loud for you.

Her eyebrows draw together as her voice cracks. "Please."

Would it be worth it, though? I'd have to lie to them until she gets back, and it's not something I'd have to do for a few days. This would have to go on for *months*.

What if she doesn't last? What if I make this sacrifice only to be disappointed in the end?

What if she gets better?

My mind fills with dozens of unanswered questions, so I do what my heart is telling me to do. "You'll have to do something else in return too."

Her reply comes in an instant. "And what's that?"

"Put me on your emergency contact list in case you decide to leave earlier."

She sucks in a breath. "I won't."

I shoot her a look. "That way, I can tell the boys. But Tam?"

Tamara chews on her lip, and her eyes light up with hope. "Yeah?"

"They may be mad at me, but they'll never forgive you if you fuck this up. Especially because it involves me."

One way or another, they've become used to her ruining things with every step she takes. Me being caught up in her shit is not something they'll get over easily.

She agrees with a move of her head, blue eyes peeking up at me. A swallow bobs her throat, and I turn the music on to avoid any further conversation.

Time passes, and it doesn't take me long to realize we're getting closer. There are posters everywhere in the small town with hopeful messages for people with addictions. By the way Tamara shifts in her seat, I say they are pretty obvious to her too.

I follow the GPS and turn right, entering a big, beautiful garden. No walls are separating the outside from what this place actually is. I thought that might help Tamara ease the jail feeling.

After driving on a tight road, I park the car where the path ends.

"I'll see you in six months when I pick you up at this exact spot. I know you can do it." I give her an encouraging smile.

She lets out a weak laugh before getting her stuff and stepping out of the vehicle. "Thank you, Jellybean." She smiles at me, then closes the door behind her.

I wait in my car until she gets inside, then drive away, letting out a harsh exhale.

The best I can do is believe she'll stay until the end. After all, this place feels more like a sanctuary, and that's exactly why I chose it. So she doesn't think I'm sending her to prison.

I leave the rehabilitation center and pull into a gas station a few minutes later to fill my car. When I get back and try to start it, the engine sputters like it's choking.

The second time I try, nothing happens besides a soft vibration.

Damn it.

I have zero experience when it comes to cars, and the only person I know who does is Ares.

Ares. I should call him. I get my phone from the console, and my finger hovers over his contact when I remember—I can't call him because I have no explanation for being this far away from the house.

Shit.

Of course this would happen to me when I'm in an unknown city, doing something the boys should know about but don't.

My forehead bumps into the steering wheel.

My car broke down, and there's no doubt I'm next to fall apart.

CHAPTER EIGHT

ARES

"Are you sure she wasn't just tired? After these last few weeks, I'm sure she's exhausted."

I slide August a skeptical look, trying to determine whether he's serious or not. He's lounging on the couch in our living room, his eyebrows knitted together in the wait for my reply.

He has no idea what he's talking about.

"That's not the point," I tell him, shifting my attention back to the large window with a perfect view of Blaise's house.

"No?"

For some reason, a single-word question irritates me like no other.

Blaise was off at dinner—barely got a few words out. She smiled, but her eyes looked lost. It's something everyone could have seen from miles away, and yet it looks like I was the only one to notice.

Maybe reading a childhood book wasn't the best choice to help with clearing whatever was going through that head of hers, and it shows. There's still something wrong, and I can't figure out what.

It can't be about Catherine. It's just this feeling in my gut telling me this is more.

Her car disappeared from the street this morning, and it still hasn't come back. She missed her run with August today, and even if he doesn't think much about it, I do. Because on Sundays, she's either running with him or staying home with Catherine.

"Maybe she met a guy and, you know..." he says from behind me.

"I know what?" My eyes snap back to August. I don't really know if I'm playing dumb or if it's impossible for me to comprehend a simple sentence.

August sinks into his place. "Do I need to spell it out for you? Maybe she has a date."

A date.

When it comes to her, that word does nothing but give me the ick. It's like "date" and "Blaise" in the same sentence are an anomaly. They don't fit together. Plus, I don't remember her ever bringing a guy home.

I guess the only thing I can do is pray she won't start doing it now.

"Yeah. Sure," I say and swallow the dryness in my throat.

When I return my eyes from August to the window, Blaise is getting out of an Uber, cheeks flushed. Somehow, the idea of her having a date suddenly makes sense.

For a brief moment, she holds the door open, and I hold my breath as I wait for a man to step out of the car. My breathing regulates the second she shuts it behind her, the Uber driving off.

Before thinking it through, I put my shoes on and head out the front door.

"Dude!" August shouts from behind me.

Ignoring him, I speed-walk to Blaise's and knock twice on the door that just closed. She doesn't even have time to open it fully because I'm already talking.

"Where have you been?"

Angry eyes shoot daggers my way, but she tries a smile. "Well. Hello to you too."

I avoid repeating the same question, so I try another one. Maybe this time, her stubborn fine ass would actually reply. "Where's your car?"

She shifts her weight from one leg to another, barely holding my gaze. "It broke, why?"

My eyes squint. "You are never *not* home on Sundays."

"Thanks for reminding me." She rolls her eyes. "The tow truck should bring it back tomorrow."

With a sigh, I soften my voice. "What's wrong?"

Her head tilts to the side, and I just know she won't tell me. "You just can't stop with the questions, can you?"

I give her a look. "Not unless you answer them."

Blaise takes a deep breath, closing her eyes for a second, probably praying I'll buy every lie she will get out of her mouth.

"Nothi—" she tries to lie to me.

"Bullshit," I cut in.

Her shoulders drop, and so does her face. "Okay, I'm not in the mood to deal with you."

Without any other word, she slams the door shut. Since she didn't lock it, I take it she wants me to follow her.

I enter the house, leaving my shoes at the door—for Catherine's sake only—and keep my eyes on Blaise as she starts running toward the staircase. I walk quicker, taking sight of Catherine in the living room from the corner of my eye.

"Hi, Catherine," I greet her as I walk past the sofa.

Blaise sprints up the steps, and I reach her right before she sails into the room. She draws in a frustrated breath when my fingers grip her elbow, stopping her from running.

Protruding green eyes skim across my face in a twirl of uncertainty.

"Where. Have. You. Been?" I ask quietly, carefully stressing each word.

Blaise turns to face me. "Not that this is any of your business, but I went on a drive to clear my head."

My shoulders roll back with inexplicable relief.

So she was alone, after all.

It makes sense. I do that sometimes, too.

What doesn't make sense to me is the way she's acting and why she didn't ask for my help before calling the tow truck.

"And why are you all..." My eyes wander over her as I try to find the right words. "Pissed today?"

"On my period," she says, hugging her chest.

She's not. "You're lying."

She frowns, removing my hand from her arm. "I'm not."

"You wear sweatpants and that annoying heating pad that squeaks every time you move when you're on your period, so stop lying to me."

Her big eyes analyze me, mouth parted open in question.

"Everyone knows," I explain half of the truth.

Everyone knows, but I remember.

"No, they don't." She fights back, a weird look playing on her face.

"What?" I ask.

"What's that?" She points her finger behind me.

I turn and face an empty hallway.

Classic Blaise.

When I whirl around, Blaise already has her hand on

the doorknob and is halfway in her room. Fortunately for her, I'm not quick enough to grab her in time.

She closes the door and, this time, she locks it.

"Are you going to open the door so we can talk about this?" I try.

"No." Her reply comes firmly.

So be it then.

Downstairs, Catherine is murmuring something indecipherable, and I stop to give her a kiss on the forehead before striding out of the house.

At home, August is still drawing on his iPad.

"What happened?" he asks as soon as I step inside.

I rush past him, taking the stairs two at a time to my room. I close the door softly—the opposite of how Blaise did—and vault over the windowsill, then travel the distance from my roof to hers in a jump.

At least last night, I was inspired enough to leave her window ajar.

The aperture opens in front of me, revealing Blaise's body stretched on the bed. She has her hands under her head and stares at the ceiling with what seems no intention to look at me.

Not even when I step inside.

"Are you going to talk to me now?" I ask and drop to the floor, leaning my back against the wall.

"Do I have a choice?" She's still looking up.

"No," I say because it's the truth.

Blaise releases a long exhale, sitting up. She gazes

down at me, pursing her lips together. "I just had a bad day." Her murmur sounds exhausted, and so low that I almost miss it.

I turn up the volume of my hearing aids a little, shifting in my seat. "Can I ask why?"

She lets out a small smile. "You just did." She drops on her back again. "Does it even matter why? Can't you just, like, be here and nothing else?"

It bothers me that she won't talk about what's upsetting her. Not because I need to know but because I know who Blaise is. She never lets anyone ask so many questions with no replies. She spills out everything.

Now she's doing none of that, and it only proves something is indeed wrong.

"Sure."

We sit in silence, her breathing evening out with each minute that passes until she's close to falling asleep. I stand on my feet before she does and walk to the edge of the bed, shaking her body a little.

"What?" she mutters, her eyes fluttering.

My hand sneaks under her back, lifting it until she sits up. Her brows question me, but I carry on.

When I'm sure she can support herself, I get on my knees—the second time in two days—and slip her socks off. I unbutton her jeans, struggling not pay attention to the whimper she releases at the touch of my fingers. I must do a shitty job at ignoring it because the sound shoots straight to my cock.

For both of our sakes, the jeans slide easily off her legs.

Big eyes shine in the darkness as I grab her by the waist, then hook a hand under her knees before tucking her under the blanket.

I circle a strand of hair behind her ear. "Good night, Moon," I say, ready to leave.

She clings to my arm, and I peer down at her.

"Good night." Blaise smiles, then lets go of my hand.

I slip out of her room at the same time my phone pings in my pocket. I take it out to find a message from Tamara. I don't even bother to read. If I were her, after so many texts unread, I'd simply stop reaching out.

Before locking the device, I delete the chat.

Tamara doesn't deserve anyone's attention, but she'll drag it with her teeth if they won't offer it.

The last time we accepted her back home was almost a year ago. Tamara was cooking every day, waiting for us with food on the table, insisting that Catherine needed to rest. I enjoyed the home-cooked meals but kept my distance.

She stuck around for two months, and August and Blaise lowered their walls. Not me, though. I knew things could never go back to normal, and after all, I don't think *normal* was even that good for me to wish it'd return.

She made my life a living hell and broke Dad while at it too. A few years after she cheated on him and ran away, Dad moved to Texas and hasn't come back since. We still talk regularly, and I guess we have what you'd call a "fine" relationship.

Pushing the thoughts swirling through my mind to the side, I take one last glance at Blaise and walk back to my room.

Once I'm changed into more comfortable clothes, I saunter downstairs.

"What?" August asks when he notices me, but he keeps his eyes on the tablet, brows close.

"Have you heard from Mom lately?"

He stops drawing but doesn't meet my gaze. "No. Why?"

"You sure?" I push.

It just doesn't sit right with me. Why would she text me nonstop and not her favorite child? "Sunshine," she used to call him. Is it because of remorse or some shit?

Funny because I don't think Tamara's capable of feeling that.

"Yeah. Did something happen?" he questions.

"Nah. Go to sleep. You've been killing your eyes with that iPad of yours." I pat him on the back, and he shoots me a smile.

CHAPTER NINE

BLAISE

This is our busiest day since I came back, and it's a welcome distraction from the mind I've been a prisoner in for the past weeks. It's refreshing to be separated from my thoughts, even if only for a few hours before they ambush me like a merciless tsunami.

I take a deep breath and let my gaze wander over the crowded bookstore. People push each other inside, choosing to be packed like sardines instead of waiting in line outside. Some struggle to get a glimpse through the windows, and others sit down in the booths, people almost falling into their lap.

Rhodes tries to remedy the situation, but it's like he's talking to a wall. They won't even spare him a glance.

It appears Teressa Kimberly's newest release made a local frenzy, and if there's one thing I know about excited readers, it's that they walk over dead bodies to get what they want.

I look over at Ares, who's preparing a few drinks behind the bar. His grip tightens on the cup in his hands, matching the strong twitch in his jaw.

Knowing he's not a people person, I distract him. "What's taking her so long?"

Ares looks at the clock behind me, shaking his head. He probably didn't realize how late she was. "She calls herself the 'queen' of romance. Of course she'll make us wait."

With a sigh, I place my elbows on the counter.

Soon enough, everyone will start losing their patience and ask questions. And who will they ask? Us. Do we have the answers they are looking for? No.

Ares slams a glass on the bar, drawing some attention to us as he pours milk with his other hand. He peers down at my breasts—which I probably squeezed between my arms—while filling the glass.

When I woke up this morning, I felt like choosing a shirt with a deeper cleavage and my best bra. I'm still trying to figure out if it was a good choice.

Ares raises his eyebrows, and his gorgeous dark eyes finally rise to mine, not at all ashamed of his obvious staring.

I fidget in my place, trying to escape the shiver running down my spine.

"Does your bra match those pink panties I can't

stop thinking about?" Ares asks, looking down at the glass between his hands, a serious look on his face.

My heartbeat triple in speed as warmth floods through me.

I take a brief moment to take him in and gather as much confidence as possible before talking. "They're red, actually."

The corners of his lips curl into a smirk at the same time I release a quiet exhale, and I find myself in the position of smiling without intending to. I turn my back to him, biting my bottom lip to keep the thoughts swimming through my mind silent.

What would it be like to show him instead of telling him? Drag him into the bathroom. Trace my palm along his chest. Tease him until he can't resist me anymore and—

This is wrong, Blaise. So wrong.

Luckily, Teressa enters the bookstore, distracting me from my rich imagination. She's smiling at everyone, a pair of glasses resting on her nose.

I turn to Ares, praying my cheeks aren't burning red. "It seems like the *queen* decided to show up after all."

We're all thrown into work for the next few hours, making sure the event goes as planned. And it does. Teressa signs every book and takes a few minutes to talk with each person. She's charming, I give you that.

At some point, when I'm heading to the back room

to bring more water, a hand squeezes my arm. I whirl on my toes and smile when I find Ares.

"I'll wait until you're done," he says.

"My shift ends in three hours. You don't have to wait for me." I smile. "Selah will give me a ride home."

"I didn't ask." Ares sets my hand free, then goes behind the bar and sits down on a chair.

On my way to the back, I brush my fingers over the skin his palm has touched and wear a smile at the memory my entire shift.

Time passes quickly, and the closing hours surprise us in a rush. Every employee is cleaning, the mess people left behind outnumbering us—something that I think Ares notices too because he joins us soon.

"I need to talk to Rhodes, and then I'll take you home," Selah says once we're done sobering.

"It's okay." I lean down and kiss her cheek. "I'll go with Ares."

She nods. "Text me when you get home."

"Will do."

Ares gets up from his seat, opening the door for me. "After you," he says.

I shake my head, smiling, and continue to walk as he follows close behind.

When I get to his car, I place my hand on the door-knob, waiting for him to open it. He doesn't, at least not immediately. So I look at him, ready to tell him something, but I swallow any words that were about to escape.

His eyes have darkened ten shades blacker, thick brows shadowing over them. He clears his throat. Unlocks the car. No words addressed.

We both occupy our seats, and I have to clench my thighs together when he throws me one last look before driving off. It's not until we're close to the house that he talks again.

"I'll fix your car this weekend," Ares announces out of nowhere.

"No need to," I say, looking out through the window. "I'll get a mechanic to take a look at it." He snorts, and my gaze snaps at him. "What?"

"You've been saying this for weeks. And again, I didn't ask."

"Well, it's time for you to learn how to ask," I counter.

Ares laughs. A laugh I love to hear so much that I replay it a thousand times in my head.

"Demanding is better. Plus, it usually spares me some time."

I smile. "Usually? Meaning it doesn't always work?"

He nods, flashing me a knee-wobbling grin. "With everyone else, yes. With you, no."

Ares parks the car, and I have my hand on the handle when he stops me. I swirl my head in his direction, trying not to let my gaze slip to the place where his palm is lingering. As if he just realized, he removes it from my leg.

"I'll fix your car," he says, his eyes cascading over my body.

"Yeah." A shaky breath unchains from my throat. "Sure." I get out of the car. "Yeah, I'll see you tomorrow."

And I really, *really* want to leave, but his voice nips my wish in the mud. I inhale deeply, forcing out a smile.

"I'll talk to Rhodes about our schedules, but from now on, we'll go to and back from work together."

Deep breaths, Blaise.

"Cool." I nod and ignore the knowing grin on his face. "Night."

Before I have time to close the door, his voice winds outside. "Good night, Moon."

CHAPTER TEN

ARES

It's not until Blaise exits my car that I notice the familiar black Toyota Corolla parked close to our house.

I swallow the dryness in my throat, knowing it can only mean one thing: my dad's here.

The last time I saw him was years ago when I was nothing but a child who had the responsibility of an adult. He took his shit and left, keeping in touch with us through text messages or phone calls, talking about how he was going to visit soon, but he never did.

Until now.

The only reason why he might be here is to deliver some bad news. I can't wrap my head around what it could be, but Dad coming back home after five years can't be good.

When I open the door, muffled laughter fills my ears. I slide my shoes off and make my way into the kitchen, where Dad's sitting at the table, that cocky smile never missing the opportunity to be on his face. August is sitting in his usual chair with his back facing me.

Dad looks up, clearing his throat as I sit down, and August's eyes quickly follow to land on me.

He could've at least texted to warn me. I don't think it would've really hurt his fingers to type two simple words: "Dad's home." That would've been a hell of a lot better than finding his car parked in front of the house.

"Ares." Dad gives me a broad smile. "It's good to see you."

He looks different. Good different. He sits taller, he's shaved, and I'm pretty sure he got a new haircut too. Definitely not something Dad would do.

It's been a long time since he bothered to take care of his appearance. That stopped after Tamara left.

The Court who's standing in front of my eyes brings back memories from when he was more than the man who abandoned us, from when the word "Dad" actually meant more than a three-letter word.

I remember how I used to say that I wanted to be my dad when I grew up. Funny how, now that I've actually grown up, I want the polar opposite.

"How was work?" Dad asks, trying to fill the silence as he opens the box of pizza that's already sitting on the table.

It feels impossible to come to terms that this is really him. He's so... Dad.

When I realize I've been staring for too long, I clear my throat and shrug. "Like work." Once the words leave my mouth, I feel there's a better reply that doesn't make me seem like a total asshole, so after a few beats of silence, I try again. "It's been a long day," I say, and even if it doesn't feel like enough, Dad's lips turn into a small smile, his mustache moving up and down as he chews his pizza.

He swallows his bite, then puts the slice down and looks at the two of us with a grin that makes the corners of his eyes wrinkle. "I have some news."

Too happy to be something bad.

"What's up?" August asks, shifting in his seat.

"First of all, I'm moving back to New Jersey." He looks for both of our reactions, but I keep mine blank. August widens his eyes but nothing more.

"And second?" I ask, taking some pepperoni off the pizza and throwing it into my mouth.

Dad smiles. "You know that things between Caroline and me are serious." He stops for a second, probably waiting to see if one of us would disagree about his relationship with the thirty-something woman he's been dating for a few years. I mean, she could probably be my sister, but who am I to get in the way if half his age is his type?

"Sure," August says between bites.

"She's pregnant." Dad smiles softly.

"Is it yours?" I ask, cocking a brow.

It's true I don't know Caroline personally, but the age difference between them makes it hard to believe that the thing she's looking for is love.

He, on the other hand, would never cheat.

"Of course," Dad says calmly. If he's offended, he doesn't show it.

"Congratulations." Maybe saying it right away makes it feel dishonest, but I mean it. As long as their choices don't affect my life, I don't give a fuck.

"Do you know what you guys are having?" August asks.

"A girl. She's due in December," he replies, a sparkle twinkling in his eyes. "And I'd like you both to meet Caroline when you're ready."

Dad gradually relaxes, and I can see how sharing this with us took away a weight that was hanging heavily on his chest. Honestly, I'd be that way, too, after telling the kids I left to raise themselves that I'm having another child.

I hope at least he doesn't fuck it up this time.

CHAPTER ELEVEN

BLAISE

"There," I tell Nanna, helping her onto the bed.

Today's walk ended with a smile on our faces, both of us aware of the enormous progress she's made. Her physical recovery is on the right path, but there's no improvement with her speech or the left side of her face. It's as though her words are locked in her throat, unable to be released.

A lock of hair lies atop her forehead, and I carefully sweep it away, my heart swelling at the sight of the woman who raised me.

"I love you a thousand lives," I murmur.

The corners of her mouth curve upward, and I dip my head to kiss her cheek. Her soft, warm palm rests on mine, and my eyes close as a natural reaction to her comforting touch.

Nanna's fingers brush over my skin before she talks. "I love you a thousand more."

It seems like it was ages ago when I first heard Mom and Nanna say that. There was something about it I loved so much that I couldn't stop repeating it to them and my father. Now, it's just between the two of us.

And I cherish it with all my heart.

My eyes flutter open, a lump forming in my throat. Like every other family, we had beautiful moments— moments I'd give anything to live again, especially now that the memories are beginning to fade.

Sometimes, I doubt it was even real. Maybe it was that kind of dream you can't decide if it was real or not. Or maybe it happened too long ago to stay forever in my mind.

After making sure Nanna has everything she needs, I take the steps to my room.

I draw my phone out of my jeans and toss it on the bed, the display lighting with a text from Ares. I pick up the device, prepared to type the regular reply, but I pause when I see the message.

ARES

dad's having another kid

Oh.

I was certainly not expecting this.

Court rebuilt his life from the ground in another state,

and it seems like the wound Tamara left him with has finally healed. When she left, he was a walking disaster, broken enough to run away from his kids when things got hard.

He's the one who taught me how to kick a boy in the balls if they ever hurt me and the one who showed me without intention how much love can hurt because the love he had for Tamara was the love I used to dream about. Now, I pray to never know his pain.

My free hand loosens the ponytail I have tied up on the top of my head.

> **ME**
>
> do you want to talk about it?

Is it a stupid thing to ask? Yes. Do I know what else to say? No. Not at all.

> **ARES**
>
> No.

> **ME**
>
> rooftop?

Not waiting for a reply, I crack open my window and squeeze myself out.

I'm not surprised to see him already here the moment I step out. He's so fast, I wonder if he was here before even texting me.

"Penny for your thoughts?" I inquire, then take a seat beside him.

His eyes twinkle with amusement as he gazes into the dark night sky. "It'll cost more than just a penny."

He's always been like this, mysterious in a way. Reserved. Quiet. It's challenging to figure out how to console him. Or if I should do it at all.

The difference between us is that I don't have a filter between my mind and my mouth, and he chooses not to have it. There's something powerful about deciding on purpose how you speak instead of just blurting out whatever comes to mind like I do. It's something out of my control.

"He seemed different," Ares says after a few minutes of silence.

I wonder what he's like now. He wasn't the best father in the universe, but there was a time when his love for his kids was greater than his hatred for his wife.

"Good different?" I ask.

"Yeah." Ares shrugs, letting his hands fall between his legs as he stares into the distance. "I wasn't expecting him to come back to Cape May."

This must be difficult for him. Out of nowhere, his dad shows up and says he's having another kid. It can't be easy to digest.

I place a hand on his shoulder, trying to show him I'm here whether he wants to talk about it or not. If he pushes me away, I'll pull him back harder. No matter what, I'm right beside him.

Exactly how he's always been for me when I need him.

He looks at me. "He can have a horde of children for all I care, but the question is, is he going to be there for them?" He clenches his jaw. "That's all I can think about."

Ares's concern is something I can understand. He was just graduating high school when Court left him to raise a thirteen-year-old on his own.

I slowly scoot closer and rest my head on his shoulder.

"He might," I whisper. "Try to remember how good he was before."

His chin rests on my hair, and I feel him breathing me in. "I can only remember how bad it was after."

CHAPTER TWELVE

ARES

Try to remember how good he was before.

He *was* good before everything went downhill with Tamara.

Whenever we went fishing, he made sure it was during the week so we could skip classes. Dad would relax in his chair, drinking his beer, while we ran around in the muddiest water before finishing the day with grilled cheese and pork.

Court was a great father most of the time. Until he fucked it up.

Why would it be any different with this child?

There might be a chance he didn't even realize how messed up his decision to leave was. And considering the only reason he came back after five years—during which we never saw him in person—was to deliver the news about the pregnancy, I'd say he doesn't realize it now either.

But I've learned to leave the past behind, and I know Dad deserves to be happy. Even though I don't know what the fuck happiness means for him, I want Dad to have it.

For some time, I thought I was happy until I was proven otherwise.

I have a roof over my head, a job, and a girl I can't stop thinking about. Still, it's not enough.

Besides work, I'm not doing shit with my life, and that's not how I imagined my life would go.

I used to think I'd have someone by now. Yet, besides a rare night with a stranger, I can't bring myself to take it further with anyone. Every time I go on a date, I keep comparing them to Blaise.

With Blaise, it's easier to talk. Blaise would've understood this. Blaise would've laughed at this.

It was hard to bring myself to understand that it's impossible to get along with a stranger as well as I do with a girl I've known for years. Eventually, I stopped searching and decided to leave it to destiny or some shit of that sort.

A long time ago, I promised myself that my only real relationship will be with the girl I want to marry, and even though I think it's fucking stupid right now, there's a part of me that can't unglue itself from the idea.

A squeeze on the shoulder brings me back to reality.

I glance at Blaise, and a cute smile plays on her lips, which somehow succeeds in raising my own.

"You never changed, you know?" I nudge her with my shoulder.

Blaise is the type of person who offers anyone her help on a silver tray along with bits of her heart. Luckily, she's got a big one.

She tilts her head, squinty eyes peering at me. "You did."

"I had to."

"It's still so damn hot outside," my brother says in a breath the moment he walks into the house, then gulps a whole bottle of water from the fridge.

"I could fry an egg on the pavement if I wanted to." Blaise's voice chimes in from the hallway, her light steps drawing closer.

She saunters into the living room and sinks into the couch, with uncontrolled breaths lying heavy on her chest.

My eyes move on their own accord to Blaise, roaming over the black sports bra supporting her bust before dropping to the tight running shorts she's wearing. A drop of sweat slides from her neck down to the path between her breasts, and I barely find it in me to avert my gaze.

Blaise stretches her legs on the small table in front of us and holds out her hand to August, who throws her a water bottle and then drops on his chair. After taking a few generous sips, she attempts to put the cap back on, but it slips through her fingers and glides right down her bra.

A swallow gets stuck in my throat as I follow the motion of Blaise's hand, taking it out and closing the bottle shut. Only then do I breathe again.

Fuck, what I'd give to be that cap right now.

Out of instinct and because I don't want to be caught staring like a freak, I look away to where my brother happens to be narrowing his eyes at me. I ignore him.

"Dinner tonight?" Blaise asks, looking at both of us. "I'm thinking of making some steak with baked potatoes."

"Mmm." August touches his stomach and lets out a satisfied hum.

"I can come once I'm done with your car if you need any help," I offer because that's my plan for today anyway. And that way, I'll have time to sober up, and she won't be wearing only a bra anymore.

Her gaze snaps at me. "I told you, you don't need to do it. It's Sunday. Enjoy your day off."

I shoot her a look to make her understand that there's no point in fighting me right now.

She rolls her eyes and stands up. "I'm going to take a shower."

"Do you have everything you need for dinner? I can run to the store," August asks, getting on his feet.

Blaise thinks a little, looking like she's mentally checking every ingredient. "I'm not sure if I have garlic, but I'll text you."

On cue, my stomach growls. Blaise grins and pats me on the back before she turns on her heels and leaves.

"Great, now I'm hungry," August says, and I crack a laugh because God, so am I.

He walks toward the stairs but stops and looks back at me. I cock a brow, waiting for whatever he has to say.

"Did you think about what we should get Blaise for her birthday next week?"

I shrug. "I'll be working."

My brother squints his eyes, judging me for not taking the day off. Of course I know how much Blaise loves her birthday. It's not like she keeps it a secret.

"Right." His tone is rough, but I ignore it. "I have an idea for my gift."

My eyebrow lifts in question.

"It's for you, too, so I can't tell you."

Then why the fuck did you bring it up?

He walks up the stairs, and I stand up, put my shoes on, and go next door, letting him be. I don't knock. I only open it enough to snatch the keys from the entry table and close it right after.

I unlock her car and sit in the driver's seat. The key turns in the ignition, but all I hear is silence. I pop the hood and poke around, but everything looks fine. I try starting it again, but still nothing.

The problem seems like an easy fix.

Working at a garage when I was sixteen taught me a lot about cars. I didn't go there because it was my passion, even though I was damn good at it. I did it out of the wish to be able to support myself and gain some independence.

Once I grab what I need from my house to fix the car, I walk back to Blaise's and head straight to the kitchen.

My feet stop in their tracks as soon as I see her coming down the stairs. A towel is wrapped around her hair, while another one that's far too short hangs on for dear life around her body. My eyes travel from the valley of her breasts to the place where the material ends.

I can't help but wonder if she has any panties on under it. Would they be white? Pink? Maybe a red lace thong. Or maybe she doesn't have any.

Blaise notices me staring and hugs herself. My curiosity worsens as her breasts squeeze together, the towel rising one more dangerous inch. She clears her throat, and I finally look at her face.

"So? What's the diagnosis?" she says in an undistinguishable tone.

Her cheeks have gained a new shade of pink, and she holds my gaze, probably thinking I can't see how she wiggles her bare feet nervously.

"I think the battery's dead," I say and catch a silent, shaky breath slipping past her lips.

"Oh." Her eyes size me up in one quick move. "Okay. Did you... need something?"

It takes me a second to remember why I came here in the first place. "Yeah." Blaise's eyebrows shoot up. "Baking soda."

Blaise frowns at me but doesn't ask any questions as she heads into the kitchen. She rises up on her heels, and the white towel lifts again, the bottom of her ass now peeking out.

My mind wandered to every color of panties she could be wearing, but I was fucking wrong about all of them. She's not wearing any.

Fuck me.

Her hand grabs the hem of the fabric, dragging it lower. I look away—try to, at least—as my jaw clenches.

She opens a cabinet and moves stuff around, all the time getting closer and closer to losing that fabric. When she turns around and hands me the box, her gaze lowers to my stone-hard dick, then snaps back to my eyes. She squints, her lips quirking upward, not at all ashamed.

My eyebrows rise in an unspoken challenge, and she quickly glances away.

I take the box from her, intentionally brushing my fingers over the skin of her hands. Blaise sucks in a breath when I head for the front door. I take one last look at her with a slow turn of my head.

"Wear red," I say, looking at her lower half before leaving.

I spend the next few hours struggling to work on her car. I hardly make any progress because all I can think about is if Blaise will do as she was told.

I take a break to sober up, then walk inside Blaise's house with a hungry stomach and uncontrollable thoughts.

We sit at the table, and the decision to tell her what color to wear seems like my biggest mistake so far. The entire dinner, all I can think about is what hides under those jean shorts.

After I try to get her attention several times, she finally looks at me, eyes swimming in lust. Her breath hitches, and a soft blush spreads from her neck onto her cheeks and nose. Blaise swallows under the touch of my not-so-subtle glance. She does it so slowly, parting her lips when her throat bobs and that's it. That's the last drop of a glass full of water that is already overflowing.

I need to know.

My phone is in my hand in two seconds.

ME

What color?

A victorious grin breaks free on her face when her phone buzzes on the table, and I realize this is what she wanted.

But she'll pay for it.

She makes no move to grab it, and I find myself in the position of needing to give her a push. I act like I drop my fork on the floor.

August makes a stupid remark. Blaise's eyes widen before I even get under the table. She knows what I'm about to do.

Good. Waiting will make it better.

As soon as I have the fork between my fingers, I spread my fingers over her thigh and give it a tough squeeze. She clenches them, squirming in her seat. When I return to my place, the device is already clutched in her palms.

Catherine and August carry on with their conversation, and I focus on my phone, seeing the three bubbles jump on the screen.

BLAISE

Red.

One. Single. Word.

One single word that sends all the blood rushing straight to my cock.

BLAISE

A red lace thong.

My eyes snap to her. I expect to see her smiling, but she's as affected by this as I am.

ME

I don't remember asking for so many details.

I feel her eyes on me, but I continue.

ME

Go to the bathroom, then be a good girl and show it to me.

She clears her throat, and I simply lock my phone, placing it on the table face-down. I continue eating, giving her a few seconds to make a decision. She stuffs her iPhone in the back pockets of her jeans and takes a bite of her food.

I'm ready to drop something else as an excuse to give her another motivation, but she stands up.

"I'll be right back." She smiles before speed-walking out of the kitchen.

The three of us eat in silence as excruciating minutes pass with no sign from Blaise. I give my throbbing dick a squeeze, not resisting the urge. One more, and I'll come here, for fuck's sake.

She knows what she's doing so goddamn well. Unfortunately for her, so do I.

In no more than two seconds, I send her another message.

> Don't make me come after you, Moon. I'll rip them off and keep them in my pocket for the rest of the dinner.

The threat works because her next message is one of the sexiest photos I've ever seen. I have to bite back a groan as I zoom in on the photo where her jeans are unbuttoned, and she lets me see half of the fabric that sits so tight on her. I keep moving my finger up and down the image like that will delete the existence of her unwanted pants.

I might just follow her into the bathroom after all.

BLAISE

What did I tell you about asking?

A smirk finds its way on my lips as I relax in my seat, my eyes glued to her panties.

Fucking red lace thong.

CHAPTER THIRTEEN

BLAISE

The days are rushing to the end of July, and if I thought time would wash away the moments I relive the dinner with Ares, I was wrong.

So wrong.

At night, when my eyes close and I'm ready to be enveloped by complete darkness, it's him I see. Black pupils gleam with a hint of light. A smirk stretches on his beautiful lips, and I touch them, asking myself if it's real.

It can't be real. It feels so real, I tell myself.

Then his eyes darken even more as he slowly lowers himself on me, aiming for the throbbing between my legs that won't go away. He doesn't take my panties off, pushing them to the side as he eats me. And because I'm weak when it comes to him, I stop wondering if I'm having another dream or if he's truly with me and let myself sink into the touch that lingers on my skin even when I'm not sleeping.

I can rarely rest, and it definitely has something to do with wet dreams I shouldn't be having about my best friend.

It's consuming. Extremely hot and consuming. It's like I'm all wrapped up with a constant need of getting a release, and no matter how many times I pleasure myself, it's only getting worse.

Since I can't figure out a way to get rid of the dreams haunting me during the day, I keep my mind busy. I work and without intention, avoid Ares—he and Selah give me weird looks, which makes me believe they suspect something—and spend the evenings with Nanna, celebrating every little improvement in her recovery. And the boys never stop coming for dinner.

She's happier when they are around. I can see it in the way she looks at all of us. Her eyes shine and so does her soul.

Nanna asks me about my novel a few times, but the truth is, it's been pushed to the wayside. Looking back at the conversation I had with her about taking a break, I realize she was right. Forced by the outer factors, I take one without thinking it through.

It's something I *need*.

I'm not in the right mental state to finish the book, and today is only pushing me further away from that goal.

While others might spend their birthdays celebrating another year's passing, I spend it mourning the
day my parents died.

This time, though, there's someone else on my
mind, along with the memory of my parents. The realization that Tamara's close to her second month of
rehab hits me when I'm at work, putting a hint of a
smile on my face as I carry on until my shift ends.

Before I can leave Westnook, Rhodes comes behind
me with a little birthday cake that says, "21st, kill me
with kindness." Selah cuts the cake, Ares stands behind
me, giving me that handsome smile of his, and they all
sing "Happy Birthday" to me.

Under Ares's intense gaze, I can barely hold the
blush creeping up my neck. For one stupid second, I
think he can read my mind and see how far it goes.

Surprisingly, I find it in me to leave without embarrassing myself and head to the beach like every year.

The beach is the place I come to be closer to Mom
and Dad. When I stay here, it's almost like I can see Dad
running after me into the water before giving Mom a
chaste kiss on the lips. He always snuck me some sweets
when Mom wasn't looking.

I smile at the memory.

Grace and James were good parents. They were a
little bit of everything. Funny, kind, and demanding
when they needed to be.

They'd always bring me here on my birthday, just

the three of us for a walk. We used to talk for hours, and they shared with me everything they were proud of. Last time, they were proud of me for doing well in school, for making new friends, for getting a tooth out on my own —all trivial things that I'd kill to get back.

Is there something they'd be proud of this year? Probably my heart. I know I have a big one, but would there be anything else for them to find pride in?

I hope so.

After their death, Nanna brought me here and told me to talk to them. Even as a kid, I thought she was crazy, but then she walked away from me, and the idea didn't sound so bad anymore.

Since that day, I come here every year, and instead of talking to them, I write a letter and send it to the sea only if I find an empty bottle. People always throw their bottles into the sand, so I decide if I find one in ten minutes of searching, it's a sign to throw it in the sea.

Stupid, I know.

But it works for me. It helps me feel like I'm still keeping the tradition going, and I'm not reliving my seventh birthday, waiting for them to get back from grocery shopping. It wasn't until later that night that Nanna received a call from the hospital confirming they died in a car accident.

I release a shaky breath at the echo of that day, and I let my feet sink into the sand as I look for an empty bottle, the cork hanging heavy in my pocket.

Soon enough, the time's up, and for the first time in years, I don't find one.

This letter isn't worth sending, anyway. It's shitty, full of bad thoughts and bad news.

My heart thumps in my chest, and my throat tightens until it feels like breathing is a luxury I can't afford. My trembling hands release the paper I rip in pieces until there's nothing left but particles of paper in the trash.

I leave and cry the entire drive home.

Once I park in the driveway, I wipe off the tears that were flooding down my cheeks just mere seconds ago as fast as an angry river. Even though I love the beach, it also makes me incredibly emotional every time I go there.

With a heavy sigh, I walk the steps to my house. The door squeaks open, revealing the space covered in darkness as Nanna's soap opera plays in the background.

I take off my shoes and make my way through the short hallway to the living room but stop the moment Nanna appears with a big cake in her hands.

A smile builds its way on my face.

Of course, deep down I knew she'd never let my birthday pass without some kind of celebration. Yet my skin prickles with surprise.

"Happy birthday to you," she tries to sing, the left part of her face still hanging low.

My chest squeezes, and my eyes water, the image of

her holding a cake being something I wasn't expecting to see so soon. Close to the second verse of the song, the voice of a boy joins, and I giggle, the happy child in me screaming.

August, Ares, and Selah join us from behind Nanna.

I smile so wide my cheeks hurt. Four of my favorite people are standing in front of me on my birthday. My special day.

They find some way to surprise me every year, and even if I know they'd never miss it for anything in the world, I always keep making scenarios in my head.

I guess I'm just waiting for them to disappear as my parents did.

After they finish singing, I get to hug each one of them. And those hugs... I hold on to them for dear life.

"Shouldn't you be at work?" I ask Selah, grabbing her by the shoulders.

She shrugs nonchalantly, giving me an innocent smile, and I can't help but feel grateful for having her as a friend.

My eyes snap to Ares, who's taking the cake from Nanna's hands.

"And you?" I press my lips tightly, barely keeping in the grin that fights to break free on my face.

He shifts his body weight from one leg to another, tightening his grip on the cake as his eyes soften on me before he talks. "I'm always home for your birthday."

CHAPTER FOURTEEN

ARES

I wouldn't miss her birthday for anything in the world.

She bites the inside of her cheek, building a perfect image of someone simply trying to fight a smile—which is credible enough for others to believe. But to me, it's clear there's another reason for that. I know Blaise better than my own reflection. She's nervous about something.

My eyes are drawn to hers, and they tell me all I need to know. Blaise swallows, well aware her theatrics don't work on me.

After one more beat of silence, her armor starts to shatter. I turn around to switch the lights on, then make my way to the kitchen.

Blaise is happy to see us, that's for sure. It's the tracks of sadness betraying her that I'm worried about. She had tears dried on her cheeks before Catherine even started singing.

And that's why I needed to leave the room. Because seeing her cry... does something to me.

Knowing I have to recollect myself, I decide to cut the cake and take it to the living room.

Footsteps follow close behind, and it's weird, but I know it's her. She closes the door after us, her uneven breaths hanging heavy in the quiet room.

"I'm glad you came," she says softly.

I place the cake on the table, inhaling a deep breath. My body rotates toward her, and there has to be something on my face because her cheeks are now painted in a light shade of pink.

Without thinking it through, I close the distance between us and tower over her as she takes two steps back out of instinct. It does nothing but pin her on the door, offering me a sweet proximity.

My hand settles next to her head, the other scratching at my chin.

When I speak, she avoids my gaze. "Why were you crying?" I ask, my jaw twitching so hard it could pop.

Blaise takes a gulp of air, a spark of indefinable emotion reflecting in her pupils. Even the smile she was wearing loosens a little.

"What do you mean? I always cry." This new tug of her lips is forced.

My head drops between my shoulders.

There's no birthday Blaise won't cry on, but she's not telling me anything about the *why*. All I get is her coming home with tears dried on her cheeks, then acting like it didn't even happen.

That pisses me the fuck off.

"Do you not trust me?" I breathe out and look at her straight in the eyes. "Is that why you're not telling me?"

Blaise places a hand on my chest, gazing up at me, sympathy blazing over her features. "No." She shakes her head. "Of course not."

The control slips between my fingers, and I lower the palm I had on the door, putting it behind her ear instead. I could lean down just a bit... It would be more than enough to crash the distance between our lips.

So close.

My thumb brushes over her cheekbone. "Okay," I say when I get out of my own mind.

She flashes me a genuine smile. One that feels so fucking good to see.

"At least is it safe wherever you're going?" I watch her from under my eyebrows.

Blaise nods her head, and then a knock on the door interrupts us. I take a step back, and she goes behind me to cut the cake and put it on plates.

Selah appears from behind the door, the smile that was on her face earlier brushed away. "Oh." She stops short, her eyes darting from her friend to me.

Before she can say anything else, Blaise gives her a

few slices of cake and drags her to the living room. I walk after them, and we all sit down to eat.

They chat and laugh, but I can't do anything else but concentrate on Blaise.

Does Selah know where she's going? I hope so. The thought would lift a shit ton of weight off my shoulders. She should talk to someone, even if that person isn't me.

"You look like you're getting stronger and stronger with each day, Catherine." Selah compliments her with a warm smile.

Once everyone's done eating, August disappears into the hallway and comes back a second later with a box between his hands.

"Is that for me?" Blaise asks, acting surprised.

Her eyes widen at the gift between my brother's palms, roaming all over the red wrapping paper. He cracks a laugh and holds it out to her. Blaise snatches it from his grip, giggling.

I catch her throwing me a quick glance before thick, black lashes lower over her eyes as she struggles to keep her excitement in. Shaky hands fight to open the package, and when she actually manages to get to the actual gifts, she pauses, then glances up at her grandmother, eyes shining as she takes out three little boxes.

Catherine looks at my brother and then at me. I don't react, not wanting to give her the wrong impression. I didn't buy her anything.

"Why so many?" Blaise questions.

"Come on, open them." Selah nudges her shoulder. "I want to see what's inside."

Blaise laughs and unpacks the first one. Her mouth automatically parts open when she sees the thick bracelet with the initials ABA accompanying it. The next that follows is a necklace.

I don't know what's in the last one. August refused to tell me anything about it, mentioning something about wanting to surprise me too. The only thing I know is that it's for me.

Blaise takes a ring between her small fingers. A sharp breath escapes me, and when they both peer up at me, I avoid their gazes.

Because I fucking like it.

My hands are full of rings, and my brother knew that is something I would wear.

"Wait." Her brows draw together, and her lips pout. "This one doesn't have ABA written on it." She twists it between her fingers, lost in deep thought.

When we were twelve, Blaise gifted each one of us a necklace with ABA—Ares, Blaise, August—written on it. Not long after, she lost hers and was devastated. August and I decided not to wear ours anymore if she didn't have it. There was no point. I was only wearing it for her because she would've cried if I said no anyway.

"Look inside," he guides her.

She puts the boxes down and lays the jewelry on her palm.

"Let me guess," she starts, sobering. "Necklace for me, bracelet for... you." She points her finger at August, and he nods. "Ring for him." A big smile settles on her face as she hands it to me.

"Exactly." He grins, threading his fingers through his hair.

"Thank you," Blaise whispers and hugs August tightly.

He pats her on the back, faking a choking sound. "Strangling me is not a way to thank me, but I'll take it."

Blaise laughs and smacks his arm, then stands up, arms open to me. I stop her before she has the chance to hug me with a raise of my palm. She halts in her tracks, studying my face unhurriedly, feature by feature.

"I had nothing to do with it."

"Oh." Her mouth sets into a hard line, and a flash of disappointment takes over.

Fuck, that upset her.

She sits down, plastering a smile on her face as she looks down at the necklace in her palm. "It's gorgeous," she says, running her thumb over it.

I sigh, studying the way her face drops into a pool at her feet, and knowing I'm the one who let her down makes me feel sick to my stomach.

For the second time today, I try to get her attention. My eyes are screaming for her to look at me, to let me console her, but she covers her ears from my pleadings, ignoring me.

I let my back slump to the backrest of the couch as silence surrounds us.

Selah helps Blaise put her gift on, then takes out a small bag from under the table, separating the chairs from the couch.

"My turn."

I've been on her roof by myself for twenty minutes now, watching how the night settles, the moon hanging low in the sky.

Guilt spirals through me, and I can't stop thinking that maybe I should've given her the gift instead of waiting for a moment alone with her. Now, she might not even want to see me, and it's only fair, but everything is arranged already. There's no going back, so I might as well try.

What I got is for her and her only, not for everyone else to see. It's selfish, I know, but when it comes to Blaise, I can't help it. I *need* to be selfish.

I want the happiness she's going through in that moment to be mine. I don't want to share it with anyone else. Not my brother. Not Selah. Not even Catherine.

My phone vibrates in my hands, taking me out of my own mind.

BLAISE
give me 5

It takes her longer than that, but I don't mind the extra time alone to put my thoughts in order.

Blaise is difficult to handle sometimes, and it's not a bad thing; it's just that it brings me into a situation I don't know how to escape from. Like today, when I managed to upset her by trying to keep my distance and not give the wrong impression. I did, though.

She thinks I didn't get her anything when I've planned to surprise her on the roof for weeks. And I don't blame her because now, looking back, I realize how that might've looked.

The window squeaks open when Blaise steps outside dressed in pink shorts that leave nothing to the imagination and a white T-shirt with no bra underneath. Her hair is tied in a bun, and I try to focus on that as she makes her way to me.

Blaise sits down next to me, dragging her knees to her chest and hugging them.

"Hi," she says, looking at the sky above us.

I smile at her cute ignorance. "Hey."

"Everything okay?" Blaise asks despite her being mad at me.

I turn my head a little, taking her features in: her small nose that turns up slightly at the end, high cheekbones, perfectly arched brows, and full lips that I like to see pouting.

She finally returns my gaze, chewing on her bottom lip.

"Yeah. I wanted to show you something," I tell her, looking down at the phone in my hands.

She doesn't say anything during the time I search through my photos and sits next to me in complete silence. When I find what I'm looking for, I hand her the device. Her eyes widen at me before she taps the play button, and the video starts running.

"Happy birthday, Blaise North. May all the inspiration come to you. A bird told me you're pretty talented." The woman smiles, and I do too, watching Blaise's eyes getting wider and wider. "I can't wait to read your book and see what that birdie was going on about."

Every time the video comes to an end, she replays it, and I enjoy seeing how she's entering her happy bubble.

Last summer, when Sylva West—Blaise's favorite author—had a signing event at Westnook, I asked her for a favor. It seems she remembered me when I sent her an email two weeks ago for the video.

She turns to me, an uncontrollable smile stretching on her face. "Pinch me?"

My mind wanders to her nipples that were poking through her shirt minutes ago.

Fuck, do not pinch her there.

Slowly, I let my hand fall down between her breasts,

barely touching her shirt before I nip the skin of her waist. She whimpers as her chest falls and rises with rapid breaths. I hold my exhale.

The only reason I tweak it harder is to sober out of this mood.

Blaise smiles. "What?" she asks like she still can't believe it. "How did you know she's my favorite author?"

"I know everything about you, Moon," I admit.

She swallows at that, and then her eyes drop to my lips. I clear my throat when I realize mine do the same and move back to her eyes.

"There's something else," I say and tuck a strand of rebellious blonde hair behind her ear. Her breath quickens.

When I set the hair free, I take my hand away with a brush of my knuckles over her cheeks.

"Yeah?" she murmurs so low, I barely hear.

I nod. "Do you still want to get a tattoo?"

Her eyes snap at me so fast, I'm scared they'll roll in her head. She takes me by the shoulder, round and big green eyes watching me.

When Blaise was analyzing my tattoos a few months ago, she mentioned how much she'd like to have one. She never brought it up again, so she might refuse, but at least the video of Sylva was a total success. I think.

"Yes!" Her grin is wide, the corners of her mouth almost touching her ears. "Can I hug you?" she asks.

"I'm gonna hug you." She does it before I have time to protest.

I let out a sigh of relief.

Her arm circles my neck as her body pushes into mine. She's squeezing me harder, her intoxicating scent filling my nostrils. She stills there, and I find myself responding to her hug, my hand palming her silky, smooth hair.

"Did you make an appointment? When is it?" she asks when she removes herself from the embrace, eyes frantically looking from one of mine to the other.

"Tomorrow," I say and take a mental picture of her jaw falling to the ground.

CHAPTER FIFTEEN

ARES

"Already?" Blaise asks from the chair as she turns her attention to Killian, waiting for his confirmation.

In return, he gives her a nod and a low smile I don't appreciate plays on his lips. "You didn't ask for something big, you know?" He shrugs, changing his gloves.

I peer to the other side of Killian's studio, hoping to find something to focus on besides their conversation.

The first time I stepped in his salon was over six years ago, and it's like no one has laid a hand on it since then. It's still the same small place full of sketches, papers, and pens everywhere, along with splashes of his weird collection.

On a rustic table that has nothing to do with the rest of his decor, a stuffed cat watches me as a broken clock ticks on the wall behind her.

I fidget in my seat, looking away.

"That was fast," Blaise murmurs and my eyes find her again. She makes herself comfortable as he applies some after-care cream above her elbow.

Fast my ass.

The ten minutes he worked on her tattoo passed as painfully as a sunny day at work.

When I picked her up this morning, she refused to tell me what tattoo she was going to get, claiming it was a surprise. Since then, I've brainstormed anything she'd do on that part of her arm and came up empty-handed in the end.

Blaise asked me to keep my distance while she got it done, and no matter how many times I tried to peek up, the guy's hand was in the way, blocking my view.

It's small, that much I figured out.

And now I have to wait until Killian finishes telling her how to take care of it and all the boring stuff I could've told her. But I know it's important for her first tattoo to hear it from a professional. Having it infected is the last thing we need.

Blaise sits up and nods at what he's saying, but I'm more focused on getting a glimpse of it.

"It looks cool," he says, his gaze wandering all over her body the moment she stands up.

There's a chance I might be a bit too extra, but I don't give it a second thought before walking behind her and throwing Killian a glare. I didn't bring her here to have him gape at her like a horny animal. The only thing he has to do is his job.

He ignores me, continuing to talk to Blaise, and the twitch in my jaw increases.

Fuck this guy.

Just because I can, I throw my arm over her shoulders. "Your money's on the counter," I tell him and gently tug Blaise's elbow towards the exit.

She turns to Killian, and I swear she's giving him an apologetic smile as she speaks. "Thank you again."

We exit his studio and stop face-to-face. There's no way I can wait any longer to see the ink on her skin. She drove me crazy with all the teasing, and now it's time to see what all that was about.

Blaise gives me a frown, then hugs herself, probably bothered by my attitude. It's on her if she didn't see the way he was looking at her. Or maybe she liked it.

"Can I see it now?" I ask to change the course of my thoughts and gently grab her hand in mine.

Her eyebrows slowly ease the tension, and a smile takes over, laugh lines stretching around her eyes. I turn her hand around as she bites her bottom lip in excitement, barely standing still.

A swallow passes tightly in my throat, freezing my bones in place.

She notices the shift right away because when I look at her, her brows are knitted, and her lips are a little more plumped than usual. Her eyes travel over me as I do the same, trying to figure her out.

Why would she tattoo this?

The ink embedded into her skin is the most significant thing in this world for me. It's what, many times, kept me going, giving me the fuel I didn't know I needed. It's what now is part of both of us.

"You don't like it?" She searches my eyes, but I'm too busy tracing my finger around it.

Do I like it?

I fucking love it.

My finger trembles on her arm, taking in the meaning behind this.

Seeing it there makes me feel like I'm forever marked on her. And I don't know why, but the thought burns deep in my chest.

A single etching of a tiny moon, and it's the most incredible thing I've ever seen.

"It's fucking epic, Moon."

At that, we make eye contact once again, both of us smiling like fools. I slowly let my grip fall down her hand, not once interrupting the touch. Her breath quickens, green eyes staring deep inside my soul.

"Where did you get the idea from?" I murmur, playing with the tip of her fingers without taking my gaze off her.

Blaise opens her mouth once, but nothing comes out. "I told you I'd only get something that's meaningful to me," she murmurs, her eyes not leaving mine as I try to find the right words.

Her arms circle around my waist, and she hugs me tightly, invading my space with her scent. I breathe her in and let her squeeze the shit out of me as I kiss her head.

Because the feeling of her hug feels unreal.

"It's meaningful for me, too," I whisper in her hair as I wrap my hands around her.

She inhales sharply, then removes herself from the hug. "Can't wait to see what Nanna and August think." She claps her hands together, the corner of her mouth rising.

I laugh. "Come on."

We get in the car, and for half of the ride, Blaise listens to the radio, singing loudly until she gets bored and starts running a marathon with her words, clearly nervous about showing the tattoo to August and Catherine.

"It didn't hurt at all." She shakes her head at herself, looking out of the window. "I barely felt it. And he got it done so quickly. When are we going back?" She turns to me, and I can't help but crack a laugh.

"Not too soon if he continues to look at you that way," I joke.

Not really.

I steal a glance at her from the corner of my eye,

noticing the wide grin on her face. "I don't know, he was fine."

It's clear she's messing with me, but I still bite.

I snort. "You know laser tattoo removal is a thing?"

Blaise flips me off, laughing when we park in front of the house.

"Let's go to your place, and then we can all spend some time with Nanna." She gets out, leaving me behind, but I quickly catch up.

I open the door for her, and she runs to the living room, once again forgetting about me and about taking her shoes off. After I put mine by the front door, I join my brother and her.

"Close your eyes," she tells August, who's on the phone.

He looks at me, silently asking for answers, and then his gaze flicks back to Blaise.

"I'll call you back," August says to whoever is on the phone with him, slowly putting it on the table. "Don't hit me in the balls, alright?" he jokes but obeys.

As soon as his eyelids are closed, Blaise turns around, facing me. Her eyes are squinted from how hard she's smiling, barely holding her excitement in as she tells him to look. I stand there, hands in my pockets, a smirk on my lips.

My brother gets closer, trying to get a better view. His mouth parts open. "Holy shit, you really did it."

At that, Blaise quickly turns back to him. "What do you mean?"

"I could've sworn you were going to chicken out." He laughs, turning her around to look at it again.

"Well, you were wrong." She covers her chest with her arms but still lets him see.

"There's a difference between wanting something and actually doing it, but this looks so, so good, Blaise. I'm not even kidding."

I let the two of them be and sit down on the couch. As I lower my legs, his phone on the table lights up with a notification I would've rather not seen.

The world stops around me, tension weighing hard on my temples as the only sound in my ears is the sporadic beat of my heart.

Boom. Boom. Boom.

The temperature in the room increases by a hundred degrees. It's so hot, I can barely breathe. My body shakes with anger, and for the first time in my life, I don't know how to control it. It's escalating at such a fast speed that I don't have time to comprehend what I'm doing. Or come to my senses and stop.

So, instead of punching my brother like I'd like to, I walk away, clenching my fists while imagining it's his head I'm crushing between them.

CHAPTER SIXTEEN

BLAISE

If there's something I want to say, it's swallowed by the sudden shift in the room. It's almost palpable, raising hairs on my arms as steps edge near me.

Both August and I stop talking, words long forgotten in the back of our minds.

A cold chill runs down my spine as August's eyes squint a few inches above my head. I can only guess it's Ares who caused this change in the air, and judging by the look on his brother's face, he knows it too.

Whatever the hell just happened is serious.

For some reason, I don't dare to glance behind me until Ares passes me, and when I do, the deadly stare in his eyes catches August in a tight grip.

"Ares." August's voice lacks the usual confidence, and it's replaced with a shaky exhale.

The way he says his name is like a guilty call for

forgiveness. His tongue clicks over the end of the word, content there's no good explanation for whatever just swept between them.

Ares walks the stairs, ignoring him. To me, the disappointment and fueled anger in his eyes express everything August needs to know.

Our heads are tilted towards where he disappears, and we break from the trance the moment his door closes shut.

"What happened?" I whisper-shout, kind of thrown off by this entire silent interaction.

"Go talk to him," he murmurs, massaging his temples.

I like to think I know Ares better than the majority of people, and it's clear as day he doesn't want to talk to anyone.

Since he was a boy, Ares'd lock himself in his room rather than feed an argument and lose his temper.

I always liked that about him. The control he holds is sometimes scary, but most of the time, I know to appreciate the way he handles things. It's obvious he's fuming with anger, yet he chooses not to let anyone be the victim of his rage, no matter what they do. That takes a lot.

He and August will talk this out eventually. They always do.

My head shakes before I even get the words out to refuse. "He's too pissed right now."

"Go." He nudges my elbow, forcing me to take a few steps towards the staircase. "He needs someone."

"What happened?" I demand, cornering him in the search for answers.

August certainly knows how much his brother hates unwanted attention, and the fact that he's pushing me to step over that boundary only confirms the severity of the situation.

There's only one answer to this: he fucked it up badly.

He turns his back to me and heads to the kitchen. "He'll tell you if he wants to."

Hah.

Then, I already know I'm going there only to come back empty-handed.

I follow him, throwing my hands next to my body. "Why can't you tell me so I know what to help him with if he really needs me?"

"For fuck's sake, Blaise. Just go." August pushes me away from him.

God, he's insistent.

It wouldn't hurt me just to give it a shot. Right?

I sigh, dropping my shoulders. "Fine, but you owe me," I tell him before whirling on my toes and taking the stairs one by one.

That's a lie. No one would owe me anything for being with Ares.

It's clear as day I'm not walking to him right now

just because August told me to. I'm going because a part of me wants to be there for him, even though there might be a huge chance he doesn't.

Either way, I'm doing what my heart is telling me to do: be there for him.

I release a breath before laying a hand on the doorknob and twisting it open.

Ares is sprawled out on the bed, vacant eyes avoiding me as I step closer and take a seat next to him. His left arm stretches behind his head, playing the role of a pillow.

Despite the heavy air filling the room, Ares still sends a sense of calm through me. And it appears to be so effortless I'm starting to ask myself if it's a natural reaction to him.

My eyes travel from the folded arms in my lap to the loose curls resting on Ares's wrinkled forehead.

I remove one with the tip of my finger. "What happened?"

He throws me a look that says I should know better than to ask, but I shrug it away.

This is who we are—who we've always been. We share everythings and nothings, we have silent conversations, and we always look out for each other. Our friendship never gets to know what a secret is. We're transparent like that.

What about Tamara?

"You know, I remember when you guys had your

first fight." I laugh at the memory and push the Tamara thought away. Ares's gaze moves on me, and I call it a victory. "You were running in the garden, and I was standing in your way. One of you knocked me down, mostly because I was clumsy—still am—and you just couldn't stop throwing the guilt at each other. It was—" Ares sits up, and I swallow my words at the sudden shift.

He doesn't waste any time, taking advantage by catching me off guard, and before I get the chance to comprehend what's happening, warm lips touch mine.

It lasts no more than two seconds, but somehow, it's enough to make me feel like I'm fifteen again, sitting on my rooftop mere moments before my heart was broken.

Only now it's worse because we're not just two kids who have no clue what they're doing anymore.

"What was that?" I ask, resisting the urge to touch my lips.

Deep down, I hate myself for letting it get to me. If anything, it proves I never actually got over it, which hits me like a goddamn wrecking ball.

My stomach twists in knots, making it hard to breathe, and when Ares gives me that look I know too well, it simply stops.

"Making you shut up," he says coldly in a voice I can't recognize.

A loud exhale shudders out of me, and I don't know why, but I don't leave right away like my gut is telling me to do. I stay there, glancing from one eye of his to the other as if that will give me the answer I'm looking for.

Please, tell me you're not serious, I beg with my gaze.

Ares stays still as a statue, dark eyes distancing me with every second passing. When I'm certain he won't let me breakthrough, I give him what he wants.

I walk away, slamming the door on my way out.

Come after me. Don't let me go.

For a few moments, I wait in front of his room, hoping to hear steps coming as my breath evens.

I don't.

All this time, I took Ares's age as an excuse for our kiss and the way he handled things. I found it in me to forgive him, even though he was the person I was expecting the least to hurt me.

He was only seventeen, I kept telling myself.

What's the reason now?

I'm twenty-one; he's twenty-three. I thought we were adults in charge of their own feelings, capable of making decisions that wouldn't hurt either of us.

Turns out I was wrong.

When I get downstairs, I don't bother glancing in August's direction, I just aim directly for the door.

"What's wrong?" he asks, and I stop.

"You two can handle your own shit," I say, conscious I'm overreacting. But no one knows how much a kiss means to me, except for him.

He doesn't get the chance to reply because I don't stop until I'm locked up in my room.

Ares used my weaknesses for kisses to his advantage, knowing it would freak me out and silence me. The way he did it was just... It's not something to do when you care about someone.

Before kissing Ares, the only man who showed me affection was Dad. He used to tell me the guy who'd someday get what was his has to be the guy I'm marrying. Not because he was a strict father but because he wanted me to have the kind of love he and Mom had. And believe it or not, that has stuck with me to this day.

My phone buzzes in my pants, and when I take it out, it lights up with a message from Selah. I release a relieved breath, eager to talk to her and get all of this off my chest. I have to calm down before spending some time with Nanna.

I dial her number and throw myself onto the bed.

"Heya," she replies quickly. "I'm washing the dishes right now, but I need to see your tattoo once I'm done. How was it?"

"Freaking great," I mutter, and the background noise on her end disappears. "Until we got home. Ares and August had a weird and silent argument."

"Weird, silent argument? Tell me more."

With a sigh, I tell her everything that happened today, from the experience of getting my first tattoo to how Ares kissed me to make me shut up and how I left like a bat straight out of hell.

"He kissed you?!"

"Yeah." I breathe out, not knowing what to say anymore.

"How was it?" she asks, and I can hear the smile in her voice.

I sink my face into the blanket and talk that way, not caring if she can make out what I say or not. "Are you seriously asking me how the kiss was?"

"Well..." She pauses. "Yeah."

Turning on my back, I look at the ceiling and exhale harshly. "It was more like a peck."

"No tongue?"

"No tongue."

She laughs. "Ares needs to step up his game and watch more romance movies because when a guy kisses a girl to make her shut up, he usually doesn't stop there."

CHAPTER SEVENTEEN

ARES

I knock on the window, a tight feeling tugging at my chest as I replay her reaction in my head.

There's no way I can put into words what she made me feel with a single look. Her not bursting out in rage, throwing things, or making sure I understood how pissed she was at me only confirmed how badly I messed it up.

Blaise's silence was so loud. She stared down at me like I couldn't disappoint her more than I did. And that hurt like a motherfucker.

When I realize she won't open her window, I knock harder, the patience in my veins slowly running out.

It's clear she heard me. She's just being stubborn, and while she has every right to, it doesn't mean I want any less to talk to her.

"Blaise." I wait a couple of seconds before shouting,

not giving a shit if anyone can hear me. "Blaise, open the fucking window."

A part of me thinks I should've stayed in bed, not giving a fuck if she's pissed or not. But I can't. This isn't who we are. We come to each other when we have problems, even if we're the ones causing them.

Kissing her like that was a dick move, but at that moment, her lips were moving at such a high speed that they were the only thing I saw. It's weird because it was more like a natural decision. I didn't even think twice about doing it before smacking my lips to hers.

"Blaise North," I yell. This time louder.

At this point, I think it's better to head downstairs and enter the house, but there's a muffling sound in the room, so I decide to wait a little before doing that.

She finally opens her window, hair free on her back as my eyes automatically roam over her shape. Blaise is wearing her usual pajamas, but they do nothing more than distract me, tightening against every curve of her tempting body.

I know I could go on watching her for hours without a single ounce of guilt in my chest. Yet I avert my gaze from her and step into the room the moment she lets me.

The window closes behind me before she speaks. "What?!"

When sexy, angry eyes widen on me, I find myself struggling to get a hold of the situation, especially because her arms fold over her breasts, giving them a natural lift that's pretty fucking hard to ignore.

She clears her throat, not once feeling shy about my obvious gaping.

"What?" I ask, placing my hands in my jeans pockets, mostly because I forget what she previously said.

It's a bit stupid if you think about it, but I also enjoy playing with her. She's so easy to piss off, and I think I'm doing it only to prove myself we can still regain some sense of normalcy after what happened between us. That I didn't fuck it up entirely.

"What do you mean, *what*? I just asked you that! You can't reply to a question I asked with the same question." She raises her hands in the air, then lets them flop back on her legs.

I crack a laugh at her tirade and the speed she's talking out, somehow at peace with how familiar this Blaise is to me.

She's the kind of girl who will throw in a rant when you least need it, and in the end, she'll make you ask for more because the silence afterward feels... wrong.

Whenever Blaise isn't with me, I unconsciously search for some background noise to keep me sane. Silence used to be the thing I treasured the most. Now, when I'm surrounded by it, I'm close to opening our chats and playing one of her voice messages just to get rid of the weird feeling.

I've done it a couple of times, and it freaks me the fuck out how much it helps.

Her eyes widen at me. "Look at him. He has the nerve to laugh at me."

It's difficult to explain how I know this is all an act of hers, trying to induce feelings she doesn't really have. There's nothing she'd love more than to hate me in this moment, but what she wants, it's far away from the truth.

Still, I'm aware I hurt her.

I take a step forward, not liking the distance between us. "I'm *so* sorry, Moon," I admit, letting my shoulders drop.

"You're not." Blaise hugs herself, staring me down as she taps her foot on the floor.

She has every right to doubt me. That doesn't mean the ache inside my chest stings any less at the thought, and because I don't know what else to say to have her trust me, I walk on the safe path.

I sigh, then thread a hand through my hair. "Do I ever say things without meaning them?"

We both know I never do. I share very little of what I actually think, and when I do, I make sure it's honest.

We stand in silence for a moment. Blaise's eyes roam all over my face, almost as if she's searching for a hidden reason behind my question. There isn't any besides wanting her to know I'm being genuine.

Her body visibly relaxes. "No."

A relieved breath falls past my lips. "Alright, then trust me when I say I'm sorry for hurting you," I say in a low voice, brushing my knuckles over the bare skin of her arm.

Blaise shivers under my touch, swallowing a lump in her throat. She inhales deeply, closing her eyes in an attempt to get control over her feelings. It's no surprise she can't, and I don't mind it because I'm not done with this conversation. Not now and certainly not until she understands my reasoning.

I open my mouth to say something, but she talks before I do.

"What happened between you and August?"

As if on cue at the mention of his name, my body tenses. Talking about August is the last thing I want.

"It's his mistake. He'll tell you," I reply, eager to get over this and be back to where we left off.

Blaise steps back from me, sitting down on the edge of the bed and rolling her eyes in her head. "He told me you'll tell me, but if you don't want to, that's fine. At least talk this out with him."

I nod, knowing later on, I'll have to sort things out with him, whether I want to or not. And while it might not seem like the best option at this moment, I'll come to my senses soon enough. I always do.

I take a seat too, and hook a finger under her chin, forcing Blaise to meet my glance. She gulps but looks me in the eye. This is so much better than having her look at the ground.

"But that doesn't mean I'll forgive him," I say, wanting to make this clear.

Her mouth sets into a hard line as she takes me in. It's clear that she doesn't like my answer, but I know I won't.

At least not yet.

"He's your brother," she whispers like that should change something.

I grind my teeth, feeling my pulse speeding.

That's the point. He is my brother. I trusted him with my life. And what did he do? Lied to me. He took my trust, threw it under a bus, then came to step on it like it was fucking nothing.

Blaise defending him makes it worse.

"Why the fuck are you taking his side?"

My tone is calm, utter betrayal finding its way through me. It's not right to feel like this, but I can't help it.

Her eyes widen as if I'm being stupid to ask her that. "Because he's like my little brother, Ares. I'll always be on your guys' side. No matter what."

I tilt my head, knowing full well I'm acting foolish. "It seems like you chose him this time."

Blaise rolls her eyes, hugging herself harder. "I did not. I just think no matter what he did, you should give him a chance to justify before deciding you're not forgiving him."

She looks so certain I should listen to her that a twisted part of me wants her on my side to show her how bad what he did was.

"He kept in touch with Tamara," I say and watch the way her brows rise. "He lied to my face when I asked him weeks ago if he heard from her. He said no."

Blaise smooths her hair down, her gaze pointed at the desk in front of her.

"When I went to sit down on the couch, he got a text from someone named Rick. But I know it was Tamara. She was saying how sorry she was for not replying to his message last week," I say with a breath.

"How do you know it was Tamara?" Blaise asks, peering at how our knees brush together.

"She called him *sunshine*," I tell her, and she nods her head, knowing as well as I do that August was always Tamara's little sunshine.

He could've just told me. It wasn't like I was going to lock him up in his room with no access to his phone so I could split them apart. With all the shit Tamara did, she's still his mother, and August not telling me anything only shows how little trust he has in me.

Of course, I wouldn't have been thrilled to know he'd kept in touch with her all this time and hid it from me, but in the end, it was his choice to make. Not mine. I would never stop him from seeing his fucking mom, no matter how cold my relationship with her is. I could've forgotten about it if his happiness was at cost because that's more important than anything else.

After all these years, Tamara still manages to fuck things up from a distance. It doesn't take a lot to realize it's her manipulative nature making her way between August and me, always finding ways to hurt me.

Every time I have the impression she's gone for good, she comes back like a plague.

I just need a goddamn break.

Our hands touch when I lift mine to shuffle it through my hair, and Blaise scratches her elbow, stealing a quick glance at me as she bites her cheek.

A smile sneaks its way on my face at her not so obvious way of making it well known she has something to say.

"Just say it," I encourage her when she keeps sighing dramatically.

She parts her lips open and closes them a few times before speaking. "Why would you kiss me, Ares?"

Blaise slides me a guarded look, releasing a sharp exhale through her open mouth in the wait for my answer.

My grin wipes off.

Why would I kiss her?

Because I thought about it often. Because I wanted to. Because I couldn't stop myself.

But I still used it against her.

"It was shitty of me," I admit, my head lowering between my shoulders.

"It was." She's eager to reply.

"I'm sor—"

She stops me with her hand in the air. "Don't tell me you're sorry you kissed me. It'll make it a lot worse."

Blaise climbs into the bed, tucking herself under the blanket and putting it on top of her head. "Turn off the light on your way out," she says, sniffling.

CHAPTER EIGHTEEN

BLAISE

As soon as the sound of a window clicking shut sneaks into my ears, I throw the blanket off my head, finally breathing properly since the moment Ares stepped into the room.

With my eyes closed, I stretch onto my back and inhale deeply.

It's hard to be mad at him, especially when I know he's so sincere and open with me, but saying he's sorry for hurting me is a completely different thing than being sorry for kissing me.

I couldn't let him finish the sentence. Not when it meant that nothing had changed since the first time our lips touched. That his feelings remain the same.

After that night, I learned to push our kiss far away in the back of my head so we could be ourselves around each other again without hatred or awkwardness between us. Of course, I was aware of its existence—it never stopped haunting my dreams and thoughts—but I acted like I forgot, and slowly started to believe it.

Today's event, though, only brought that to the surface.

Since I don't feel like going to sleep anymore, I decide to take a shower and sober up a bit from this mood. When my eyes peel open, I have to bite back the scream in my throat because the second option would involve waking up the entire neighborhood, including Nanna. Giving her a heart attack is the last thing I want.

"Sweet Jesus and Mother Teresa," I hiss, touching my heart like that would slow down the speed of its beating right now.

During my struggles to even my breathing, Ares sits down on the bed, utterly oblivious to how badly he scared me. And something tells me he doesn't give a shit about it either.

I do care. He was supposed to leave me alone instead of sticking by to make this even more embarrassing than it is.

"Why are you still here?" I grumble, then drop my arms in my lap after I sit up on my butt.

Being a bitch isn't my intention, but I can't stop the frustration from slipping into my voice. Ares made his point. I don't need to have him gape at me while I dissect everything he said.

He stays quiet and continues to watch me with

those deep eyes of his until it becomes *more*. He removes layers of me with his gaze, leaving me unarmed and with the impression I'm standing naked in front of him.

I'm not against it as long as he doesn't stop tracing paths on my skin with his eyes. It's oddly reassuring and calming.

"I'm mad at you," I tell him, just because I can't keep it to myself.

A faint smile stretches on his lips as if he was expecting it. "I know."

He knows, that's the problem. Ares knows me better than my reflection, inside out, flaws, and all. Yet...

"You don't kiss a girl to shut her up, and you especially don't apologize. No one should be sorry for kissing someone else. That's why, before doing it, you need to—"

"I'm not," he interrupts.

My heart stops beating, and my eyes blink under furrowed brows as I attempt to read him and find out if he truly means it or if I'm getting it wrong. But his face is as stern as a concrete wall.

Did he really say what I think he just said? Because if he's serious about this... It changes everything.

He has to feel sorry for me. There's no other explanation for the unexpected shift after all these years of denying his feelings.

Internally, I hit my chest, and my heart starts beating again. "I don't need your pity, Hart." I make a show of crossing my arms over my chest with a raise of the chin, then look away.

He snorts, tilting his head to the side. "Hart? Where did that come from?"

I shrug because I don't know either, but I'm too busy being mad at him to process anything else. Does he even realize him saying that is only making it worse?

"I'm not sorry for kissing you."

My eyes flash at him as I let his words sink in for the second time.

He's not regretting it now, but what about later? What if he wakes up the hope blooming in my chest, and when he decides he was wrong, it's too late for us?

Breaking what we have now would break me too, because I fought for our friendship to be like this—easy-going, honest, and true. Complicating it isn't on my checklist for the week.

I turn my back on him to signal the end of the conversation. I try not to think about how much of a bitch I am for ignoring his confession, but I know it's the right thing to do. We can't ruin everything again. I don't think we'll survive it this time if we do.

He places his hand on my back, and I move further away in the bed.

"Don't," I snap.

"Blaise," he murmurs.

I turn abruptly, propping up on my elbow, staring into his soul. "Don't say that to me, Ares. It's not fair.

You're only saying it because you *think* you feel something—just like you did when I was fifteen. You know I'm—"

"So let's do it right this time."

"Can you stop interrupting me every two seconds?" I say, but his last words echo in my mind. I squint at him. "What?"

He's goddamn serious about this, isn't he?

Ares sighs, then messes his hair with his fingers. "I said, let's do it right this time."

It's what I've wanted to hear from him for so long that it almost seems like an illusion made up in my head. Only it's not.

If we're not going to be honest with each other, we're having this conversation for nothing, so I let my doubts speak for me, being as transparent as possible. "The only way this could end is with you figuring out that I'm not what you want."

Ares stops for a second, beaming at me. "I think I spent too much time trying to convince myself that you're not what I want, Moon."

Hearing he wants me does something to me, heat gathering between my legs and a blush staining my cheeks.

He shakes his head, the little smile I love appearing on his lips. "Let's redo everything, starting with our first kiss."

A laugh I can't keep locked in slips past my lips.

Thankfully, it takes away some of the warm feeling buzzing in my body at his proposal and helps me back on my feet so I won't say yes with the next breath I take.

"You mean the one you pretended never happened?" I ask.

He doesn't know how hard it hurt to act like something didn't exist when it was consuming my existence. It was even more difficult to see how easy it was for him to forget it when I had dark circles under my eyes for weeks. My ranting disappeared, and still, he remained the same. Unaffected.

Ares sighs, and the muscles in his jaw flex, defining his cheeks sharper than usual. I look away once again, swallowing to untie the knot in my throat. Every time my eyes are set on him, it's painful to take them away.

Everything about Ares puts me under a spell I can't escape—I don't want to escape.

"I was a kid," he admits, his head tilting towards me a bit. "You were a kid. We know better now."

"You were seventeen," I whisper, casting a glance over him as his features soften. "Almost the same age August is now."

Ares's teeth tap against each other, his mouth setting into a straight line, and he rakes a hand through his loose spiral curls.

"I think you can find a way to forgive him," I say, taking advantage of his silence.

He sucks in a sharp breath. "Stop changing the subject, Moon."

Before he has the chance to say anything else, I drop back onto the bed, gawking at the ceiling. "What do you expect me to say?" I ask in a low tone.

Knuckles graze against mine, and then his fingers open my palm, tracing it afterward. An audible exhale fills the quietness in the room, and it takes me a second to realize it was mine, not his.

"It's not about what I expect you to say because if it was, it'd be you agreeing to start it over," he mutters, still playing with my hand. "But it's about what you want."

What do I want?

For the past weeks, the only thing I could think about was Ares.

I've always wanted him, but I got so used to not getting anything back that I simply pushed away every idea, every scenario, and every expectation that he'd reciprocate one day. My thoughts were buried deep.

Until now.

And there's no difference from how it was then. I still want him. Always have.

"Did you ever think about how it would've been if you stayed?" I question after I sit up, his hand slipping from mine.

He's quiet for a few beats. "Every single fucking day."

I nod and listen to our tangled breaths before

speaking again. "I do want this," I say and meet his raw, hungry eyes. "But I have one condition."

It might seem like a stupid one, but I'm not taking any risks, no matter how badly I want him. He can't have me wholly just yet.

"No kissing."

That's a solution to keep my feelings locked in. It's something that won't let me fall completely unarmed in his arms.

At that, his breathing stops. "You can't just ask me not to kiss you when that's exactly what I want to do right now."

His hand lifts, and he brushes his thumb over my bottom lip, my insides quivering under the touch. I inhale sharply and allow myself to enjoy the feeling before removing his palm.

"I'm not asking you to never kiss me. I'm asking you to wait until you're really serious about us. Until you're sure I'm what you want."

Ares shakes his head, then tilts it back as his tongue clicks against his teeth. "I hate that rule so fucking much right now," he murmurs.

I smile at him because I can easily relate to that when every ounce of me desires to have him. "Think of it as... safety measures."

The moment his eyes harden on me, I can practically hear thoughts roaming through his mind. "Why would you need those?"

Ares doesn't need me to explain it to him. He sees it all in my gaze and hates himself for the way I need to protect myself from him. I d, too.

A few minutes pass by. Minutes I keep swallowing like that would help my dry throat, with him clenching his fists like I've imagined him gripping my neck.

"Then what am I allowed to do?" he asks out of nowhere.

I shrug. "You can sneak into my bedroom tomorrow night and find out."

CHAPTER NINETEEN

ARES

I had to go through today's shift at Westnook in the company of a very determined and energetic Blaise, who made it her mission to convince me to fix things with August, and while her concern is highly appreciated, I need to step aside for a second before that happens.

She's right about calling his decision to lie to me a small mistake. That's why I didn't even attempt to argue with her, but it's more the *why* that I'm worried about.

Trust and honesty have always been essential for the two of us, so finding out he'd go behind my back like that has naturally been a surprise, but I know we'll figure it out like we always do.

Not right now, though.

Blaise and I walk into our kitchen, both of us stopping the moment we notice Dad and August at the table. They stop midway through the conversation I was too distracted to hear from the hallway, and a smile brightens on Dad's face when he sees us approaching.

"Pizza's still warm if you guys want a bite." He pushes the slices to the edge of the table before straightening to his feet and opening his arms to Blaise. "How long has it been since the last time I saw you?" Dad asks, taking a quick glance over her face. "I barely recognize you."

Blaise laughs and accepts his hug. "You're still pretty the same to me."

"With a bigger stomach," I joke, then drop on the chair in front of August's, not once peering his way.

Dad pats his stomach proudly after stepping away from the embrace he caught Blaise in. "How's Catherine?" His eyes soften as he sits down. "The boys told me."

Blaise takes the chair next to me, her body tensing in an instant at his question. "She has a hard time talking, but other than that, she's good."

The good part is that her condition is only getting better. From needing to have someone to feed her, she now gets to her own feet after the daily walks with Blaise. Progress is slow but still incredible.

"I'm sorry," Dad murmurs, the remorse reflecting in his voice. "Is there something I can do?" he asks, tilting his head, gray strands of hair sticking out as the sun washes over them through the window.

She glances at us, then back at him. "I think we got this, but thank you."

A sympathetic look takes over Dad's face, but he doesn't insist. He turns his attention back on us, squints his eyes, and darts them between August and me.

"Why are you two acting so weird?" he says after a few moments of silence.

It's always been a mystery to me how he can easily tell when something is wrong between August and me, even with no interaction on our part. Now that I'm thinking about it, that might be what gives us away.

My fingers drum on my knee under the table while I hold Dad's eyes without any intent to reply. August chooses to ignore him as well.

"Okay." He raises his shoulders, then cups his chin between his fingers. "I stopped by to see if you guys are up for dinner sometime soon?"

"Sure," August finally speaks for the first time since we got here, and I raise my brows without looking at him.

"Great." Dad stands up, but I interrupt him.

"You and Caroline can come here," I suggest because going out doesn't really delight me.

We don't need a fancy restaurant to meet. I'd choose privacy a thousand times above dressing nicely for the night and eating in an expensive place. We could sit on the couch with a movie on and order some takeaway, and the day would still end with happy faces.

Dad looks around the house that holds all of our memories, good or bad, and his expression flattens a little. I don't blame him, especially because the kitchen was Tamara's favorite place to throw things around or blow off some steam at the both of us when August was sleeping. "I think a change of scenery would be good."

Since he isn't looking, August takes advantage and acts like he's scratching his nose with his middle finger. I simply mouth back a "fuck you." Out of love.

"Right, boys?"

"Huh?" August glances at him.

"I was saying I'll text you the details, and you'll do your best to make Caroline feel welcome." He cocks his brows the same way I do but doesn't wait for our reply. "I have to go. Caroline went to some business in town, and I'll meet her there." Blaise tries to rise too, but Dad pats her on the back. "Don't bother."

August gets up to lead him out, and because Blaise can't let the chance slip away, her fingers wrap around my arm to get my attention. Interesting how she hasn't realized yet that when we're in the same room, she gets all my attention.

"Talk. To. Him," she whisper-shouts, eyebrows raised.

When the door clicks shut, indicating Dad's gone, I unfold her palm from me and stand up to walk upstairs. I get to twirl on my feet for a second before Blaise's arms turn me back to face her, a tiny fist clenching at my T-shirt.

"You have to," Blaise murmurs as a frown takes over her features the moment she registers the proximity between us. We're so close our noses touch.

Her cheeks are painted a light shade of pink when she catches herself stealing a glance at my lips, her grip slowly easing the material, and I lean down to her, a smirk stretching on my face. Blaise raises her chin up, which only brings us closer, creating the perfect distraction for her to forget about August.

"Want a taste?"

If possible, Blaise blushes even harder as she dips her chin into her chest, like she's embarrassed by my question, and seeks a place to hide away from me.

I tuck a finger under her jaw before placing my mouth next to her ear. "Never be ashamed for wanting me, Moon. Because I'm not."

I step back to give her some air, ignoring my pulsing cock, and as if on cue, August clears his throat behind us. I give her a reassuring smile, then turn to my brother, knowing that Blaise'll most likely hide behind me until the red in her cheeks disappears.

For some reason, I'm protective of that and enjoying that she's keeping it just for the two of us.

August runs his tongue along his teeth, gazing down at his legs. "Didn't mean to interrupt," he says, then looks at me with that stupid face of his I can't be mad at.

"You didn't interrupt anything," I tell him, then whirl on my legs to leave, but Blaise stops me once again, and I'm surprised to see she recovered this fast.

"Ares," Blaise practically begs.

I don't know what her voice tone does to me, but I fucking obey and rotate on my legs, even if I don't make a single move to talk about what happened. We just sit there, watching each other like fools.

Until he speaks. "You hate her."

He's saying I hate Tamara, but it's not even about that. It's true I *did* hate her when I was a child who knew nothing else than to embrace the fury beside the bruises all over his body. In time, though, that hatred consumed me until I was nothing left but a reckless boy who later on decided she didn't deserve his anger.

Because Tamara was feeding on it, she loved whenever I'd snap, turning into a mini-her—smashing things with every chance, screaming from the bottom of my lungs, doing everything a bad example would do. And since it meant she was right about how defective I was, she loved it more than anything in the world.

Now, after everything she did, I simply don't like or trust her. She's nothing more than a stranger to me.

I snort. "What I feel or don't feel doesn't give you any pretext to lie to me." It's beyond me how it doesn't hurt him as much as it hurts me.

"Can't you see why I didn't tell you?" he asks quietly. "You freaked out over a text."

Blaise is quiet. Having her next to me transmits a sense of calm through my body, and I cling to it. "What I can see is you not trusting me enough to tell the truth."

August sighs, treading his fingers through his hair as furious eyes watch me. If I knew saying that would piss him off that much, I would've kept my mouth shut. It's like the idea can't even filter through his head.

He doesn't say anything else, just steps back and walks away.

"Where are you going?" I ask. Just because we fought once, that doesn't mean I don't care about the idiot anymore.

August doesn't stop. "To clear my head."

A few moments later, I hear his car's door shutting close.

CHAPTER TWENTY

BLAISE

I need to tell them the truth.

It's the first thought that occurs to me the second I step out of their house. I know without a doubt it's the right thing to do because the unspoken words are already burning in my throat, making it clear the time has come.

With Ares being this shaken about August keeping in touch with their mother behind his back, it doesn't take a genius to realize how mad he'll be at me for doing far worse than his brother. I didn't just *talk* to her, I helped her do something without their knowledge, risking their trust for someone who did nothing to deserve it so far. Still, she succeeded in making me go her way.

Agreeing with her was a first mistake, but I won't let

Tamara take away what I have left or allow myself to take another wrong step.

With that decision cemented in mind, I walk into the house and take two stairs at once to my room, seeking the safe place in it. The moment my hand touches the doorknob, Nanna's low murmur passes through the hallway, calling me to her like she knows there's nothing more I want than to be alone now.

Well, she's clearly not eager to let me spend some time in the great company of myself.

Because there's no bone in me that could ever refuse Nanna—not in her current state or ever—I inhale a deep and much-needed breath before heading out to her room.

I find her lying on the bed, a long floral dress hugging her body as she rests her freshly washed hair on a pillow, eyeing me with no restraint.

"How was work?" It takes her a while to get the words out, but she smiles, the corner of her blue eyes wrinkling.

My chest hurts like every other time I have to face the disaster her stroke left behind, the pain and worries still etched on her features, almost like an echo of what happened. She's still a little pale, but I know better than not to be grateful for what I have, so I find myself smiling at her obvious progress, a spark of pride buzzing through me.

"Busy," I say because I desperately want to be

dismissed instead of having her pumping secrets out of me that will do nothing but increase her stress.

When she pats the seat next to her, I come to terms with the fact that I never really stood a chance.

Damn it.

She's going to suck the truth from me, and I avoid that happening as hard as I can. "No thanks. I need to shower."

She grimaces, not at all surprised. "Sit."

"I stink," I say in an attempt to convince her to let me go.

Nanna shoots me a look, and it takes a high level of willpower not to sigh, roll my eyes, or run in the opposite direction. I do as she asks, praying she can't smell my bullshit too.

"Now." She tilts her body enough to face me, taking the hands I let hang in the gap between my legs into her shaky palms. "What happened?"

The stroke woke me up to an ugly reality I didn't want to have to face so soon—that my time with her is limited—and I choose to tell her rather than hide behind my own hand, knowing when she isn't here, I'll regret it deeply.

Plus, she's very good at making me spill the beans. And everyone else, for the record.

So I tell her. Everything from the day Tamara appeared to the present day.

"Then Ares kissed me."

She gasps at that, her wrinkles tightening around the furrow of her brows, and her eyes flash at me. "Oh?"

"Well, if you're asking me if there was any tongue involved, there wasn't, but—"

"I don't think I want to hear the rest." His voice meets my ears in one painful second.

As if on command at his presence, my back arches, skin prickling at the sensation of his eyes on my body. It's no surprise my treacherous Nanna smiles at him with half of her mouth, always happy to see him.

I turn to him, too, taking in the way his shoulder is leaning on the doorframe, his ankles crossed. I swallow at the sight.

"Hi, Catherine." He gives her that boyish smile of his. "Can I steal her for a second?" He asks Nanna, but the question is directed at me.

My stomach sinks at the thought of everything we need to talk about, but I know it needs to be done sooner rather than later.

Nanna pinches my arm, and I sit up straight, nodding. "Yeah. Sure."

"You can keep her." She grabs the remote and turns up the volume, giggling like a five-year-old.

I roll my eyes at her, and Ares places a hand on the small of my back the moment I reach him, a smug look carved into his face. Before I can make a sarcastic remark, he speaks.

"Only if she lets me." Ares winks at Nanna, and we walk to the corridor.

He gently tugs on my elbow, and I follow the path his hand leads me to, standing face-to-face with a broad chest.

"Actually, I was wondering if we could talk in private?" he whispers.

"Yeah, let's go in my room." I look up at him, ready to whirl on my heels, but he stops me before I can.

"Let's go talk at my place instead. August just left." When he notices me hesitating because we could easily say what we have to say here, he continues. "Please."

Ares pleading isn't something I can refuse.

Goddamn it with those eyes of his.

When I go to kiss Nanna's forehead, she throws me a questionable gaze but lets me go without another word, probably knowing she'll get everything out of me the moment I get back.

We make our way in silence out of my house and into his, the conversation that's about to be happening hanging heavy on our shoulders.

I can feel he's nervous. I just don't know what could possibly make him feel this way. Or maybe that's my own uneasiness speaking.

Once we get into the living room, I throw myself on the couch and cross my arms over my chest. Ares doesn't bother to hurry as he comes from behind me with calm steps and then sits on the chair in front of me.

He exhales sharply, threading his fingers through his hair, and then big, dark eyes watch me, stripping me down to nothing but my secrets.

"Are you mad at me?" he asks, not even once moving his gaze off me.

"Mad?" I raise my brows and wait for him to nod before shaking my head. "Why would I be mad? Unhappy about not fixing things with August? Yes." His jaw ticks a bit, and I feel the urge to explain this further. "You shouldn't be worried about me being mad because the way you two handle your problems is none of my business. Not until one of you asks for my help, anyway."

Relief washes over his features, and he smiles brightly when he speaks. "You've always been the only one who could convince us to make peace."

It's true. No one could get these nut heads to come to an agreement—not even Court and especially not their mother—without their huge egos standing in the way, though I can say they are smaller now that they've grown up.

A smile stretches on my face at the thought, and I scan the man who only got bigger and bigger under my eyes with every passing year, unable to believe for a second how much he's changed.

There's no touch of the little boy left in him. That little kid was cold-hearted, quiet, and unfriendly, but I loved having the caring, lovable side of him when no one else could have it. The Ares standing in front of me now is so much different, and despite having nothing in common with his old self, he feels like *home*.

I take a deep breath, my expression faltering a little when my subconscious screams at me, not content with keeping the Tamara issue away any longer.

Ares notices the shift the second it happens, his scrutinizing eyes analyzing every depth of me.

"I... I have to tell you something too," I blurt so I won't change my mind.

He clears his throat, coming back from wherever he went inside the abyss of his mind. "Okay."

I swallow to gain up some courage, telling myself it's better to say something than stay quiet.

Honesty above anything else.

"The day Nanna had the stroke, I found Tamara in front of your house." Even if I see him inhaling deeply, he doesn't attempt to interrupt me. "I told her to go away, but she kept telling me about how badly she wanted to see you both, how she's doing well, and that she was two months sober."

Ares shakes his head, an expression full of disgust taking over his features. One that I know is not aimed at me.

"She was fucking with your head, Blaise."

"Maybe." I shrug, recalling how I thought the same. "But I told her she can't see you guys until she's sober for at least six months. I know it wasn't my right to send her away, but—"

He raises a hand to stop me. "No buts. We tried to explain it to her several times already. If any of us were in your place, we would've done the same. You did the *right* thing."

I glance at the window on my left and the sun shining through it. "For you, yes. For August, I don't know."

Because if he kept in touch with her after all this time and didn't say a thing to us, I'd say he would like to have her back.

Ares wipes his mouth, a loud sigh falling past it. I'm sure he thinks the same.

"She agreed after she made me promise I won't tell either of you about it." With that, his head snaps back up, looking at me. "She said she wanted to get better for you."

He cracks a laugh. More like a snort. "Bullshit."

"She's in rehab right now."

His jaw twitching, fists clenching, foot bouncing, Ares stares at me for so long that I think he'll get up and leave. "How could she afford it?" When I give him a shaky smile, his face twists in understanding. "Goddamn it, Blaise."

I laugh. "Let's just hope she'll stick to it."

"I don't want you throwing your money around for people that did nothing to deserve it." Ares stands up, messing his hair with his fingers. "Especially on her. Didn't you get used to her being always two months sober?" he asks, and it's hard not to agree with him.

"I did, but I also want to give her one last chance before I stop trying, and you can't blame me for that."

He would've done the same if this were about my mother, I'm sure. No matter what my relationship with her would've been, he would've wanted to help her because she's still my blood.

What I'm hoping is Tamara'll keep her word, spend six months in rehab, and come home to fix the mess she left behind.

If not... I might have to finally learn not to have this much faith in people anymore.

CHAPTER TWENTY-ONE

ARES

Blaise's big round eyes stare my way, a silent demand swimming through them. She's begging for my rage, almost as if she's expecting me to be flaming mad, and while in other circumstances I might've been, this isn't the case.

I know how hard she must've judged herself already for keeping this from me, so I won't put on her shoulders something that was never her fault.

The way she handled things makes me appreciate her more than ever. While August lied to me and waited to admit it until he had no other option, she hid it and told me the truth even after she was manipulated by Tamara.

That's a big fucking difference, but I'm also mature enough to know people can't react or deal with whatever life throws in their way in the same manner.

That doesn't mean August has any excuse for what he did. It means I can't blame him for not knowing how to manage a situation he's never found himself in before.

Because I can feel Blaise's worry increasing with every passing second of silence, I decide to spare her of it. "So, no tongue involved, but...?" I ask, wanting to step over Tamara's topic. One of my brows lifts in a cocky way, eager to draw a blush out of her and get an innocent smile in return.

Her shoulders shrug. "I guess you'll never find out."

It's a surprise not to face her crimson cheeks the moment I mention our kiss, and I find myself grinning at the sudden confident shift in her attitude.

That "no kissing" rule is fucking killing me now that her lips form a smile that begs to be kissed. Damn me for being the good guy who wants to respect her boundaries.

Blaise grazes her palms over the material of her jeans, sensing the change in the air when my eyes shamelessly tighten over every inch of her. The fingers on my knee squeeze, stopping themselves from reaching out and clenching around any of her sweet curves.

It's hard to resist the temptation when not only her body but also the heart beating in her chest lures me like a siren's call.

"Can I touch you?" I'm surprised my voice comes out so steady, camouflaging the impatience running through my veins, but I'm almost sure the white tips of my fingers gripping my legs give it away.

Her nod is quick to come, eyes flashing with pure lust. "Please," she croaks, and the sound makes my cock jolt in my pants.

I'm not even ashamed of the relieved breath that escapes me at the urgency in her voice, eager to give her what we both want. I get up to my feet and don't waste another second before picking her up in my arms.

Her legs wrap around my torso, securing themselves in a tight grip that does nothing but close the little proximity left between us. I grab a handful of her ass, pushing her into my dick, and her palms automatically find shelter on my shoulders as a moan echoes in the room.

"*Fuck*, you feel so good already, and I'm not even inside you." I sneak into the crease of Blaise's neck, inhaling her addictive scent. She tilts her head, responsive to the kisses I place on her skin. "Why didn't we do this sooner?"

It's a question that, now that I have her, will become a constant one to ask myself.

My hands encourage her to press harder, to do something with this unbearable pleasure I don't know how to resist, and she surprises me by grinding on my shaft.

I nibble on her neck, sucking it in a slow, painful move that sends shivers down my throbbing cock. My head empties when I think about how I could possibly name the way she makes me feel—close to losing my mind and snapping out of this world at any second.

My cock slides between the heat of her pussy, and her hips slow down a little before she speaks to me in a panted, sexy whisper, "Take me upstairs, Ares, or I'm going to come before you even get a taste of me." Blaise continues to move on me, her hand crawling from the back of my head to my hair.

Fuck.

The picture of my head between her legs, as I lick the juices rushing out of her, is enough to make me take the stairs, but with each slow step I walk toward my room, I fight to regain the control I know I'll need when she's sprawled out on my bed.

It's impossible to ignore the tremor in my legs, and I'm certain even if I wanted to go faster, I couldn't. Because that's how fucking bad I want her.

Blaise isn't great at helping me hold back before I rip her clothes apart and have her here in the middle of the staircase. Her nails scratch my back, sharp teeth catch my lobe the moment I give her the chance to, and she grinds on me faster, surely making the decision to come.

I let out a guttural growl before grabbing her hair and yanking her head back so she can look at me. With hooded and almost sleepy eyes, Blaise gives me a raise of her brow. I know she's enjoying this, and when I open my mouth to make a comment about it, she speaks first.

"If this is your way of torturing me, it's working, Ares." A frustrated moan falls past her lips, and then she buries her teeth into my skin.

"Torturing you wouldn't end up with you coming all over my face," I murmur, then open the door with my foot and close it behind us. I tuck one of her strands behind her ear, enjoying the drunk look on her face. "So fucking beautiful, Moon," I say, then trace the curves of her breasts with the tip of my finger. She shivers under the touch, palming my cock through my pants.

Such an inconvenience right now.

Because I decide against torturing us both, I walk the two steps to the bed and slowly lower our bodies onto it.

"Do you want to know what I was reading back at the hospital?" I ask, pressing my dick into her.

It's a challenge to keep my control right now, knowing I can touch her anywhere the same way I imagined many times. It's like, for the first time in ages, I can finally breathe properly. It's even better when she nods her head at me.

I take a second to watch her, to make sure that this isn't all in my imagination, that she's actually here, in my bed.

Blaise arches her back at the same time she bites on her bottom lip, and a smirk stretches on my lips as I recite and improvise a part of the chapter that I pictured doing with Blaise.

"He traces her silky skin with the top of his fingers, palm disappearing under her T-shirt and cupping one of her full breasts through the material of her bra. The only thing he can think about is getting rid of it." I continue doing exactly that, and the moment our gazes collide, I know I haven't been the only one touching myself with her in my mind.

Blaise lifts her body under me, forcing her center into my hips and quietly agreeing with the idea of taking clothes off her. When she's finally naked in front of me, I take a mental picture of it.

Her hand buries in my hair, fingers grabbing strands of it. "He teases her thighs with kisses," I say, kissing her thighs. "With his fingers." And I do, not once touching her where I know she wants me the most.

"Please," she begs again already, pushing her head into the blanket in the most sensual way that brings the valley of her breasts into view.

I grab her by the chin, forcing her to watch me as I speak. "This is how I'd torture you, and I can keep going like this for hours." I clench my jaw, tracing her wetness up and down with my finger. "I could write a thousand stories about worshiping you, and I'd never get bored of it, Moon."

As soon as the tip of my finger teases her insides, she whimpers, and her head falls back when I shove it inside, the motion making her breasts bounce. My finger twirls.

Blaise lowers her hand and puts it on top of mine, pushing it to go in deeper.

The urge to kiss the lips I can't stop thinking about is so dangerous that I stop myself from going for her nipples, deciding to twitch them between my fingers instead. Simultaneously, I thrust my finger in and out, her low moan meeting every pump.

The scent of her dripping pussy is what makes me finally take her clit in my mouth. Her taste is to fucking die for.

My tongue swirls over her heat, the speed of my fingers increasing until it's fast and deep enough. Her flavor makes my mouth water when I literally have it on my tongue, pleasure pulsing in my veins as I continue to eat her like my fucking favorite dessert.

With each sound of pleasure that slips past her lips, my dick gets harder and harder, only making it more painful to lie on my stomach.

She begins to clench around me, the moment she'll give in getting closer with every sweep of my tongue. Initially, her palms and toes curl on the bed, but then she grabs my hair in a death grip, hanging on it for dear life.

When she looks at me through hooded eyes, I almost come from that alone. Her eyes flutter, fighting to stay open as she pushes herself harder into me.

"Come for me, Moon," I say, mouth still on her.

Blaise's body shakes, and all she needs is one last

pump of my fingers until she soaks them wet in a bath of her juices. I can smell her arousal from here, and I still haven't removed my fingers.

Her breath comes out in soft pants, eyelids closed as she struggles to open them.

My plan was to get up to give her some space to get back to Earth, but she stops me, eyes still shut. "Do you have a condom?" There's a whimper when she says it, and never in my life did I think this question would be so fucking hot.

"Yeah," I stand up, looking down at her.

She opens her eyes, and while I was expecting her to be shy about being the only one naked between the both of us, a sexy smile forms on her lips. Blaise crawls to me, stopping on the edge of the bed.

It's *way* hotter than how I pictured it.

My cock throbs in my pants, and I give it a squeeze to release some of the tension there. Without breaking eye contact, she pulls the T-shirt over my head and unbuttons my jeans. And when she drops to her knees, her breasts bounce, stealing a groan from me. I pinch her nipple playfully before she raises her lips into a teasing smile in response to my touch.

For some reason, she chooses to keep my boxers on, her hot breath touching my dick through the material. I throw my head back, letting her lips size every inch of it, and I'm ashamed at how much pleasure is rippling through me from the innocent contact.

And for fuck's sake, she's not even touching me skin to skin, but I'm already so close to finishing it's fucking embarrassing.

"Fuck, Blaise." I groan, grabbing her ponytail, loving how it feels in my hand. "This hair of yours..."

I've imagined this so many times. Fantasized about her hair. About how it'd be to have it in my hand.

She giggles and without warning, takes my dick out, her palm covering only half and her mouth taking the rest of it like a fucking expert. Part of me loves it, and the other part wonders how much experience she's had doing exactly this, but I push the thought away.

My knees wobble when she wipes my tip with a long move of her tongue. I look down and find her looking directly into my eyes.

Fuck. Me.

I yank her hair, making her head fall back as her tongue is still out. My legs move half a step further, and I cover her throat with my dick in one quick move, taking it out as soon as she gags. She knows what she's doing, and she's so proud about it too by the glistening of her eyes.

"Get on the bed," I demand, not resisting any other minute without being inside her.

She sits up slowly, seductively, and her thumb reaches to swipe the wet corner of her mouth in the most lustful way. She brings it to my own, and I open it, letting her slide it inside, my tongue twirling around and sucking it.

"Sure, officer," Blaise teases, turning around.

I slap her ass. "Do you want me to handcuff you too?" I cock a brow, excitement running through my veins at the idea. The look she throws over her shoulders tells me she wouldn't mind it a bit.

Goddamn it.

After I fish a condom out of my drawer, I let her take a step forward before grabbing her by the waist and dragging her on top of me. My hands grab her ass, squeezing it until my fingers turn red. She grins, then lowers herself on top of me. She moves my head aside with her chin, going back to taunting my neck.

Her hand sneaks between us, takes my dick, and teases me by moving it up and down between her wet lips. She bites my skin, stroking me before licking my neck, then tightens her grip on my cock when she pushes it inside just a bit.

If having the tip of my dick at her entrance feels this good, I wonder how it'll feel to dip it all. Only one push and I could be fully inside her, with nothing between us.

Blaise lifts her head, watching me through dazed eyes, and I quickly tear the wrapping with my teeth, giving it to her before I do anything stupid. She takes it, raising her brow in challenge.

She lifts her butt, rolls it on me, and sits up on her knees with a confident glance my way.

"What do you want, Moon?" I ask.

"You," she whimpers, trying to lower herself on me, but I sink further into the bed.

"Tell me what you want me to do." My voice is demanding as I gently grab her throat with my hand.

She grabs the bottom part of my dick with her hand to keep it still while working herself on it from side to side, bumping her butt into my stomach.

Her head snaps to me, eyes full of lust. "I want you..." she starts, stopping from moving, and then she lowers herself just a bit, enough for my cock to feel her warmth. "To fuck me."

One sentence, one demand, and I'm done for.

I smirk and grab her neck in a tight grasp. "I'll fuck you until you scream loud enough for the entire neighborhood to hear."

CHAPTER TWENTY-TWO

BLAISE

A raspy groan brushes against my ear, and the firm grip around my neck tightens as goosebumps cover every inch of my skin. Ares enters me fully, his teeth grazing along the lobe of my ear in a gentle swipe. I instantly arch into him, seeking his warmth that somehow doesn't seem enough.

In reality, I'm glued to him, but my body needs more. *I* need more. He's too far away and at the same time so close I bet he can hear my thoughts.

I've lost count of how many times I went to sleep with this exact image in my head—us wrapped up in each other, barely containing our loud breaths—and yet I never anticipated the desperation I'm feeling right now.

Having him like this isn't enough. I want his heart and soul, and I want his scent with me every part of my day. I want to get through this beautiful moment faster, the wait being too much to bear, but at the same time, I want it to last forever.

What I don't want ever again is to live without *this*.

The hand around my throat flexes, every vein on my forehead pumping with adrenaline the second he pushes himself into me again, and I begin to ask myself how the hell it fits inside me. Ares thrusts in and out with slow movements, giving me enough time to adjust to his big size.

He trembles with me in his arms, catching my skin with his teeth while moving at a painfully slow speed.

"If you want me to scream, you have to let it go," I whisper, not liking the way he's holding back now that I got used to him.

I don't want him to do that. I want him all. I want to have him unleashed of any control.

He quickens his pace, but it's not enough. "You sure?"

"Yes," I moan when he puts me on my side and quickly places himself behind me, lifting one of my legs in the air and supporting it with his hand while slipping in and out of me. "Fuck me, Ares. I'm not made of glass."

He slams into me so roughly that I feel my toes curl, ready to give in to another orgasm. Ares drags me by my ponytail, my back arching in a way I never thought I'd be capable of, bringing his lips to my ear.

"I take it you like it rough," he murmurs, slapping my ass, and I let out the loudest cry of pleasure, biting it back from going louder when he moves to circle my clit. "You want everyone to hear what a dirty little girl you are, don't you?"

"Yes," I agree, loving the place I just arrived at.

His fingers work my clit, sending shivers through my body before he takes a good amount of my arousal and puts it on his dick. The only thing I know is that I've never been this full. His dick and the hand on my clit move in synchrony, chasing what's theirs.

No matter what he's doing, it feels like it's not sufficient, but at the same time, I can't handle it.

The release I've been dreaming about finally happens, and he doesn't even let me take a breath before he has me pinned on my back. Ares lifts both of my shaky legs in the air, grips them together by the ankles, and slams into me until there's no ounce of space between us. Not even air. Nothing.

He takes his hand away, then forces a gap between my legs that offers me a perfect view of him.

His curly hair is stuck to his forehead as dangerous eyes darken on me. I don't know what I look like, but by the expression on his face—like he's going to devour me —I think I look good.

I can't even keep my eyes open to fully understand what he's doing. My second orgasm isn't even over yet, and he's ready to build another with his words next.

"Look at me," he speaks in a husky voice, and God, I love that. He eases his pushes, and I groan in protest.

"Please," I beg, not recognizing my own voice, needy of more already.

"Keep your eyes on me." My eyes snap to his dick stretching my entrance. "Good girl." I can hear the smirk in his voice, and then he starts moving like he couldn't be buried deeper.

Our bodies move in tandem, roughly slamming against each other and taking away every rational thought from our minds. We become one, and the moment he finishes off in the condom inside me, a shiver runs down my spine. He stills, his hands gripping my breasts as a sensual groan slips past his lips. A low and pleased hum warms my blood at the ruthlessness of his clenched hands on me.

Ares sets my legs free and drops his head onto my chest, his breathing erratic.

I keep my eyes closed, waiting for our bodies to stop trembling. It finally happens after a few minutes, and when his weight disappears from on top of me, I try not to think about the loss of his warmth. I can hear him getting out of bed, throwing the condom into the trash, and a second later, he sits back down next to me.

He made my fantasies happen and more. Ares fed my appetite, and I don't think I'll ever get enough. Even now, as sore as I am, my clit throbs at the thought of having him inside me again.

I decide to calm the hell down and think about other things that are not sex-related. It's pretty hard with the smell of sex filling the air, but I manage to send my thoughts in another way.

When I feel the urge to snuggle into his chest and fall asleep to the rhythm of his beating heart, I regret ditching the idea of having him one more time.

Because it scares me.

My throat squeezes at the memory of his hand circling it, and heavy rocks weigh onto my body, stopping me from breathing. Everything smells like him. *I* smell like him.

I sit up, making the sudden decision to go home and distance myself. I look for my clothes, but I can't even concentrate on doing that with the feeling of his gaze on me. Ares stands up, and I try my best not to look over the tattoos on his beautiful, muscled chest.

"Why are you being weird?" he asks, putting his boxers on.

I'm still naked, with my back to him. "What do you mean?" I try to act clueless, and I fail miserably because of the hitched tone of my voice. For a second, I forget what I'm searching for and simply let my eyes wander over the floor.

I'm not weird, though. Am I?

"Did I do something wrong?" he asks, and I hate the guilt in his voice.

Did he do something wrong? No. That's the problem. He was tender but harsh, too. He was thoughtful but let go of his control, too. He was *perfect*.

And I'm already falling for a few stupid gestures that might get me hurt in the future.

It's only after I find my clothes and get dressed that I talk. "No, of course not."

He puts his T-shirt on. "Then..."

I peek at the door, eager to get out. "I need to take a shower. That's all."

His eyes squint as his mouth sets into a hard line. He points his hand at the other door in his room. "Use my bathroom."

The idea of washing myself with his shampoo and smelling like him for days delights me but freaks me out, too.

My shoulders drop, and I notice his features lowering. Ares runs a hand through his hair, tugging the ends a bit between his fingers. He walks further until our toes touch, and he's so close that every breath we take collides into a single one.

"I don't have any clothes here or anything," I whisper and peer at the ground.

A finger scoops my chin up, and that's all he needs to do because his eyes do the rest, begging me to *see* them.

"What happened?" he asks, tilting his head to get a better view of me, his brows furrowing.

Why does he have to act so... perfect?

I catch the inside of my cheek between my teeth, struggling to find the right words. But when he looks at me like that, no matter how many words there are, I forget them all. My mouth glues shut, and my mind empties.

"Do you want to leave?" Ares questions, moving his palm behind my ear as his thumb strokes my jawline.

With a shaky exhale, I close my eyes and lean into his touch. I shake my head, giving him honesty because that's what he deserves.

"Then stay," he mutters.

"I can't." I look at him, finding my voice in a whisper.

He frowns when I step back but doesn't say anything. I walk towards the door, and he stops me with a grip on my elbow before I get past him.

"Why can't you stay?" His eyes are nothing but gentle, burning every part of me with one single look.

I peek up at him with a small smile. "You know that I feel a lot, and I'm feeling too much right now."

CHAPTER TWENTY-THREE

ARES

I let her go and regret it as soon as I hear the door clicking shut, her footsteps echoing away from me and what we just shared.

My feet itch to chase after what's mine, to carry her back into my room and force her to talk about whatever happened in that head of hers, but my mind makes two connections I hate.

One, I know how she felt all those years ago when I left after our kiss, and two, she doesn't trust me either.

It's not like I gave her any reason to confide in me. Every time things got serious, I removed myself from the situation, thinking I was protecting her, when in reality, I was breaking her to the bones.

Blaise's choice to leave the moment feelings got too intense was her way of doing what she had to do—guard herself around me because I was the one to fuck it up when she handed me her heart on a silver platter.

Now I understand why I couldn't bring myself to kiss her when she told me I could do it only when I have feelings for her. And it's not because I don't have feelings for Blaise—I *always* have, no matter if they were innocent or not. It's because deep down, I knew that rule was meant to mirror the little trust she has in me.

It would've been so easy just to kiss her and pick it up from where we left off, and maybe if she didn't leave now, I would've. But there was a chance that doing it was a sign-up for failure and a replay of our past, something I'm not going to risk happening ever again.

In a twisted kind of way, I'm glad she left because, after this wake-up call, I know I have to do something about regaining the trust of the most important people in my life.

I reach for my phone on the nightstand to dial August but stop midway when the door to my room opens.

"Can we talk?" my brother asks from the doorframe.

His question releases some of the tension in my body, being a confirmation that he hates us fighting as much as I do. It also proves how mature he is, and my chest blooms with pride at the thought.

"Yeah." I lean my elbows on my knees. "Come in."

He walks in and takes a seat on the chair before clearing his throat. "I know I shouldn't have kept this from you—I'm sorry for that. It's just that I never hated Mom like you do." I huff, but he continues. "I know the bad stuff kind of outweighs the good now, and I won't try to make you forgive her, but I just wanted you to know why I talked to her."

Tamara's a great manipulator with toxicity ready to burn to ashes everything she touches, so I don't blame him for falling for her theatrics and lies. She's still his mother after all, and I have to give her credit for how believable she can be sometimes. She has fooled men older than August, so I don't think August's age determines his blind trust in her.

I warned him many times, but he needs to learn how she is on his own. And I'm not saying it as an act of irritation because he didn't listen to me. I'm saying it because that's how life works. We have to make mistakes and learn from them.

August doesn't remember a lot of the shit she did. I do. I remember when she broke an empty bottle of beer on my head because she couldn't find anything to drink and decided it was my fault. I remember how she used to act so innocently whenever my brother was home, but as soon as he left with Dad, she used me as a punching bag. I remember when she pushed me down the stairs, and I wanted to hit her so badly. But I couldn't bring myself to do it because if I did, I would've only been a male version of the woman I loathed so much at that time.

With August, she was showing her bright side, and

I'm glad he got to know his mom that way. Even so, an alcoholic can't be nice all the time.

He was too little to remember, but she got drunker than her usual limit, brought a man home, and fucked him in Dad's bedroom, next to ours. I gave August his headphones and let him listen to his favorite songs, stroking his hair with my fingers after taking my hearing aids out.

"I don't hate her," I say, knowing I have to clarify this for him. "Let's say I just saw past her façade, and I don't want anything to do with her anymore."

He sighs. "I just thought you'd freak out if you found out I was still keeping in touch with her."

I shake my head. "She's your *mother*. What I think shouldn't change what you feel about her." I stand up and look down at him. "And I would never stand between you two if that's what you want. Never." I place a hand on his shoulder. "Do you understand?"

August nods his head. "Yeah, I get it. It was stupid of me to think that way."

"Good." I give his back a light smack before returning to the edge of the bed.

"What's up with you and Blaise?" he asks like our previous conversation doesn't even exist.

I smirk. "That obvious?"

He cracks a laugh. "From *miles* away."

There's no point in hiding, so I tell him. "I think

we're still figuring out. We both want something, but it's hard with our history."

"Just kiss and make out, you know?" August jokes and snaps his fingers like that's all it takes.

We did make out. No kissing yet. I find that pretty hard to explain to him, so I leave it out.

"Is that what you're telling yourself whenever you're with a girl?" I cock a brow.

"No." He relaxes on the chair and puffs his chest out. "More of, like, shoot and go."

We both laugh and when the laughter fades, a calming feeling settles into the room. I don't like to be mad at him, to walk around the house like he isn't there, and I know that in this fight, August was the mature one.

"I'm glad we talked this out," I say, wanting him to know.

He nods and stands up, looking lighter than he did when he entered my room. "Me too." He smiles and walks toward the door but stops with his eyes locked on my trash. "And at least wrap that before you throw it in the trash."

CHAPTER TWENTY-FOUR

BLAISE

I finish telling Selah everything that happened, talking without taking a second to breathe or process if what I'm saying makes any sense.

When I was walking out of Ares's place, I texted her, and it literally took her three minutes on the clock to get here. Maybe it was my fault and the way I wrote the text to make it seem like it was a big emergency, but it feels good to have someone by my side.

"And he just let you run away?" Selah raises her brows at me, squirming on the edge of the bed in wait for my reply.

I nod, and she scoffs like that was the stupidest thing he could've done. "But I'm glad he didn't run after me."

Her face scrunches, and I know she's fighting with herself to not call me out for what she thinks is bullshit, but she manages to drop it for now. "How come?"

"Everything was..." I start in a sigh before stretching down on my bed, Selah joining me right after.

"Too much," she says at the same time I do, a smile growing on our faces as we stare at the ceiling.

"Look." Selah puts her head in her palm, staring at me while she speaks. "I know you're afraid to get hurt, but as far as I see, you're hurting yourself more by keeping him at arm's reach."

My heart sinks at the truth of her words, sad I'm staying away from someone it yearns to love. She's right. It is hurting me, but what about what's at stake? There's nothing I treasure more than what Ares and I have, and jumping with my head straight into the water would only show the exact opposite. I have to be careful with how things develop between us, with slow and sure steps that ensure we *will* be alright.

"Your thoughts are so loud. Get a hold of yourself, girl," my best friend jokes, getting back to sitting on her butt and most likely ready to give me a lecture. I don't move. "Just shoot your shot. If he isn't *the one*, at least you know you tried." She punches me lightly in the arm, and I laugh.

"It's not that simple." I shake my head, and I don't have to look at her to know she's not buying it for a second. At that, I sit up, too. "If it's that simple, tell me why you and Rhodes are not together."

In terms of friendship, she technically has no right to judge me about something she does herself or give me some advice she should be following as well. For years, Selah and Rhodes have been playing this cat-and-mouse game, running after each other but stopping the second they get too close.

She shoots me a look. "He's my boss, and besides our *completely platonic* love-hate relationship, there's nothing between us."

I crack a laugh. "Did I hear something about love?"

Selah groans and picks up one of my pillows, then throws it at my head. I don't bother shoving it away. "Fuck off."

After Selah left exactly three hours ago, I stepped into the shower and only came out when I was entirely soaked. I'm not sure how much time has passed since I got out, but I shouldn't still be wearing my robe or the wet towel on top of my head, and I certainly shouldn't stare at the phone clutched between my hands for this long.

The conversation with Ares is on display, but my fingers make no move to text him.

What should I say anyway? Something close to: *Hi, sorry for practically running right after we had sex. I was just protecting my feelings and didn't think about hurting you*? I type it and delete it right after.

A sigh falls past my lips as I swipe up and down through our chats like that'd magically strike the right words on the keyboard and eventually hit the send button. Then, three bubbles appear. I act on instinct—close the conversation, lock my phone, and throw it beside me like I wasn't just thinking about what to text him.

I pick it up two seconds later when it buzzes and try to hold my disappointment in when I see the text is from the wrong brother. I click on the chat with August's photo and read his message.

AUGUST

Dinner with Dad and Caroline next week. U still coming?

August barely texts me, so this catches me off guard. There's only one reason I can think of that might explain why he's sending me messages.

ME

Did your brother ask you to text me?

When he doesn't respond, I send another one.

ME

He did, didn't he?

Blue bubbles jump for the second time today, and I sit up straighter, waiting to see what he has to say. I see him disconnecting from the app, but he calls me right away. Of course, I pick up.

"He thought you needed some space and wanted me to check up on you," August murmurs.

Damn him for being so sweet and understanding about it.

I sigh into the speaker, hating that he's somehow right and wrong at the same time. Space is the last thing I think about when I'm with him. It's what he makes me feel that's making me ask for some distance.

It's weird how I wanted two parallel things at once. I wanted him to let me leave so I could calm down, but I was utterly disappointed when he let me go. He didn't text. He didn't knock on my window. Despite how many times I prayed before reaching his door that he'd get up, grab my elbow, and stop me, he didn't.

"We talked too," he says.

"I figured." Because if things weren't fixed, Ares would've never asked him to text me.

It's good that they clarified everything. They are brothers. They should be there for each other, not against each other.

"Why don't you come over?" he asks after a while.

Come over. Right.

"Who's asking? You or your brother?" I want to know if he wants me there before I go.

August is silent for a second, and then there's a

muffling sound before I hear his voice. "Both," Ares says, hanging up the phone.

I get rid of my robe and my towel, not bothering to dry my hair. I just put on some shorts, and when I think about what T-shirt to choose, my eyes wander to the white top. Knowing Ares could see my nipples through it is tempting.

I wonder if he'd like it.

No bra.

No nothing.

Instead of the white one, I choose the complete opposite and throw it over my head as I head toward the door. I tiptoe out of the house, not wanting to wake Nanna up. She gets up every morning at six and keeps telling me her brain is so old that it has a clock alarm on its own.

After taking my shoes off and rounding the corner of their hallway, I see Ares on the couch, stretched with a book in his hands. Curls fall over his features, his brows furrowing at the pages in front of him, and if I didn't know better, I'd say he doesn't even notice me.

August sits on the chair on the other side of the room, sketching on his iPad.

"What's up?" I ask, jumping over the couch to my usual spot.

August glides his pen onto the tablet one more time, then turns it off and offers me all his attention. Ares closes his book shut, putting it on the table as I take a deep breath in, ready to tell August about his mother, too since we are here.

Maybe for Ares I made the best decision to send her away, but I don't know if I can say the same thing about August. He still keeps in touch with Tamara, and maybe he would've loved to see his mother.

I look at August, my features softening. "I have to tell—"

"She told me the day you brought her to rehab. I know." I freeze. "It was nice of you to drive her there. Thank you."

Color me shocked.

No.

Pissed.

She had the nerve to ask me to keep it quiet until she gets out, but she ran straight to August and spilled the beans as soon as we met?

What a sneaky bitch.

This is Tamara we're talking about, and I still followed her request blindly like the fool I am. My mouth parts open, words struggling to come out of my mouth. "What?" I stand up, my eyes widening at him. "Why didn't you tell me?"

He lets out a sigh. "She didn't want Ares to know, and she was sure you'd tell him."

"She begged you not to tell us, but she told him right away." Ares laughs sarcastically, taking a curl that fell on his forehead.

"Wait, what?" August stands up, too.

"The fucking bitch," I whisper to myself, dropping back on the couch as I stare at the floor.

She pulled the "I want to get better for my kids" card, and I was stupid enough to believe her. I lied for her for months, fighting sleepless nights and ugly thoughts, and she betrayed me like what I did for her meant nothing.

"She played both of you like puppets on a string," Ares says while August is still in shock she made both of us hide everything from Ares with ease.

I don't know why this is even surprising for us anymore. This is what she's good at.

"I feel like an idiot." August finally talks, sitting back on his chair.

A laugh slips past my lips. "That makes two of us."

Ares walks to the kitchen and takes a bottle of water out of the fridge. "It's not your fault she knows how to lie."

It is my fault because I decided to trust someone who broke my trust countless times instead of doing what was right: telling the boys, or better, not sticking my nose into other people's business. Especially in hers when I knew, *I knew*, that she does nothing other than disappoint us every time she comes back. But I still did.

It's not even about being a good person anymore. It's about being naive enough to fall into a trap you fell for a thousand times before.

"Why do you think I never reply to her texts?" Ares asks and comes to sit next to me, directing the question at August.

He looks up at his brother, waiting for him to continue. Ares doesn't say anything, but August still stares at him and raises a brow in question.

Ares sighs. "Because of what's happening right now."

CHAPTER TWENTY-FIVE

BLAISE

The last few days slipped through my fingers as if time itself was in a hurry to pass.

Now that I finally wrote the last chapters of my novel, I sent it to Ares to see what he thinks about it since he's the expert. He should be able to read it this weekend, which makes me *so* nervous that I have to stop myself countless times from bugging him about it. I just have to be patient.

Right.

After finding out Tamara played us all on her fingers, Ares and I agreed transparency is important if we want this to work out. There wasn't much I needed to tell him about the reason I left because he knew it before I walked out of his room, but explaining it all over again freed me from some kind of weight and brought us even closer.

Ares can't keep his hands off me as much as I can't keep my hands off him. They are innocent touches but still present—at work, whenever he walks past me, whenever we hang out at his house, when he drives—and it's no secret I enjoy them the same way I enjoy a fresh breath of air.

He's charming, and it's getting harder and harder to be composed when I'm around him. It seems like every small action of his—a stolen glance, a smirk, a wink, anything that comes from him—is destined to drive me crazy.

A sigh falls past my lips as I stare at myself in the mirror, leaning my elbows on the edge of the sink.

Tonight is the night we're going to meet Court and Caroline for dinner, and for some reason, I'm a little bit nervous, though it has nothing to do with them. More with the man waiting for me outside.

My hair is tied into a bun, two strands falling over my cheeks, and a golden, silky dress barely touches my knees, opening towards the white stilettos covering my soles.

I look good.

After spraying on my favorite vanilla perfume and raising my chin up with one last look in the mirror, I leave my room in a hurry, knowing the boys are already at the doorstep.

Nanna forgets about the show she's watching, and

her eyes sparkle the moment she sees me. "You look gorgeous." She smiles, and her eyes do too.

While it's still difficult for her to talk, it's much better than it was before. Slowly having her back only taught me I need to appreciate everything I have while I have it and value every second like it's the last one.

"Thank you." I walk towards her and lean down to kiss her cheek.

She purrs happily. "Have Ares keep you warm." She points her fingers at me from the couch once I straighten my back and look down at her. "And have fun."

"I..." I open my mouth to say something about her mentioning Ares but change my mind. "You know what, I don't even want to ask."

"What?" She relaxes on the bed. "Do you think I'm blind? You're not even trying to hide it."

I laugh it away. "The one hundred degrees outside are going to keep me more than warm, Nanna." I kiss her one more time before walking downstairs and getting out of the house.

Ares's car is parked in front, and I take quick and small steps since the dress is pretty tight. I open the back door and get in, which immediately makes Ares look into the rearview mirror, smirking, hands on the steering wheel as I make myself comfortable in the middle. He drives onto the street, and August puts some music on before getting the air going.

"Look at you, all dressed up." I playfully slap their shoulders as they sit clad in nice T-shirts and jeans.

The look he shoots me through the mirror delivers the message very clearly that he's not happy about it, but it goes straight to my core. I clear my throat and focus on everything else but him because now is certainly not the time.

August turns back to me, looking down at my shoes and then back to my eyes. "Damn, Blaise. Looking hot tonight."

Ares's murderous glare snaps to his brother. I don't want to overanalyze his expression right now because my stupid mind considers it jealous. And I like it. *Too much.*

August chuckles, threading his fingers through his hair as he lies back on the seat. "Well, someone should tell her," he says calmly.

To that, Ares doesn't reply, but I know he's watching me. I can see from the corner of my eyes how his head slowly rises from time to time, checking me out all the way to the fancy restaurant.

We enter the parking lot, and it's pretty crowded, so Ares barely finds a spot in the back.

"Jesus, is Shakira here or something?" August asks while his brother is parking the car in a tight lot.

Ares kills the engine and gets out, closing the door after him calmly. While angry people would slam it, that's how he gets control, by not letting the anger dictate to him. And for some reason, that's extremely hot.

August throws me a look over his shoulder. I clear my throat, and we both follow Ares. He is standing in front of the car, hands in his jeans pockets, jaw twitching. My first instinct is to thread my fingers to his and lead us into the restaurant. Instead, I place a comforting hand on his back, and he nods as we all walk toward the entrance.

"He wasn't wrong, you know. You do look hot as hell," Ares whispers in my ear halfway to the restaurant, sending a shiver down my spine.

August opens the door for me, and we walk into Battello's, the loud chatter filling my ears. The first two steps I take inside are enough to make me certain I have never seen a room this full before. There's not even an empty chair.

We glance around, trying to figure out where Court is, but it's pretty difficult to find him in this madness. Ares stands next to me, his hand lingering close as his skin brushes mine like we're in a dance no one is leading yet. This time, I grab it in a gentle hold, giving it a squeeze to show him support.

A hostess finally comes, apologizing for the wait. The young girl leads us to the table where Court and Caroline are waiting, then places five menus on the table and murmurs another apology before leaving.

Caroline's smile radiates all over her face as she gets

up, arranging her skirt over her small bump in the process. While the boys say hi to their father, she comes to me, blue eyes sizing me with delight.

"I'm Caroline." And the corner of her mouth tugs up even more, if possible.

This woman is gorgeous. Green eyes, sharp cheeks, beautiful lips, and a body that every girl would envy having while being pregnant. She's dressed classily, and there's something about her I like. I can't put my finger on it quite yet because this is one of those moments when I have a feeling about a person, and I'll keep it until proven differently.

I smile warmly. "I'm Blaise."

"Blaise, what a wonderful name," she says as we slide together on the bench while the men sit across from us. "I heard you're a writer?" she asks, trying to make conversation.

"Yes, I actually just finished my last book not too long ago."

"I bet that wasn't easy." She laughs, and I do too because she's right. "I'd love to read it one day."

"Thank you, that's so nice of you to say." I smile.

We're interrupted by the waiter and pause our conversation as each of us tells him what we want. Once he's gone, Caroline moves her attention back to me.

"What about you? What do you do for work?" I ask, taking from where we left off.

At that, her features brighten, and I already know

that whatever her work is, she's doing it with all her heart. It's all over her face.

"I'm not doing anything right now since we just moved to New Jersey, and I'm still adjusting." Caroline smooths her skirt, pride shining in her eyes. "But back in Texas, I worked at a school for the deaf."

I smile. We're going to be such great friends.

CHAPTER TWENTY-SIX

ARES

The only good thing about tonight is having the table placed as far as possible from the center of the room. Blaise and Caroline start talking about something I can't hear, and I try not to let that ruin the night.

But it already has.

It's loud. Too many people speak at the same time.

Just a simple night out, and I can't, *I can't* even have a conversation, a good time. I had to turn my hearing aids down because the room is too goddamn loud.

I sigh. At least I'm not fully deaf, and there's no music buzzing in my ear to make everything ten times worse.

But it is bad enough.

My throat tightens. My skin burns and prickles, and I don't know if it's all in my mind, but it's suddenly

warmer in here. So warm. Unbearable. Like a hand gripping my neck, stopping me from breathing. The blood
goes to my head and—

"How's work?" Dad places a hand on my shoulder,
and it's like I've taken a breath for the first time since we
sat down.

After a shuddery exhale, I give him a nod, not in the
mood to talk. He catches on quickly.

"We can leave right now and eat some burgers." He
cocks a brow at me, offering me a way out I didn't
ask for.

I clench my jaw.

"It's fine," I say a little more harshly than I intended
to.

He massages the back of his neck. "Okay. Just say
the words, and we're out of here." He turns to August,
knowing that he shouldn't insist.

The last thing I need right now is his pity. He
wanted us to have dinner together, and we will. I'm not
going to ruin this for him just because I'm not comfortable here.

Dad asks him something, but the words sound
muffled in my ear, mixing with the other voices. I look
around, my pulse quickening.

Whether I want it or not, in cases like this one, I'm
an outsider. That's why I choose to get myself out of any
conversation before I'm unintentionally left out.

My leg bounces as I focus on the crowd, and a light

touch on my calf brings my attention back to the table. Caroline is now talking to August while Dad silently takes part with a nod or a smile.

I look at Blaise.

The world quiets. The voices fade.

She's all I see. She's all I hear.

Blaise smiles sadly. "She's beautiful," she mouths, then wiggles her eyebrows toward Caroline in excitement.

I mouth nothing back. I just stare at her. She wants to help me feel better like she always does, coming to my rescue whenever she notices a shift in my attitude. I just nod because I like Caroline, too. She seems good for Dad.

In a quick moment, she sobers, her palms clasping on her lap, a movement that squeezes her breasts together. Gritting my teeth, I watch how her nipples harden under the silky material like I just ran a finger over them. That's how responsive she is.

"Do you like my dress?" she asks innocently.

Of course, I do. I stared at her in the car's side mirrors, at how she swayed her hips like she was a fucking walking temptation. Those legs that I remember being smooth, the curve of her body. It took all my power not to cancel tonight's plans. And my brother being next to me turned me off a little, too. But definitely not enough because my dick is growing in my pants, and Dad is right beside me.

I shake my head because I want to mess with her, not once moving my eyes from her round breasts. She fake pouts, and I look at her as she mouths, "Why?"

My chin lifts, pointing at the nipples that are poking through the material.

She's taunting me. And she knows it's working.

My chin rests on my right hand, imitating a position that won't give away what I'm about to do. Slowly, I slip one of my shoes off and raise my foot. In one quick move, I'm tracing Blaise's leg. In the meantime, I fully focus on others, acting like I'm paying attention to whatever is happening there. Only in appearance because the truth is, all I focus on is her.

She doesn't even try to escape, but I can see from the corner of my eyes how those breasts of hers rise and fall with aggravated breaths. The spell from the silky skin under my touch makes it so much harder to cage in every single thought that runs through my mind about what I could do to her right now.

And I hate that fucking stupid rule so much. If she'd let me, I'd excuse us for a second, steal her, and kiss the shit out of her with my dick buried deep inside that pussy until she learns to never tease me again in public.

But I know what she wants. She wants to come.

That's not going to fucking happen after she tempted me with her perfect nipples. Even though I know it was all to save me from my spiral, I don't need to be saved. What I need is to teach her a lesson she'll never forget.

I force her crossed legs open, but she grits her teeth at me. The second time I try to push my foot between them, they're open. When my foot touches her thighs, she sucks in a sharp breath, hiding it in her fisted palm. With slow movements, I get to her panties and rub her clit through the material. I move my toe up and down in circles, and at the feel of my toe lightly pushing into her, she clamps her thighs shut over my foot.

Finally, I take my gaze off everyone else and look her directly in her eyes. Her cheeks are flushed. Eyes watery. Jaw clenched.

"Open," I mouth, and she raises her chin, closing her eyes as if defeated. As soon as I touch her wetness, they snap back open. This time, I don't take my gaze off her. I watch her as silent whimpers escape past her lips, and I feel her panties wetting with each stroke of my toe.

I can practically feel how every muscle in her body tenses with expectation, quivering with desire. How her lips tremble, locking in screams of pleasure I know she wants to set free. How her fingers twitch in her lap, mourning to touch something. To squeeze something.

Her lips part, and I imagine a soft moan escaping. I pull my foot away and put my shoe back on. There's no way I'm giving her an orgasm after she teased me.

I know she's wearing that dress for me. But we are

not alone now, and I can't get rid of it for her. Or better, rip it off her.

I take my phone and type her a message, a smirk growing on my lips as I hit send and put the device back. When her iPhone vibrates, she peeks at me cautiously but takes it. She unlocks it, and her big eyes meet mine.

ME

you're fucking soaked, Moon.

Caroline turns to say something to her, and the device slips through her fingers, landing on the booth between them. Caroline reaches it first, and she's polite enough not to glance at it as she hands it to her.

"I'm sorry," I read on her lips as she laughs, putting it facing down on the table. Caroline brushes her off, smiling.

Her panties must get wetter and wetter with each passing moment. Somehow, being here makes everything feel sexier. Knowing that I was just between her legs mere seconds ago...

Fortunately, the server brings our drinks and appetizers. A much-needed cold shower.

"Can you reserve a copy of *Ina May's Guide to Childbirth* for Caroline?" Dad asks. "She wants to pick it up this week."

"Sure." I meet her gaze, and she gives me a smile. "I can check if we have it."

A grateful smile forms on his lips as he pats my shoulder. "Thank you."

After our food comes, time passes pretty quickly. Blaise texts me about everything they speak of—they chat about August's plans to major in architecture, and Dad brings up my specialty in literature too and makes sure to turn to me as he speaks so I can hear him, and they talk a bit about their time in Texas.

When the waiter comes with the check, we've all finished eating for a while and are ready to leave.

"Where did you guys park your car?" Dad asks after paying the bill.

"The back parking lot," August tells him as we stop in front of the exit, the noise lowering.

My stiffened shoulders gradually relax as we walk outside.

"Thank you so much for coming. I really appreciate it." Caroline smiles at us, and Dad puts an arm around her. "It was so nice to finally meet you."

Dad looks down at Caroline before clearing his throat. "After things settle down with the baby, Caroline and I are going to get married, and I'd really love to have you all there."

Blaise squeals, then hugs her tightly, and I already know they are going to be good friends. "Congratulations!"

I give Dad a smile, and I notice his shoulders relaxing. "We'll be there."

August gives him a pat on the back, and Dad's lips turn upward. "Thank you."

We say our goodbyes, and I place my palm on Blaise's lower back, struggling not to think about her ass and how much I want to squeeze it between my hands right now.

It doesn't work.

CHAPTER TWENTY-SEVEN

BLAISE

We pull up in front of the boys' house, and my knees shake with anticipation as I step out of the car, the burning glances Ares threw me all the way home still fresh in my mind.

I close the door behind me and smooth my dress, choosing to ignore how unnecessary that actually is. My dress looks perfect, the same as it did all night as I kept playing with it.

Ares rounds the vehicle and comes to a halt beside August and me. His hands are stowed in his pockets, his beautiful jaw twitching, and he has no shame eye-fucking me with August standing directly next to us.

"Imma get going," August says, throwing his thumb back toward the house.

Ares has no reaction to that, and I only manage to give him a small nod, my gaze locked on the dark eyes staring back at me. A slow, painful swallow slides down my throat, the sound of steps fading in the distance.

The door closing echoes into the quiet night, and Ares is here in one second, so close that his nose touches mine. His breaths are controlled, while mine have been stolen away as one of his strong hands lifts and gently touches my cheek. I instantly sink into the feeling.

"I want to kiss you." He says it so nonchalantly while my heart's close to hammering out of my chest, growing legs, running on the street, and never coming back.

I let out a warm breath reaching his face. "Don't," I manage to say, lowering my head into his hold.

Only God knows it takes me all the mastery in the world not to let my knees give in to one simple sentence.

He takes a deep breath and places his forehead on mine. My shoulders fall into a heavy sigh, his hand squeezing my hair into a gentle fist. Almost as if he's repressing himself.

I don't dare look at him.

Ares nods at whatever he just agreed to with himself and straightens his back until he takes away every evidence of his body on mine. Just like that, that quick.

I have no more than a second to think about how much I yearn to feel his touch again because he already knows or needs it as much as I do. Ares takes my hand into his and brings it to his lips.

Soft, sinful lips.

"I won't," he promises, resting his chin on the top of my palm.

Click.

I take a mental picture of him. A gorgeous picture.

The lust in his eyes from earlier has melted into pure tenderness as a light touch rests on my cheek, fingers brush over my lips, and breath is warm on my neck.

Too *much*.

I step away from him to put some distance between us, and he's quick to draw his hand back, placing both of them in his jeans pockets. I stare at my stilettos. Balance my weight on them. Hug my chest.

The hungry look on his face has returned. I can feel it.

"Were you thinking of me when you chose this dress?" he asks, his voice bathing in a new shade of black as he takes the silk between his fingertips. His tone is so thick and grave that I can feel it vibrating through my whole body.

My thighs clench.

"Yes," I admit, making sure to look at him when I say it.

He curses under his breath, a guttural growl leaving his throat when his full attention is caught by the peak of my nipples. I shudder, loving the way his eyes darken under the dim light of the night sky.

"Go home, Moon," he suddenly says, sobering me.

I part my mouth open. "What?"

Him rejecting me in any way after he literally toe fucked me at the dinner with his dad would be rude as hell now that my own libido wants to come out and play. Plus, I just admitted I wore that dress for him, which is a very good reason for him to take me upstairs.

Ares takes a step forward. "Go home, or I'll bend you over right here, right now, and punish the shit out of you." His voice is unbelievably composed. It's hard for me to believe he's actually *that* close to losing his control over a glance at my breasts.

My insides tense at hearing his threat that sounds so tempting to me, I might stay here only to see if he'll follow through on his promise. I've been so turned on since the restaurant that I might just ask him to do it anyway.

His eyes snap to my thighs, a smirk growing on his lips because he knows full well how much I enjoy when he's speaking like this. He loves it so damn much.

"Good night." I try to form a smile as I arrange the purse onto my shoulder.

He takes a strand of my hair and brings it behind my ear, his finger brushing the tip of it. He takes my breath away along with his removal.

"Dream of me," he says in a husky voice that hits me to my core.

Damn him.

Ares whirls on his feet, the growing proud smirk on his lips paling into the darkness. I do the same, but only when I'm sure he won't change his mind about bending me over the car.

Because I'd tug my dress up to give him access without a second thought.

The door squeaks open, and I close it beside me, then make my way to my room with the silence of a thief —a skill I obtained when I was in college so Nanna wouldn't hear whenever I was sneaking out. Though now that I've grown up, I think she knew anyway.

I flick the lights on and stop, glancing at the window facing my own, where Ares is staying with his phone clutched between his hands. Mine buzzes in my purse.

With a shake of my head and a smile, I whip it out and open the conversation.

ARES

Good night, Moon?

I draw my bottom lip between my teeth at the memory of how he touched me tonight. And I decide it's my time to get back at him for teasing me.

Throwing my purse onto the bed, along with my phone, I slowly take off my heels. The feeling of his gaze on me is imprinted on my skin. I *know* he's still there.

The stilettos are hanging in my hands as I walk toward the other part of the room where he can't see me anymore. After I put them in their place, I pass in front of the window and stop at the wardrobe, picking up my pajamas for the night.

Another angle he can't see me from.

Clothes in my arms, I go to the middle of the room, close to the edge of the bed. Acting like I don't know he's there, I curl my fingers under the dress's thin straps on my shoulders and drag them down. They fall onto my breasts, one hand keeping them from slipping entirely.

Just to piss him off even more—and to turn him on —I turn my back to him and let the dress free until the material gathers at my toes. I step out of it, knowing the white lace panties I have on are driving him crazy.

My phone lights up with a text, but I don't need to look to know it's him.

A victorious smirk tugs at my lips. His gaze burns into my back, demanding me to answer. Or to turn around.

But I don't do any of that.

I just make a show of swaying my hips until I reach the other end of my room. He loses sight of me again, and then another text comes.

I walk close to the wall and catch the curtain between my fingers slowly, not wanting him to figure out my next move. In one quick shift, I drag it over the window, blocking his view.

The device lights up once again.

Taking my time to find out what he said, I put my clothes on—a pair of shorts and a T-shirt that could go as a bra—and drop onto the bed, enjoying the coldness of it on my hot skin. I take my phone and place my head on the pillow as I look over his messages.

ARES

You better turn around, Blaise. I'm not kidding.

Come back. Now.

I should've fucked you against the car when I had the chance. Lesson learned

It feels good to know that he's this worked up because of me. And the way he speaks to me when he's turned on... Just how I like it, tearing my insides and making my toes twirl in my bed at the thought of him saying this to my face. I bite back a smile.

ME

Can't believe I've been friends with a stalker all this time. I know to keep my curtains closed from now on.

Night, stalker.

His reply comes in an instant, and I chuckle.

ARES

Good night, my ass. I can't sleep with a fucking boner.

How should I punch you for teasing me this time?

punch

Fuck, I meant punch

p u n i s h

A laugh erupts out of my chest, and my head drops onto the pillow.

CHAPTER TWENTY-EIGHT

ARES

The door slams against the wall, and I twist my back to look up at the hallway at the same time August raises his eyes from his phone.

Blaise walks into the kitchen with an expression on her face that makes it clear she couldn't wait until later, too excited to give a shit about coming here at seven a.m. on a free day from work.

After she teased me last night, I needed something to distract me from the circle of thoughts her little show dragged me into, and the only good idea besides jerking off was to read her manuscript.

Fuck, it worked.

I didn't close an eye all night, entirely captured by each one of her words and the world she created. At first, I thought it was because I like everything Blaise does, but I couldn't be more wrong. Blaise is insanely talented, and I'm saying that from the perspective of a man working with huge authors, not just because she's mine.

There were a lot of things I had to edit since she has never worked with an editor before, yet it's a hell of a strong start.

When I texted her twenty minutes ago, I didn't realize it was already morning, otherwise, I would've waited so she could get her rest.

I just finished making some fried eggs for my brother —who should be starting classes soon—and me, but I turn back to the kitchen and start making another for her.

"What do you mean to send it to a publisher?" Her steps follow closer to me immediately after her voice.

I whirl to her, a smile already growing on my lips.

She's dressed in her usual running outfit: a sports bra, tight, dangerous shorts, and a pair of white sneakers. Her cheeks are red, and her nose scrunches in an adorable way.

Normally, you don't want to fuck adorable things, right? Because I sure as hell would make an exception just this once.

I scratch my freshly shaved beard, twitching my jaw as I try to think about anything else besides her. "Try" being the key word because I can't *not* think about her. Not now. Not ever.

My brother clears his throat, relaxing in his chair at

the table. "So usually, when you finish a book and want others to read it—"

Blaise rolls her eyes and playfully smacks him on the head. "I know what it means." She walks towards me, her lips twitching to keep her grin from spreading, "Did you really mean it?" Her big round eyes gape at me as she waits for my reply.

A strand of Blaise's hair falls messily on her cheek, so I stretch my hand and tuck it behind her ear as I give her a smile. "Yes."

"Like, really, really, *really* mean it, right?" She lifts her brows at me, and I laugh, not able to contain it around her.

I nod. "Just say the words, and I'll get you a meeting."

Without turning my back to her, I shut off the gas cooker to make sure the egg won't burn.

She squints at me, taking her time to scrutinize every feature of mine before she speaks. "Why this one?" she asks, tilting her head, and my brows furrow. "Out of *all* the books I sent you, why this one?"

It's simple to give her an answer. "Because this kept me awake all night."

She used to send me books to read monthly, but with time, their number decreased to a point where she rarely wrote anything. And I don't know what changed or what she did because the improvement is impressive.

Blaise draws in a sharp breath, and her lips widen in a grin.

"I can send them a summary of the story, but there are a few things I'd change. I have them on my laptop," I say, and she instantly takes a step back.

"Show me." She turns around and walks towards the stairs.

August chuckles. "What about the food?"

I put the eggs on a plate and place them in front of him. "You can eat it."

He shakes his head, and I leave, following Blaise shortly and enjoying the fact that every second she's walking the stairs, her ass bounces, demanding a slap. To my surprise, I manage to keep it cool until we get to my room and close the door behind us.

She runs directly to my desk. Before she has a chance to open my laptop, I scoop her up and put her in my lap as I turn it on myself.

"Do you think they'll like it?" Her tone is lower now, and I know are doubts are starting to crawl into her head.

"Yeah," I whisper, leaning down to place a kiss on her neck. She whimpers but stays still. "They're going to beg you to work with them," I say, sucking her skin between my teeth.

Blaise shivers. "What if they don't?" She releases the question in a harsh breath.

I smile, remove myself from her neck, and cup her

head between my palms, making sure she's watching me. "If they don't, we'll start our own fucking publishing house and make them regret ever rejecting you."

For a while, we just stare at each other as I caress her cheek, letting my last words sink in.

It's hard to believe they won't love it. I've been an editor for years—a reader for much longer than that—and I know that there's a very small chance they'd refuse to work with her.

"Okay," she whispers. "I think I like that."

Leaning down, I kiss her cheek as we both keep our breath. I keep my lips there for a moment, enjoying the warmth of her skin. When I back away, she captures the side of my face with her hand.

"Help me," Blaise mutters, and when she sees the confusion on my face, she clarifies. "Be my editor."

I stay still as a statue, not knowing what to say.

Be her editor?

"If they want me or not, let's work together on this. I can always self-publish, too." Her eyes are soft as she speaks, with gentle touches stroking my cheek.

"I specialize in romance, and you need to make sure your editor can do what's best for you," I say calmly.

Fantasy books aren't something new to me since I've edited a couple of those, but I'm good as hell when it comes to romance. Helping her edit this book would also be a learning process for me, and she needs the greatest editors out there.

"What are you talking about? You edited Shelly Dante's books, a fantasy *and* romance author." She gives me a small smile. "Just like me."

A sigh falls past my lips, and she must sense that I'm slowly agreeing to this because she snuggles herself against me, throwing a hand around my shoulders and stuffing her face in my neck. She starts to kiss it wherever she can reach.

"Please, please, please, please," Blaise says every time her lips are not on me.

I laugh and move her away when it starts to tickle. "Okay, yeah." I lift my hands in the air in surrender. "We can try, but—"

She squeals, interrupting me.

"But," I continue, inclining my head and staring down at her, "if we aren't compatible, you need to tell me so I can find you another editor right away."

I could never forgive myself for not meeting her expectations or for not giving her the best because she deserves it. There are a lot of editors and so many more that are better than me.

Blaise smiles like a child and stretches her hand forward. "Deal." She grins, and I can't stop the smile from taking over me, either. I shake my head with a laugh and catch her hand in a handshake.

When she's not expecting it, I get us up and throw her on my bed. A gasp escapes her, and I quickly cover her mouth with my palm, her eyes widening.

"Be quiet because I still have to punish you for letting me go to sleep with blue balls the other night."

I leave out the part where I unintentionally said I was going to punch her instead of punishing her. Glad there's no auto-corrector in real life.

If possible, her eyes widen even more as she struggles to get away from my arms. "I'll let you go," I tell her after tracing her breasts with my finger. "Be quiet."

She nods her head. I slowly take my hand away, but as soon as I remove it from her mouth, she tries to scream for August's help, a playful sparkle dancing in her eyes. Before she can finish the word, I cover her lips once again.

Blaise arches when she feels my cock hardening, and I push it into her until I know it hurts for both of us.

"First, never scream my brother's name again when we're in this position," I warn her, then lean down and bite her neck. "Second," I say and raise my head, making sure she's looking me in the eyes, "next time my hand won't be the one stifling your scream. It's going to be my dick buried deep in your throat."

CHAPTER TWENTY-NINE

ARES

Lust burns into her eyes, her breath quickening as she clenches her thighs under me.

"But I think you'd like that, wouldn't you?" I smirk, then sneak a hand between our bodies until I reach her shorts. "I bet your panties are already wet," I say, moving a finger up and down on the fabric.

Blaise fidgets under me, trying to get more of the friction.

"What do you want?" I ask her, supporting my body on my knees so I won't touch her anymore.

I set her free to hear what she has to say. She's trembling with need, her beautiful chest rising and lowering with each breath, and then she props herself on her elbows to get a better view of me.

Her hand stretches to my jeans, playing with the

button. When I'm too lost staring at her breasts, she drags me by the material and pins me on my back.

"I want you..." she says, throwing her bra over her head, making her breasts bounce. I can't stop myself from cupping one of them in my palm. She whimpers but continues. "To tell me what my punishment is."

My dick throbs so hard it hurts at the idea of going through with my threat. I put a hand on her back until I reach her ponytail, fisting it in my palm before bringing her ear to my lips.

"You're going to make yourself come," I tell her, breathing on her skin. "And I'll just stand there watching you break down and asking for my help."

I release her and stand up, leaving her alone on the bed.

She laughs. "What? Do you think I've never come before you?"

I sit down on my chair and smirk at her as I relax on it, noticing the cockiness on her face. "I think both of us know that I'm the one you think about when you touch yourself."

She swallows, giving me the confirmation I need. I might as well die now, and I'd be a happy man because I'd forever have this image of her with me: cheeks flushed, eyes sparkling with desire, messy hair, and pink nipples hardening with each passing second.

"Does that make you feel good about yourself?" A confident smirk plays on her lips as she slowly removes her shorts. "Who do *you* think about when you come, Ares Hart?" she asks teasingly, throwing the last piece of clothing onto my lap.

Her shorts, along with a pink thong, lie on my legs, and when I glance down at her panties, they are soaked.

"Always you, Moon," I admit, then tuck her lingerie in my back pocket.

Blaise's eyes gleam under the daylight, her lips parting open when she rests her back on my headboard, spreading her legs. She never interrupts eye contact, already eager for the orgasm she's not going to receive.

But she doesn't know that.

Yet.

"I like it when you call me Moon," she says, lowering a hand from a breast to the column under her core.

She traces her slit with a finger, and the world dims around the edges when I notice how dilated her pupils are, dark with desire for what is supposed to be her punishment. Her finger parts her lips open, revealing the wetness I know is there because of me. Blaise spreads it all over, and my eyes can't look away.

My dick grows thicker and thicker, rubbing on my pants with each throb, and it takes me all the control in the world to not forget about my threat. For now, she'll get lost in the pleasure. But right when her orgasm strikes, and she fights so hard to chase it, I'll steal it right from under her nose.

"Close your eyes," she whispers in a sexy voice, and

even if I wanted to refuse, she brings the finger that was between her legs mere moments ago and licks it like a lollipop. I obey, and I can practically hear the smile on her face. "If you look, I'll stop."

I relax on the chair with a sigh, and her shorts fall on the floor when I adjust the pulsing cock in my pants. The bed squeaks under her weight, followed by the sounds of her steps.

A breath falls over my ear before she speaks. "Count to ten out loud, and then you can open your eyes."

Before I have time to grab her, she steps back. "Why?" I ask but still ready to do it as soon as she gives me a reason.

"Does it matter as long as you enjoy it?" Blaise inquires in a low, sexy voice, and somehow, all my questions disappear from my mind.

So, I start counting. "One. Two. Three. Four. Five—"

"Slower," she says, brushing a nail on my jaw. I immediately clench it under her touch but continue as she asked me to.

"Six. Seven. Eight..." She giggles, and I can't stop the smile from spreading on my face at the sounds. "Nine. Ten."

I peel my eyes open and catch sight of her now fully dressed body running away, not even bothering to close the door after her. For a second, I just stand there, a chuckle escaping me at the realization of how easily she fooled me.

She acted so fucking greedy, and I bought the entire act, too lost in my own pleasure. Because watching her is something I could do for the rest of my life. Something that makes my heart beat unhealthily faster than normal. Something that makes me wish blinking wasn't necessary because when I'm around her, I don't want to miss a single moment.

With the thud of her steps running downstairs and her laughter filling the house, I sit up and walk after her. When I get to the top of the stairs, she's at the bottom, watching me with a wide grin on her lips while my brother's eyes jump between us.

Her cheeks are flushed, and even though I've never had balls this blue, I want to kiss the shit out of her face. A staring contest passes between us as we wait to see who's going to make a move first.

"I'll give you ten seconds to come back upstairs," I say, her smile only growing. She's enjoying this so much, and I have to admit I'm having fun too. "Start counting, or I'm going to chase you before the time is up."

My brother clears his throat, and I see the exact moment Blaise comes back to reality.

She still keeps a grin on her face when she talks. "I'll be back for a movie night." She turns around, swaying her hips as she walks out of the house.

I shake my head, and even though I want to go back to my room, I notice the weird expression on August's face. It takes me a moment to realize I'm wearing a gigantic smile that's making my cheeks hurt. I wash it away.

"What?" I raise a brow, not knowing the reason behind his curious gaze and knitted eyebrows.

He shrugs. "Nothing. I'm trying to understand this shit between you two."

A sigh leaves my lips as I open my hands around my body. "What thing?"

"I don't know. I just said that I'm still trying to understand it."

My fingers thread through my hair as I support myself on the railing, waiting for him to say what he has to say and then get back to what I have to do. And that's getting Blaise a meeting with a publisher.

"Do you like her?" he asks, eyeing me.

"Yeah," I reply, knowing it's true and that I don't need to think much about it since it's pretty clear even to myself.

"Is she your girlfriend?" he asks.

"No."

"Why not?" August squints his eyes from the couch.

"None of your business."

August sighs. "Are you serious about her?"

I nod. "Yes."

"Is she?" He cocks his brows in question.

"I think so, yes."

I hope so.

I can't believe I'm standing here with my eighteen-year-old brother questioning me about my relationship with Blaise.

He relaxes but doesn't set me free of his continuous stare. "Then what's wrong? Why can't you two just be together?"

I shrug and stuff my hands in my pockets. "It's hard to explain" is all I can tell him.

"I have time." He straightens his back and walks the stairs with a smile on his face, elbowing my stomach as a joke when he stops next to me.

He's so nosy sometimes that I find it hard to believe we're even related. August is more like Blaise than me.

With a sigh, I tell him what he wants to hear. "I'm serious about her, and that's exactly why we're not together yet," I say, thinking it will be enough, but judging by the frown on his face, it's not. "I don't wanna rush things."

"Mm-hmm, right." He finally steps away, and I take it as my cue to leave. "You're being a chicken shit," he shouts, and I raise my middle finger to him before closing the door to my room. "She won't wait forever for you to make a move, you know?"

After grabbing my clothes, I enter the bathroom and

turn on the shower. It infuriates me how right he is, but I have to remember that it's better to wait and make sure someone's right for you than jump right into a wave and expect not to drown.

If she'll be mine, I want to make sure we have what it takes to get through the roaring seas.

CHAPTER THIRTY

BLAISE

He's been silent for an hour now.

Okay, maybe it's been ten long minutes, but who's counting?

The only thing I know for sure is that I'm barely keeping my cool anymore. Ares is sitting at my desk, working through the ideas I brainstormed today and adding little notes here and there while I struggle not to let the urge to bug him win. I know he needs silence when he edits.

We ended up having a movie night after all, and I hardly paid any attention to what we were watching, too busy thinking about Ares's hands on my body.

Not too long after I came back home, he climbed into my room. And even though I could tell he was here for something else, as soon as he saw me sitting down in front of my computer, he lifted me up and took the seat. He's been looking at it since.

"So?" I ask impatiently, watching him close the laptop. "What do you think?"

Ares turns so he can see me, and I straighten at the sight of his indecipherable and stern face, certain I just made everything worse instead of better. It's fine, though. If he doesn't like any of my suggestions, we can keep the initial version of the story since he liked that one so much.

He's seen a lot of glimpses of my work over the years, but this is the first time I showed him the first draft of my book. It's a vulnerable, unpolished part of it, and I know I still have a lot to do before meeting his expectations.

I want to make him proud, and I will, even if he thinks my ideas are bad.

Big, dark eyes stare at me. "I think these changes, along with the suggestions I have on my laptop, are going to make a huge difference. Good job," he says, and I let out a small smile.

"But?" I push, knowing Ares doesn't think anything is perfect. Ever.

I've seen him editing, and it's not pretty. Red marks and question marks are all over the place. He's very precise. Strict. Critical. Involved. He's thinking from the reader's point of view and helps the authors create the most beautiful story.

"But the main thing you need to work on is Cecily and Devil's connection. We have a few things to develop before it can be edited."

My thoughts carry me away, and I imagine how it'd feel to see my book in bookstores, to see people reading it, to sign the books I poured my heart into. The words are mine, the feelings are mine, and the darkest wishes are part of me. It's everything I have to give transferred into ink and paper.

"I also talked to my boss after I sent her a summary," he tells me, covering his chest with his arms. "She knows someone at Coral's Publishing House and thinks she can give me an answer tomorrow morning."

"Thank you," I say because I know none of this would be possible if it wasn't for him.

A shaky breath sews its way past my lips. The thought excites me, but I'm also nervous to hear what they have to say about my book. The publishing house works with many well-known authors. They host events all over the world and helped Sylva West turn one of her bestsellers into a movie.

I wonder how that feels—to see your story and your characters being brought to life when you know you're the one who created them in the first place.

I think I'd cry, but that might be just me. I always cry.

"Which character do you relate to the most?" Ares asks after a few moments of silence, the chair squeaking under his weight as he sits up and walks towards me.

I look up at him, trying to come up with the best and sincerest answer. "I think, in some way, each of the characters has something that's part of me," I say, and he doesn't seem pleased about it. I roll my eyes playfully. "But if I had to pick, I'd say Cecily."

He nods and sits down next to me on the bed, our knees touching. "So her desires are technically yours?"

It's clear what he's asking me. I crack a laugh, watching his serious face. "Do you mean how she likes it rough?"

"Yeah. I want to know what you like," he says so calmly it gets me all hot on the inside, my breath hitching with the way his eyes darken, undressing me with one glance.

"Yes," I admit.

A low guttural sound escapes his throat before a muscular hand slowly rises and catches my neck in a reserved grip, which seems the last ounce of control he has left. I like that. I like to know he's so desperate for me that he has to hold himself back from ripping my clothes open and being done with the excruciating wait in one second. I also like how he prioritizes my pleasure and how he makes sex less about satisfying needs, trans- forming it into a deep and intimate place where we simply worship each other with uncontrollable hunger.

His eyes focus on my lips, and like an automatic

reflex, I bite my bottom lip, clenching my thighs when his hold on my throat tightens. A last attempt to keep it together. For a moment, I think he'll kiss me, but it's a fast thought that disappears as if it were never there.

Ares moves his hand lower, closer to my breasts, and he leans forward to my neck to give it a kiss, his other hand holding tightly on my back. My palm is plastered on his, seeking support so I won't turn into a puddle of pleasure when his teeth bite my skin through little sounds of frustration. I can't help but throw my head back and give him more access.

His fingers pinch my nipples so hard I think he'll rip them off. Pain strikes through my body, and I swallow a moan, doing my best not to let it out. The more aggressive he gets, the wetter I become. I arch into his hold, letting him suck the skin, teasing it with his tongue as his palms cover my breasts in a squeeze.

I shudder and feel his smirk shadowing my throat, hungry kisses and bites tracing it.

He feels so good.

Because the anticipation is too much to handle right now, I push him on his back and straddle his thighs in one quick move. I grin, noticing his dazed eyes watching me back. His fingers catch my chin as I stare at him, blinded by the shift in his attitude.

"You're fucking beautiful, Moon," he murmurs, and I just look at him, not knowing how to react to this kind of compliment.

Ares has always complimented me through the look in his eyes, and until now, I thought it was enough and better than any other words. I was wrong. Hearing him call me beautiful does something to me. It's like I was waiting for it subconsciously, and now that it happened, I never want him to stop. The flutter in my chest couldn't agree more.

I smile, my heart purring happily as I lean down and leave a chaste kiss on his cheek. At the same time, I take his belt off and unbutton his jeans, eager to get his cock out.

"Do I need a safe word?" he jokes, cocking a brow at me.

I rise on my knees, giving myself enough space to allow myself to get his jeans and boxers down to his knees. From there, he takes them off by himself.

"Do *I*?" I tease, wanting to know where his mind's at.

In one quick movement, he has me on my back, arms pinned above my head, caught under his grasp. His cock pushes into my center, and like an instant response to his body, mine arches into his.

"No," he whispers, hooking his thumb under my shirt and removing it.

His fingers force my back upward, sneaking a hand to unclasp my bra. I get rid of his T-shirt and feel him tensing on top of me as I trace his tattoos with my palm. With each swipe, his muscles harden under my touch.

"What a shame," I say teasingly, but my voice fades when I notice the tiny moon on his chest. I trace the ink with my finger, his eyes silently watching me the entire time. "Did you get this for me?" I ask, looking directly at him.

I can hear every thud of my racing heart in my ear, my breathing stopping as I stare at his beautiful face and the way it softens when he brushes a strand of my hair away.

Ares smiles softly. "Yes."

He has a tattoo. For me.

While it's not supposed to shock me the way it does since I have one for him as well, it feels surreal to see it. And the smile on his lips only makes it clear how proud he is to wear it...

I don't know how I even missed it.

He can't have gotten it done after I did. It's completely healed.

I bite the inside of my cheek. "When?"

Ares gives me his gorgeous smile. "Last year."

Without permission, my eyes widen in surprise at his words. I can't believe he got it a year ago, and I haven't noticed until now.

But how is it possible to have the exact same tattoos? I never saw his, and he couldn't know what I would get, so how did this happen?

The thoughts roaming through my head pause. My erratic breaths travel his skin, along with the finger that just can't stop circling the space where ink's engraved in his skin.

Just like the one I have, thin lines form the shape of a moon I wear above my elbow. And his is right next to his heart.

I look up at his lips and the way he sweeps his tongue over them, an urge I can't ignore crawling from the depths of my stomach to the surface. I lift my head a little and breathe on his mouth as I try to recollect myself. It's hard to remember why we shouldn't kiss with him this close to me.

My hand hooks around the back of his neck. I'm unsure of what to do—drag him closer or push him away.

But I don't do either. Instead, I clear my throat and stare into his eyes, wanting to escape this weird feeling tugging at my chest.

"Undress me, Ares," I whisper.

He hesitates. Nods. Yanks the rest of my clothes down, leaving me naked under the light of his eyes.

Ares captures a nipple with his teeth, biting at it until I'm pushing so hard into him it hurts. He groans, every cell that's vibrating through him reaching my body.

I move my hand to his back, and he abruptly stops, snapping his head up to look at to me. "You're not allowed to touch me until I say so. Understood?"

I agree with a shake of my head, a shudder going

through me as I put my arms back where they were, imagining a string tying them.

"Good girl," he murmurs. "Now close your eyes and count to ten."

"You know, it won't be as fun as it was when I ran if I know what's next," I say, and he cracks a laugh.

"I'm not running anywhere." He sits up from on top of me, then slaps my pussy when he sees I'm not cooperating. "Close your eyes, little tease."

My thighs clench, and I have to bite back a moan— both of pain and pleasure—but I still give him a murderous look before doing as I'm told.

"Count to ten," Ares reminds me in that deep voice of his. If I wasn't squeezing my legs enough, I'm totally doing it now.

"One. Two. Three." I hear him searching through his jeans, most likely for a condom. "Four. Five. Six." The bed moves under his weight. "Seven." He's on top of me. "Eight." His hands capture mine. "Nine." Cold metal covers my wrists.

"Ten," I whisper.

Click.

When I peel my eyelids open, he's smirking down at me.

"Did you just handcuff me?" I ask, but he's already lowering himself on me.

My head falls deeper into the mattress as he nibbles my clit with his teeth before gathering my wetness with a long swipe of his tongue. Quickly, I grab the pillow above me and put it over my mouth, stuffing the moan that uncontrollably escapes me. He barely touches me for a few minutes, using a tenderness I don't need when he's between my legs. Ares knows what he's doing, taking his sweet time until I can't stand it any longer.

A frustrated sound reverberates in my throat, and he simply laughs at me.

"You need to understand that I'm a man of his word. I always"—he stops to slip a finger inside me—"keep my promises."

And he does. He gives me bits and bits, building an orgasm that misses its wave a hundred times. It's not until I start shuddering that he lets me come.

"Fuck, Moon," he curses under his breath once I'm nothing left but pieces.

I take the pillow from my face and gaze up at him. His eyes darken around the edges as his chin shines with my arousal. I sit up and stick my tongue out, licking it away. He groans, and before I have time to register what's going on, he yanks my hair and throws me on my stomach, the handcuffs hanging heavy.

"Don't move," he says and lifts from the bed.

From the corner of my eyes, I watch him searching through his pockets. Once he finds the condom, he throws it onto my back, then parts my legs open with his and places a palm on top of my ass. He lowers himself enough to tease me with his bare tip. I moan and push into it, his head entering me by an unprotected inch.

He stops me with his hand from going forward. "What did I say?" he asks, and I feel another orgasm coming from his demanding tone.

My mouth closes shut, and I let him move his dick up and down until the need for the release is too painful.

And I just came a few minutes ago.

He pushes himself into my center, slowly entering me. I enjoy every inch of him, letting him have his way with me, but when he's almost there, I forget all about his orders and push myself onto his dick, his length touching just the right places.

"Fucking hell, you're so tight for me."

Ares immediately pulls out, rolls the condom on, and slams back into me as quickly as he left. He grabs my ass cheeks between his hands and fucks me like he can't get enough. When he's all the way in, he pushes more, my eyes rolling into my head as I scream his name into the pillow, not caring if anyone hears me.

He must love me screaming his name because the pace quickens even more, his dick tearing me apart. He places two fingers over my clit, moving them in synchrony with his cock. I come undone right there.

Ares removes the fingers, stuffing one into my ass.

His name slips past my lips a thousand times as I come harder than I ever have in my entire life. He shudders, clenching his fingers over my ass tightly.

Ares falls next to me, and we both struggle to even our breaths. "Fuck," he says, uncuffing me with trembling hands.

I look at him as he takes off his condom and throws it into the trash next to the bed, not bothering to sit up or open his eyes. He puts his hands over his chest, breathing hard.

"We should take a shower," I tell him, my breaths still heavy.

"Yeah," he agrees but makes no move to get up. "I can go home."

Before sitting, I grab his hand. "I said *we* should take a shower." He opens his eyes, watching me as I speak. "Take a shower with me, Ares."

He doesn't need me to say more because he scoops me up and walks us to the bathroom. I fight the urge to lean my head on his chest, afraid that I might never remove it from there.

Ares starts the water, making sure it's warm, then steps into the shower with me still in his arms. He sets me down gently, and surprisingly, neither of us wants to make this sexual. I wash him, and he washes me with tender touches. We relax and enjoy the company of each other, no words exchanged, only soft glances.

Once we're done, Ares steps out and grabs a towel, then wraps me in it. He grabs another for himself, and we dry ourselves before we go back to the room and put our underwear on.

He drops onto the bed, sighing. "I'll leave soon," he murmurs, and I lie next to him.

"Okay." My voice is a tender whisper.

Please don't.

Not long after, his breathing evens, and I don't know if I should wake him or not. I decide against it and drag the blanket over us, then pull his T-shirt over my head, sinking into the intoxicating scent of him. Before snuggling into Ares, I grip the lever of his hearing aids and slowly take them out.

My eyes find him sleeping on my pillow.

He has a tattoo. With a moon. For me. *His* moon.

CHAPTER THIRTY-ONE

ARES

When I'm finally able to keep my eyes open without blinking frantically at the sun streaking through the curtains, I notice Blaise sitting on the edge of the bed with a sweet smile on her face.

She hands me the hearing aids I don't remember taking out, and I look around as if that will restore the lost memory of how last night ended. Granted, instead of going home like I promised, I spent the night in her bed. And there's no one bit in me that regrets it.

My black T-shirt plays the role of a dress on Blaise's body, hanging largely towards the knees but curving on the shape of her breasts. The image of her with my clothes on, a messy hairstyle on top of her head, and a sleepy smile aimed at me makes me feel like I won the lottery.

I take the hearing aids from her and put the devices in my ears, turning them on. "Are we late for work?" I ask, my voice cracking.

Blaise shakes her head, yawning. "It's six."

Good. Because I'm not eager to get out of bed just yet.

"Come here," I say, my gaze wandering from her hard nipples to her smooth legs.

She doesn't need me to repeat it, snuggling herself at my chest with the guidance of my hands on her back. I give her shoulders a light massage while I glance at the ceiling and fight the overwhelming feeling at the touch of her skin on mine.

Blaise sighs peacefully and sneaks her chin into the crook of my neck, her body relaxing at the closeness.

It's strange how waking up next to her seems so normal, like we do this all the time, and it might be about our history, but there's no moment of awkwardness between us.

"You snore at night, you know?" I joke, lifting my shoulder a bit to grab her attention.

She laughs, removing herself from the hug and pushing a palm playfully on my chest. "No, I don't. I'm a light sleeper, and even my own snore would wake me up."

I smile. "We'll have to do it again because I'm pretty sure you did snore."

Her brows rise in a challenge, hand placed on her hip as she stares down at me. "Just say it was amazing sleeping with me, and you want to do it again."

Blaise looks like she's half joking, half hoping to hear those exact words from me, and it gives me the confirmation she loved waking up next to me as much as I did.

I sit up and hook my hands around her waist, letting my palms explore under the T-shirt. I look her directly in the eyes. "Seeing you the first second I woke up made me feel like the luckiest man alive, so yes, I want to do this again."

A blush travels from her neck to her cheeks, but it disappears the second I pinch a nipple, and lust fills her eyes. I have no problem being quick before work, and I'd do it in a heartbeat if Blaise wouldn't take my hands off her.

"I'm gonna brush my teeth before we go." She turns around, flashing me with her butt. I lean forward and slap it. Blaise doesn't seem to mind it as she walks into her bathroom.

"Hurry up, and you can come to my place to eat something while I get ready," I suggest, shifting my feet to the floor.

"Okay. I'll be quick." Her voice makes it out of the bedroom.

The door closes after her, and I get up, dragging my boxers and jeans on. When I take a look at my phone, I see the message from my boss, who's letting me know Blaise has a meeting scheduled with the publishing house next week.

"They loved it," I tell Blaise, knowing if they agreed, it's true.

She comes back with a grin on her face. "How do you know?"

"I just got a text about a meeting with them on Monday." I smile, enjoying the way the corners of her mouth widen even more.

"Awesome." She tries to keep it cool and leaves, but then pokes her head in the room with round eyes staring at me. "I can't believe you just seriously said that to me. I think I'm dreaming." She looks down at her hands. "Crap. I'm not dreaming. I read somewhere that if you want to see if you're dreaming, you have to look at your hands and see if they are blurry." Blaise looks up at me. "I'll just..." She points her thumb behind her and then disappears into the bathroom, leaving me there with a smile on my face.

When she gets out a few minutes later, I watch her looking for clothes. I sit back in the bed, arms around myself, as she removes my T-shirt off her skin and drops the material at her feet. She takes her time to put on a pair of tight jeans and a white T-shirt.

My dick hardens with every careful move she makes, well aware of the fact that I'm watching. And she fucking loves it. When she twirls on her feet, a smirk plays on her lips the moment we make eye contact.

"What?" She walks toward the bathroom, and I do my best not to stop her.

"Nothing," I say and go rest my shoulder on the doorframe, observing her as she grabs a brush and starts doing her hair. "I was just thinking about how quickly you'll regret not having a safe word the minute you tease me again."

A swallow bumps in her throat, her fingers struggling to tie her hair into two braids. These are personally my favorites.

"Oh." That's all she can get out, her movements quickening. "I was definitely not trying to."

I crack a laugh. "But you were."

And I liked it too.

Blaise smiles at herself in the mirror, biting her lip to hold in a laugh. Once she's done, she places a hand on my shoulder and gives me a shove so she can get past me. She uses some perfume and points with her finger behind where I'm standing. "Your shirt is there."

I grab it and make a show of putting it on. One that she's eating up.

"Should I use the stairs?" I ask, thinking about Catherine.

"She's sleeping. We can go." She throws a quick glance around the room, puts the blanket over her bed, and opens the door for us.

As unusual as this is, it feels good. Comfortable.

Blaise locks the door after us, and we pass the street to our house. Inside, we try to be silent in case August's still sleeping, but he's already at the table with three sandwiches in front of him. He looks up at us, biting from bread.

I guess it didn't take him long to realize where I was.

"Mornin'," he says.

Blaise blushes a light shade of pink but keeps it together, grabbing a chair and sitting on it. She takes one of the sandwiches and smiles.

"Thanks."

August nods, his eyes jumping from Blaise to me, from me to Blaise.

"I'll go get ready."

I walk the stairs, enter my room, and take a look at the clock reading six twenty. We have to be there a little before seven, so I have enough time to eat and get ready. After I grab my clothes for the day, I put them on and do my morning routine in the bathroom, which doesn't take me long because, in no more than five minutes, I'm dressed. My feet carry me downstairs, and I overhear Blaise's last phrase before I take the last step.

"I really thought she was going to do it this time." She feels me looking at her, and her eyes snap to mine. "Guess I was wrong." Blaise holds her phone between two fingers, her features lowering. "The rehab facility called me to say that Tamara just signed out."

This is something I saw coming. I knew it from the second Blaise told me about it, but I tried to keep my pessimism inside and let her have a little hopeful moment that would open her eyes regarding Tamara without hurting herself too much. Plus, I didn't want to take away a chance for August to have his mother back.

I should've followed my gut.

"Of course she did." I round the table and take my sandwich. "She better not come here this time." At that, Blaise and August exchange a look. "What?"

My brother sighs and unlocks his phone. "About that...." he says before sliding the phone to me. Tamara texted him, claiming she's excited to see us.

Great.

I give him his device back. "I'm so done with her shit," I scold and look at my brother. "Take your car and do not come back until we're done with work. Understood?"

He shouldn't be home when she gets here because if there's something she's good at, that's manipulating. And I have no doubt that she can twist August's thoughts in no time with her lies.

"Yeah, I had plans anyway," he says, then sits up from his seat.

Blaise murmurs something under her breath, her palms fisting in a struggle to keep them from trembling. Her eyes glisten with unshed tears as she brings a hand to her twitching jaw.

It's hard to compose myself when I see her this way. I knew it wouldn't be long until she'd decide to drop everything and disappoint Blaise after she put her trust in her. You can't trust Tamara. She doesn't deserve it. Nor does she do anything to earn it. She's fucking destructive, and a part of me wishes I would've been the one to find her on the porch that day. I could've stopped all of this from happening.

"I'll go change," August says and walks to the stairs.

"Leave as soon as you're done," I tell him.

Blaise stands up, and we walk to the car in silence. She gets in, and I occupy the driver's seat, bringing the engine to life. I glance at her before we take off.

Tamara won't even have a chance to play her games. I'll make sure of it. She fooled Blaise into thinking she could be trusted when she was dealing with her grandmother's stroke, taking advantage of her vulnerability, but her actions only proved who she truly is.

"I'm sorry," Blaise says so low I barely hear it.

My hand reaches her thigh, squeezing it. "It's not you who should be sorry."

She has a heart of gold. No one could blame her for wanting to help. The only person to blame is Tamara.

Even though I told myself that I'd never get involved in their relationship with Tamara, that changes today. Both August and Blaise are mine to protect, and I'll never allow her to hurt them again. She did it too many times.

Blaise stays silent the entire drive to work, and I keep my palm on her until we reach the parking lot of Westnook.

"This time will be different," I say.

CHAPTER THIRTY-TWO

BLAISE

Saying today's shift was a disaster would be an understatement because all I did was continuously mess up orders, knock a few down, and ignore everyone, thanks to the storm brewing over my head. Rhodes wanting to give me the day off made it a lot worse since that meant my clumsiness wasn't only in my head, and the rest could see it too. Fortunately, I didn't do anything that'd cost us money.

Selah tried to convince me to talk, but she didn't insist anymore when I told her Tamara's back. We'll talk about tonight during a long, *long* phone call.

The moment I step out of Westnook, I breathe out in relief, and if Ares notices the tension slowly easing away from my body, he doesn't say a word about it.

Before entering the car, we glance at each other, both aware of what's waiting for us back home. Ares doesn't seem as anxious as I am—especially after I found out she played us all. He's oddly relaxed, and I think a bit angry if I'm to judge by the occasional twitch in his jaw.

"Ready?" I smile, but not really.

Ares nods at me, and we get in, driving off in complete silence.

The drive home is tense. Ares keeps squeezing the steering wheel until the tips of his fingers turn red, and I like to imagine Tamara's neck in his grip instead. The closer we get to the house, the angrier he gets, and truth to be told, he has every damn right to be pissed.

I'm curious what she'll say when she realizes we know everything.

Will she continue to lie, deny everything, or beg for forgiveness?

Forgiveness that she definitely won't be getting from me ever again.

Too much time passed with her taking advantage of my kindness and August's naivety, but she'll soon figure out those things don't last forever. Like everything else, they have an ending, and hers is quickly approaching.

My decision to not forgive her isn't going to give me back the money I wasted or the time she used for nothing else than manipulating us. It'll help keep someone away that doesn't deserve us.

I don't have enough fingers to count the chances she

had to fix things. Chances that were undeserved but still given.

Ares parks the car behind August's, which is down the road from their house. He told him to park his car further down the street until we came back to make sure Tamara wouldn't speak with him alone.

Ares knocks on his window as soon as we're out, and August gets out quickly. Before we walk toward the house, Ares stops him. "Don't let her get into your head."

He gives him a curt nod. "I won't."

We make our way to their porch, our shoulders stiffening with each step closer. Closer to *her*.

As expected, Tamara is sitting on the front porch waiting for us. Her head snaps in our direction, and she jumps to her feet, her eyes welling with tears like a trained reaction.

"You're home." She smiles, her bottom lip quivering.

"Why are you here?" I find myself asking in a harsh tone.

She flinches as if I just slapped her. "Because I missed you all." Her gaze moves to her sons, but none of them say anything.

I've never been so rude to Tamara, but there's a first for everything, and seeing her pull out this stupid act makes me wish for nothing more than making her swallow the fake tears.

My fists clench beside my body, and I struggle to take a deep, calming breath. I'm known for my talent to lose my temper pretty quickly.

"Let's go inside before she makes a scene," Ares says, touching my lower back gently, not sparing his mother a glance as he walks past her.

August and I follow close behind, both of us getting a glimpse of Tamara's face drenched in crocodile tears. Within seconds, the sound of her footsteps echoes behind us.

In the house, she takes a seat at the table, but none of us join her.

"What's wrong?" Tamara has the nerve to ask, standing back up to return eye level with us. "Aren't you happy to see me?"

If I weren't so mad, I'd laugh at the stupidity of her questions.

Tamara takes her time analyzing each one of us, her gaze lingering on August for too long. Her eyebrows lower in disbelief at whatever she sees on his face, and that sends a flicker of satisfaction to me.

She has to finally sense that something is wrong because her shoulders drop, and she moves her hands to smooth out her long black hair.

"I think we should start from the beginning. Shall we?" I decide to speak first since this started with my attempt to help. "You took advantage of me, of my trust, of my money, and most important of all, you made me hide everything from them for *months—*"

"Jellybean..." She takes a step forward, then reaches out and grabs my hand. I yank it away, stumbling backward and bumping into Ares, who steadies me immediately.

"Let her talk," Ares tells her in a low, dangerous tone. "And *don't* touch her again."

She swallows, and I continue, thankful he has my back. "You made me swear to hide everything from them, yet you told August the day I took you to rehab," I say louder than I intended to. "Why?" My limbs start to shake, and I hate how her eyes widen in surprise, breath quickening. "What kind of mother would pit her children and their best friend against one another?"

Her gaze snaps at August, throwing him a disappointed look he doesn't deserve. If she's going to give him shit about telling us... I swear I'm going to lose it completely.

"I lied to Ares for you, thinking I was doing the right thing." August lets out both a sarcastic and pained laugh. "Now that you're not even trying to deny it, I know I should've never trusted you."

Tamara nibbles the inside of her cheek, plays with the hem of her shirt, and avoids meeting our glances.

"I hope it was worth it, Tam. Because you're nothing more than a stranger to me from now on," I say through gritted teeth, stepping closer to her. Even with me inches from her face, she won't look at me.

She barely moves when I straighten my back. Her jaw trembles, along with the hand she lifts to wipe her face.

I wouldn't be surprised if she's this quiet because of her struggles to find an excuse or a better lie to get her out of the mess she got herself into.

"Get out," Ares tells her calmly.

Her eyes glaze over, searching his face. "What?"

Ares takes two imposing steps, glaring at his mom before he speaks. "Leave, find another place to stay, and don't speak to August unless I'm there."

Tamara shakes her head, refusing to cooperate with him. "Don't do this to me." She clings to his arms. "You're the only reason I went to rehab." Tears slide down her cheeks as Ares removes himself from under her touch.

"Do you want to see August again?" he asks, and Tamara nods. She's always like that when it comes to her youngest son. "Then get out before I drag you myself."

I can't explain what I'm seeing, but the fury filling her eyes catches me off guard. I can't believe I never noticed it's directed at Ares. He doesn't seem moved by it at all. He stands in his place and waits for Tamara to do as he told her to.

Only... she never gives up this easily.

"My sunshine." She stands up, her attention turning

to August. "How can you let him treat me this way? I'm your mother." Her voice cracks on the last word, and I have to admit she's giving one hell of a performance.

August sucks in a sharp breath. "I'm letting him because if I were in his position, I wouldn't be as nice."

That surprises me. Not once has he mentioned something bad about his mother. August and Tamara have always had a great relationship, and maybe that's why seeing him against her is this shocking to me.

"If you come back without my permission, I will call the police and file a restraining order. Then you'll never see any of us again." Ares grabs her by the elbow, and she doesn't even fight his grip.

She walks toward the front door as her tear-soaked eyes are pinned on August, silently pleading for his help.

And the help she's waiting for never comes.

CHAPTER THIRTY-THREE

ARES

I'm in my car, struggling to finish a manuscript for one of my clients, but I'm distracted as hell.

Tamara's back, and I don't know how to feel. I'm not mad because that would mean giving a shit about her, and I'm not disappointed because it's no surprise she hasn't changed. Maybe I'm tired. Tired of her showing up and acting like nothing happened and definitely sick of her hurting Blaise and August.

Every time she shows up, she loves to play the loving mom, each time doing things a mother would do—cleaning around the house, cooking, being around for dinner—and it lasts less than a couple of months.

However, as promised, this time is different. She doesn't have a key to our house, and she's not allowed to see August without my permission, and thus August's.

Because at the end of the day, it's his choice if he wants to give her another chance or not.

And then there's Blaise, who's in a meeting with the assistant and owner of Coral's in his office, signing a contract if she agrees to his terms. I don't know them yet, but what I know is that publishing houses don't always play nice. If she can't meet their expectations, I don't want her to accept the deal just because of me. She shouldn't feel pressured at all.

And I hope she doesn't because it's such a Blaise thing to do to always sacrifice her needs for the sake of others.

Fuck me. I should've mentioned this earlier and made it clear to her that my help doesn't force her to take any decision.

I slam the laptop on my lap shut and put it on the car's backseat, throwing a quick glance at the time. She's already been in there for forty minutes, and I don't know if it's because they get along well or because she's trying to negotiate the terms.

The only thing I'm glad about is the empty parking lot. This was a good opportunity for me to edit in a quiet environment, but my thoughts decided to take it away from me.

I close my eyes and rest my head on the headrest of the seat. Everything is going fine inside, she'll get the deal, and maybe Tamara will vanish into thin air.

Three rapid knocks bring me back to Earth, and I

peel my eyes open. Blaise is cupping her eyes into the glass of my window, and a grin stretches from one ear to another as the wind blows her hair all around her face.

I wave for her to get into the car, but she shakes her head, cheeks red.

"Come out," she mouths.

Even though I don't know the reason behind her request, I do as she says. I climb out and close the door behind me.

"Well?" I ask, leaning against the car.

Her irresistible grin deepens as the excitement flooding through her adds shine to her eyes and colors her cheeks. Blaise sweeps the hairs out of her face, shaking her head in disbelief.

"They said I have to send them the book in five months, but I made them extend the deadline with two more." She clasps her hands together and jumps on her feet but stops when she sees me widening my eyes. She cracks a laugh. "I know, that was my inner reaction as well, but I kept it cool." She tries to sustain the fact by moving her palms in a slow move. "They loved the idea too much to let it go. Rolland suggested starting to build a social media platform to have a community before publishing. He also said working with you would be the perfect ingredient added to the mix of my story. Then we talked about the cover and..."

She stops herself when she notices me smiling, enjoying her rant and the speed she's talking. Blaise comes forward and leans against the car close to me, giggling like a child.

"Anyway," she says, laughing, "everything went *amazing*, and they asked me to send them every three chapters I have done to make sure I'm still working on it. They'll get back to me for marketing purposes and design."

My chest blooms with pride. To think I was worried about them fooling her for their benefit seems stupid right now.

"That's fucking amazing, Moon. I'm proud of you," I say because I genuinely am happy for her, and the thought of seeing her dream come to reality is a dream for me. Being a part of the process only makes it better. "And Rolland says that only because of who my boss is."

She shrugs. "No matter what, I think he's right."

"We'll do a great job," I assure her, and something about me saying it makes her throw her tiny arms around my waist, squeezing me.

"Thank you." She breathes me in, burying her head into my chest.

My hand automatically goes up and brushes her hair in long, slow strokes. I lean down and kiss it as she relaxes into my embrace. At this moment, I just know that everything else is wrong, and this is right. And I know full well it has to do with this girl in my arms who loves to style her hair as much as she loves writing.

"The merits aren't mine," I say, and she snuggles closer, remaining quiet.

We stay like this for some time—me playing with her hair and her hugging me tighter like she can't get close enough. I breathe her in like air, closing my eyes at the sensation. She shifts in my embrace, purring under my touch.

"Let's go home," I whisper in her hair after a while.

Her head lifts, and she rests her chin on my chest, groaning. "I hope she's not there. I don't want to see her," she murmurs so low I almost miss it.

Tamara should be her last care in the world now that she's getting closer to achieving her dream. And it will. As long as I'm here, Blaise will celebrate every little moment—especially this first step in her career as an author—without worrying about anything else.

"She's not, and even if she is, I'll call the police," I assure her, then take her head between my palms, her green, watery eyes not once trying to hide from me.

I love it when she's so transparent with me. Blaise has no problem showing me her real self. Every time I'm around, she acts like she's alone, and it drives me crazy to think she's that comfortable when we're together because I know how that feels too well.

Blaise nods, biting her lip. I gesture with my head to get into the car, and she hugs me one more time before getting in. I follow and bring the engine to life as she sniffles.

"She's not worth your tears. You just got a fucking amazing book deal, so fuck her." Blaise cracks a laugh, and I drive out of the parking lot. "Wanna grab something to eat?" I ask.

Food is the key to Blaise's heart, and if that's going to make her happy right now, I'll give her as much food as she wants.

"Ice cream would be great."

Soon after that, I park in front of McDonald's, get two Oreo McFlurries for both of us and hand them to her once I'm back.

"Mmm, yummy," she says, patting her stomach before sticking the spoon into it and taking a bite. "Best reward." She smiles as she swallows and points with the spoon to it. "I'm telling you. Best reward."

I don't know how she does it, but Blaise can be both a child and a mature, stunning woman when she wants to. It's a thing I appreciate about her like hell.

I laugh, take my cup, and place it between my legs. We drive off, both of us eating in silence. And when we get to our houses, Blaise's ice cream is long gone, and I take the last bite from mine. I stop the engine before throwing a glance at her.

"Climb to my bedroom tonight?" She pulls out a smile that makes my cock harden, then swipes her tongue over the bottom lip I dream about having between my teeth.

Something about my gaze makes her swallow, so I

clear my throat, realizing I didn't reply to her question and I was staring like a virgin at her breasts. "I'll be there."

She nods. "I'll come over soon to share the news with August. I have to tell Nanna first."

"Catherine is going to make you a cake as soon as you tell her," I say, grateful for the option to switch the topic to something less dick-throbbing than sneaking into her room later.

If she notices me changing the subject, she doesn't make any comments about it. "I bet there's already one waiting for me. The one with congratulations is on the table, and the one with some inspirational message about never giving up is in the fridge. Just in case." She laughs and steals one out of me, too, since it's totally something Catherine would do.

She's been a great parent figure to Blaise, always there for her, never asking for something in exchange. And then she took the place of our parents too. Congratulating us, wrapping gifts under their tree, making sure to decorate our house for Christmas as well, cooking for us, and always loving us like her own kids.

Catherine is more of a mother to me than Tamara has ever been.

CHAPTER THIRTY-FOUR

BLAISE

Nanna's thrilled when I tell her about the deal. She can't stop hugging me and congratulating me, eyes welling with tears, and because I don't want to leave, I stay downstairs to watch an episode of a soap opera with her.

Whenever we're together, every joke seems funnier than it really is, and maybe that's why we laugh even if something isn't necessarily funny. My tummy hurts, and my cheeks are sore from how hard I stretch them, but at this moment, it's too much of a blessing to care about it. I barely hear her laugh anymore, and I'm surprised to see it's as colorful and contagious as I remember.

Once the tears dry on our faces, I kiss her forehead and hug her tightly to my chest, grateful for having her here.

I dial Selah's number, and because it doesn't feel right to burst out with happiness while she's fighting her brother's cancer at his side, I hold my excitement in. She tells me how happy and proud she is, the conversation ending quickly when she has to go back to work.

Because the deal got me excited enough to start rewriting the book with the new updates, I practically run upstairs and sit in bed with my laptop until I lose track of time.

It's one in the morning, and I've written two chapters already, on my way to the third one. With the little but essential notes Ares made, I feel more confident with this story. We have a lot to work on, and I know most of it right now is shit. However, soon enough, it will turn into a masterpiece if we do it right. And I know we will. There's no other person on Earth I'd do this with.

My fingers type on the keyboard as fast as they can. I'm afraid that if I don't do it quickly enough, my ideas will get lost somewhere in a deep part of my brain.

A knock on my window interrupts me, and I stand up after I finish writing down my idea. I open the window, ready to tell Ares about how I spent my night, but when I take sight of him, I change my mind.

His curly hair is all over his forehead like he's been messing with it for quite some time, eyes dark and squinted, trying to adjust to the light in my room. His brows are slowly knitted together, a muscle in his jaw twitching as I take him in.

"Why aren't you sleeping?" he asks.

After I get out of the way, he steps in and takes his shoes off. He looks at the laptop on my bed, and I'd say he figured out the reason I'm awake.

"I could ask you the same thing," I say, walking past him and getting under the blanket.

He stares at me for a long second, then takes his pants off, folds them, and puts them on the chair under my desk, along with the shirt he throws over his head. He looks like someone just killed his dog, and it's not a pretty picture. Not at all.

Once he's done with his clothes, he removes his socks too, before gently pulling the cover from the other side of the bed, enough to give him space to get in. He fluffs his pillow and lies on his back, face to the ceiling.

"Couldn't sleep." Ares's raspy voice fills the air.

I nod to myself, place my laptop on the desk, and turn off the lights. After I get into bed, I flick on the small lamp on my nightstand. The light is enough to see him without killing our eyes. I make myself comfortable under the covers and mirror his position, thinking about how to make him feel better.

"Wanna talk about it?" I ask.

He shakes his head, stuffing his hands under it. "There's nothing to talk about. I just know I don't want to be alone."

A swallow bobs in my throat. "But you want to be with me?" Slowly, I peek at him, his dark features sharpening in the light.

293

His head turns, and his eyes find me. "Yes."

And just like that, one word brings the butterflies in my stomach back to life. This has to be my favorite thing about Ares. When he talks, he makes sure it's worth it.

"Okay," I whisper, looking straight into his eyes.

He holds my stare, and I clench my thighs, trying to come up with a way that will distract me from the thoughts I'm having.

It's not the time to think about sex when he's clearly not feeling well, Blaise. Think about anything else. Like Tamara.

Right.

That's more than enough to sober me up.

I turn around and touch the lamp two times to make the light brighter. Taking out a book I forgot I had on my nightstand until now, I sit up, resting my back against the pillows.

"Come here," I say to him. "For old time's sake."

The corner of his mouth pulls into a smile. Ares comes closer and rests his head on my shoulder as I open the book to the first page, his arm circling my waist until he's comfortable. We used to do this a lot when we were little. Sometimes, he'd be the one reading to me, and other times, I'd be the one reading to him.

"Kyra. Chapter one. A scream rips out of me at the scene in front of my eyes," I start, and his chuckle comes in an instant.

"What?" I ask, trying to get a view of him, but it's kind of hard from this angle.

He shrugs. "Bet someone's dead."

I roll my eyes. "Maybe she saw a cute dog, and the scream was because of the happiness she couldn't hold in."

Ares lifts his head and looks at me, disappointed with my answer. He grimaces, one corner of his mouth twisting to the side as he pinches the bridge of his nose, holding back a laugh. "You're a writer. Is that the farthest your mind can go?"

My eyes squint, and so do his. "Well," I say, and he raises a brow, "no." He laughs. "I just wanted to contradict you."

Ares fakes a groan and puts his head back on my shoulder, looking at the book I'm holding, reading at the same time I speak out loud. When Kyra finally reveals the scene that happened in front of her, he stops me. "See? I was right."

I ignore his comment, smiling as I continue. We stay like that for an hour, reading with nothing but my voice filling the air. It's been a while since I felt this safe. This protected and this... happy. It's overwhelming.

Soon enough, his breathing evens, letting me know he's asleep. After quietly putting the book down, I flick the lights off and reach his ear, ready to take his hearing aids off, but he stops me, his warm palm grazing over mine.

"I'll take them off in a bit." He doesn't open his eyes when he talks.

A lump bobs in my throat, and I swallow it. "Okay."

After I tuck myself under the blanket, he turns on his side, facing me. He looks at me, and a sigh leaves his lips before he takes me by my waist, bringing me closer to him. I bury my face in his chest, loving the feeling of him. He never takes his hand off my waist.

"I like you," he murmurs out of nowhere.

My leg moves up onto his, just like it was supposed to be there all the time, and a slow smile plays on my lips as I do my best not to show what his words are doing to me. I swallow and speak only when I'm sure my voice is steady.

"I like you too," I admit, and when he lifts his hand and caresses my hair, I close my eyes, enjoying the sensation.

After a few moments of silence, he talks again, his voice a low murmur that flutters every butterfly inside me. "You know why I haven't kissed you yet?" he asks me, and I peel my eyes open. "It's not because I don't have feelings for you, Blaise."

"It's not?" I arch my eyebrows.

"No." He shakes his head, the movement barely noticeable in the darkness.

My chest constricts. And it does it in the most beautiful way. My palm finds his cheek, brushing my thumb over it as I lean in and kiss his nose.

That's all that matters to me.

"Okay," I whisper and hug him as tight as I can.

"I want to make you happy. I want us to be ready to face everything together. I want to know that we *got* this. You have to understand that matters the most to me." He continues to caress my hair as his chin rests on my head. "Because I'm not playing around, Blaise. Once I'm in, I'm all in and never letting you go."

I smile in the crook between his shoulder and neck, pushing into him because the position we're in doesn't feel close enough.

"Sounds good to me," I say, loving how careful and thoughtful he's being.

He lifts his head a little to get access to his ear, takes his aids out, and stretches his hand to the nightstand next to him to put them there, not once removing his touch from me.

Ares squeezes me, and we fall asleep with his fingers brushing all over my hair.

CHAPTER THIRTY-FIVE

ARES

It's been two weeks since Tamara came back, and somehow, Blaise managed to convince us all to gather at her house, claiming we need a good distraction from, I quote, "you know what." She and Selah spend a good time in the kitchen, preparing dinner and catching up on each other's lives while my brother and Rhodes argue about whether old movies are better than the newer ones.

I think about chiming in and forgetting about Tamara for the night, but my mind is determined to stress over it regardless of what my plans are. It's odd because normally, I wouldn't care about these short-lasting visits, and I wouldn't care now either if she hadn't taken advantage of Blaise and August.

That's not something I'm going to ignore.

"Are you going to use the door tonight?" August

asks, taking me out of my thoughts when we step out of Blaise's house once everyone leaves. I give him a look, and he sighs like I shouldn't even need clarification. "Why can't you use the door like a normal person instead of your window?"

It clearly takes me a second to get it since I am so deeply lost in my mind. I cock a brow. "Shouldn't you be sleeping at night?"

He smacks a hand on my back, smirking like a fool. "So should you."

I'm ready to give him shit about sticking his nose where it doesn't belong when someone clears their throat, and both of us snap our eyes to the front porch.

Tamara has been texting me about wanting to see us, but I didn't think she'd just show up after August told her he has no intention of seeing her any time soon. I can't be surprised either because her actually listening would've been a surprise, and I think it's self-explanatory why.

She must've at least stopped messaging him because, by the look on his face, he didn't expect this as much as I didn't.

I lift my brows in question toward Tamara. She raises one back at me, tilting her head.

The fucking nerve to act like a mother right now.

"Are we late for our curfew or something?" My voice is calm, but the venom in it doesn't go unnoticed. August cracks a laugh that I ignore as Tamara sighs.

"Funny, but no." She shakes her head. "I just wanted to talk before you boys go to bed."

I look at my brother. He glances at me and raises his shoulders in a shrug. I move my gaze back to her and squint my eyes.

"The last time we talked, I made it clear I'll file a restraining order if you ever come here without my permission, and I'm a man of my word," I say before taking my phone out of my pocket and walking past her to get into the house. I stop two steps from the door. "I won't call the police to come pick you up, but I'm completing the form once I'm inside."

She drops her head into her palms. "Two minutes," she says, and suddenly I'm looking for signals that she's drunk again. "That's all I'm asking for."

It's August's choice if he wants to hear her out or not, so I simply cross my arms over my chest, waiting for him to decide. Unless he's asking me not to, I'm filing that restraining order as soon as I'm inside. It might not be necessary, but I told myself I was never going to let her harm them ever again.

And that's the only way I can make it possible.

"Be quick," August says, stuffing his hands in his pockets.

Her dark gray eyes dart between us before she speaks. "I know this isn't easy for you—"

"Get straight to the point," August interrupts her, his tone bitter.

Tamara swallows hard, playing with the hem of her shirt. "Like I said... I know this isn't easy for you both," she continues, "as much as it isn't easy for me." She stops, analyzing our faces for a second before talking again. "But I shouldn't be the only one trying. Since I've been back, you ignore my messages, don't want to have dinner together, and I have no other option than to show up here unannounced then wait for hours until you get back."

I saw every text, and August did too, but he ignored each of her attempts. When I told him that maybe they should meet and see if anything was worth fixing, he immediately shut me down.

"If you aren't willing to try, what am I supposed to do?" she asks, with tears in her eyes and trembling hands, her gaze wandering in the distance like she knows she's lost us for good.

I'm not surprised at all, to be honest. This is the card she always pulls out when things don't go the way she wants once she's realized she can't manipulate the outcome any longer.

"A good start would've been sticking to rehab and not wasting someone's money that was meant to help you." August leaves the second the words make it out of his mouth, and I follow him, knowing this conversation is over.

We lock the door behind us, Tamara's sobs blaring in our ears. I have the urge to take my hearing aids out but quickly forget about that when August's shoulders drop as if he's defeated. He drops onto the couch, roaming a hand through his hair.

"You okay?" I ask, sitting down next to him.

He nods. "Yeah, let's just get it over with on that restraining order before I go."

"Where are you going?"

The smirk on his face reappears, lighting his appearance to what I've gotten used to. A happy kid. Yet there's a tiny difference in him telling me that something changed tonight.

"I'm crashing at a friend's so you and Blaise can have the house for yourself." He laughs, patting me on the back. "Catherine must've had enough of you two fucking like bunnies."

I smack his head, but his laugh only grows louder.

CHAPTER THIRTY-SIX

BLAISE

ARES

come sleep in my bed tonight,
Moon.

His message came in twenty minutes ago, and I still haven't sent him a reply. I've been staring at my clothes, looking for something cute to wear, only to realize I don't even own cute pajamas, and the Winnie the Pooh set it's definitely not the vibe I'm going for. Usually, I just throw a T-shirt and a comfortable thong on before crashing into bed.

But now I want to dress up for him. I want to surprise him and feel sexy while his eyes travel all over my body. The problem is, I don't have anything sexy. I 100% can't go in a dress—the only piece of clothing I have that's an eye-catcher—and besides simple thongs or bras, I have nothing.

At this point, I'd go there in my lingerie. I know that would be enough to drive him crazy.

My phone rings on the bed, and I look at my watch. Shit. It's been a goddamn hour, not twenty minutes. I hurry and take it, regulating my breathing before responding.

"Yeah?" I say, happy that my voice isn't shaking.

"Get your ass here and stop trying on your entire closet." His deep voice rumbles through the speaker.

An ashamed sigh escapes my lips as I slowly turn around to my window, coming to a perfect view of Ares standing in front of his own aperture. He stares at me with the phone clutched in his hand, eyes roaming all over my body. A black underwear I thought would go well with my blonde hair pops my chest out and accentuates the curves of my thighs, making it a bit hard to breathe.

I blush. "Have you ever heard about privacy?"

His head tilts to the side, and a smile forms on his lips. "Yes, and I'm not giving it to you."

Without my permission, another sigh fills the silence between us.

Ares doesn't waste a second to find out what's going on. "What's the matter?"

I shrug, biting the inside of my cheek as I glance at him. "Nothing."

"Talk to me."

At his pleading, I turn to my closet and gesticulate a hand towards it. "I-I just wanted to wear something nice because I never do that, but I have nothing besides a basic lingerie you probably saw me in before, and I got stuck here trying on clothes to see which shirt pops my boobs out more or what pants flatter my legs better." I finish in a breath, then drop on my butt, sticking my head to the window.

"Moon, listen to me, and listen carefully because I'm not going to repeat this," he tells me, and I can't resist the urge to glance back at him. "Buy every set of lingerie on this planet, wear it every night of my life, feel sexy, and tease me, but know that at the end of the day, it's your body that I'm so desperate to see and touch. No matter what you have on, the only thing I'll think about is how to get rid of it. If you want to feel good in your skin, that's fine. We can go get something tomorrow but don't dress for me. You'll be disappointed in how fast I'll tear it apart."

His voice goes from angry to tender, touching all the right places over my heart and body, making my legs squeeze in pleasure at his words.

I don't know how he does it. He boosts my confidence with a few words, and all I want is to go there and kiss the shit out of him for being this understanding with me. I rant a lot, and sometimes it can be exhausting, yet that never happens with him.

"Okay," I whisper with a smile on my face.

"Now, come here, please."

"So it's officially done?" I ask with my head on his chest five minutes after I arrive at his place.

"Not really. There will be a few hearings going on and a lot of papers to sign, but I'm fucking ready."

I nod. "How did August take it?"

His shoulders stiffen a little, and I look at him, searching for an explanation for the sudden change in him.

"What's wrong?" My brows furrow in concern.

Ares takes a rebellious strand of my hair and tucks it behind my ear, giving my cheek soft brushes of his fingers. "He seemed fine."

"But?"

"It was nothing. It might've been in my head for all I know." He looks away from my eyes to my breasts, quick to change the subject in a way that doesn't require words.

"I—"

He cuts me off immediately, not up to discussing more about his brother. "I've teased myself for an hour, watching you change clothes and looking hot as fuck. You can't drag this on forever and leave me with blue balls so we can talk about something I've imagined."

I open my mouth to say something, but he's fast to pin me on my back, wrists caught between his firm hands. He's eager to undress me—just as promised— taking my shorts down with his teeth like a desperate man. My thighs clench at the sight, and he forces them open to fit between my legs so he can remove my panties. In no more than two seconds, I'm lying naked in front of a fully dressed man.

Truth is, I'm not feeling self-conscious at all. I like that he's yearning this badly to have me naked that he forgets about his clothes.

"No piece of clothing could do justice to this body," he murmurs as if he's talking to himself, not caring if I hear or not. But I do. And it warms me whole.

Ares catches my nipple between his teeth, and I grind into him, throwing my head back in pleasure.

"How could I see these breasts begging to be fucked if you were dressed?" he talks, still paying very, *very* much attention to my tits.

I'm so caught up in his dirty talk that I don't even feel his hand going down until it pumps into my pussy. A moan escapes out of my throat, my clit throbbing with pleasure under his touch.

"How could I feel this drenched pussy on my fingers if you had anything on?" he continues, twisting his fingers inside me.

Ares draws circles with his thumb, my toes sinking into his mattress and ready to burn a hole through it from how hard I'm struggling to get closer to him—it's impossible to do it when we're glued to one another, skin to skin. He groans, sharing wet kisses on my neck.

"I need you inside me." I draw out a breath, pushing into him as hard as I can. "Please," I plead, stretching my hands in front of me and getting rid of the shirt he has on in one quick second.

"And I need to taste you." He smirks at me, a few curls falling on his forehead as he drops between my thighs.

The moment he sucks on my clit, I'm lost. At some point, I hear a powerful sound coming from downstairs but ignore it, too absorbed in Ares. All I know is I keep asking for his cock over and over until I feel the warmth of his body slipping away. I peel my eyes open and see him standing at the edge of the bed, throwing the shirt back on, an alarmed look on his face.

I rise on my feet, my heartbeat going crazy. "What happened?"

His chest rises and falls with rapid breaths as he comes to cup my cheeks between his hands, eyes searching all over my face. I have never seen him this scared. It's like this isn't him anymore. And that makes me panic, too, but I fight hard not to let it show, knowing that's not what he needs right now.

"Ares, you're scaring me. What happened?" I ask, catching his wrist in my palm.

"Someone broke into the house. Do not come downstairs, do you hear me?" He shakes me a little, his eyes widening on me.

"I'm not letting you go alone. I'll call the police, and we can go to my house through the roof."

Ares shakes his head at me, sweat gathering at his temples. He puts his forehead to mine. "Promise me you won't come downstairs, no matter what happens."

I open my mouth in protest because if anything happens to him, I'm not going to sit around and do nothing, but then I hear it. A loud, grave scream echoing into the house.

"Why? *Why* did you do this to me?"

Tamara.

My skin prickles with dread the moment I recognize her voice, and even though I don't know what the hell she did to scare Ares this way, it has to be bad.

"Promise me, Blaise. Promise you won't come downstairs." His breath hitches when he speaks, his beautiful eyes bulging with fright, and until I shake my head, he doesn't leave my side. "Call the police."

Ares locks the door after him, and I just stand there, hugging my legs to my chest as I replay his unrecognizable face in my head. There's something he hid from us.

I know realize that Tamara did far more to him than we know.

CHAPTER THIRTY-SEVEN

ARES

When I get downstairs, she's standing in the middle of the kitchen with a bottle of vodka hanging low between her fingers and an animalistic look in her eyes. Tamara's surrounded by the pieces of the window she just broke to get in, one of them cutting through her foot, but she's so drunk that she can't feel it.

I try to swallow, but my mouth is too dry as I'm thrown back to my childhood. She came home late at night after Dad locked the door and left to drink a beer with his friend, fully aware that Tamara was out cheating on him. I was the only one home because August has a sleepover with his friend. I came downstairs thinking she must've hurt herself. I wanted to help her, but when she saw me sitting in front of her eyes, I knew I should've stayed in bed just like Dad told me to.

Because I didn't listen, I played the role of a boxing bag until breathing felt like a luxury. I could taste blood on my tongue, and my body ached everywhere, but I didn't give up. I tried to climb the stairs, and in my dream, I made it upstairs.

In reality, Dad found me in the morning. I was covered in blood and bruises. It's hard to even open my eyes, but I saw how my hand was stretched to the staircase before my father got me into the shower.

"Where is he?" she shouts, bringing me back to Earth.

I keep my voice steady, not wanting to show any sign of weakness. Even if my brain is clouded, I manage to come up with a response. "That's none of your business. Get out before the police get here."

Her nostrils flare. "How dare you take him away from me!" she screams, and my mind wanders to Blaise, hoping this isn't alarming enough to make her come here.

Her safety is the only thing that calms me down from a panic attack.

"You did it yourself. I didn't do anything," I say, regaining some confidence both in my posture and my mind.

"Tell him to come downstairs. I'm taking him with me." She walks toward the stairs, but I instantly grab her elbow.

"He's not home," I growl, twitching my jaw to stop myself from breaking her arm.

Tamara frowns. "What do you mean he's not home? Then call him!"

I drag her outside. "No."

She fights my grip, panting and crying like a kid. I don't listen to her. I let her talk until I get her out of the house, as far away as possible from Blaise. When I turn around to leave, she jumps on my back, scratching my scalp with her nails. I try to remove her from me, but she tightens her legs around my waist and continues to scratch me.

Eventually, I unlock her legs and throw her off me, touching the back of my neck, only to notice drops of blood on my fingers. My eyes zero in on it.

"This is all your fault!" she screams from the bottom of her lungs. "If we wouldn't have taken you, Court, August, and I would've been so happy. You ruined it all." She spits the words out, rage swimming through her eyes.

Weird way of saying it, but I guess she can't stand the thought she birthed me.

I close my eyes shut for a second, trying to calm down before I speak again. "Leave. We'll see you soon enough in court."

Her eyes flash with anger. "You son of a bitch!"

Without any thought to continue this and entertain her, I turn around and walk inside.

"I should've fucking let you rot in that orphanage."

That's the last thing I hear before everything goes black.

CHAPTER THIRTY-EIGHT

BLAISE

Something is wrong.

I spent the last twenty minutes convincing myself to keep my promise, but my palms itch to do something, to go after him and see what's going on downstairs before it's too late. Even so, by the time I get up and throw one of his shirts over my head, it's already too late.

The sound of glass shattering to pieces freezes the blood in my veins, stealing my breath all at once as I reach out to the door only to find it locked. My exhale comes out in a series of short, uncontrolled breaths, and all of a sudden, the only piece of clothing I have on seems suffocating.

Despair gnaws at my guts at the realization I can't go to him, and I know panicking isn't going to take me there, so I close my eyes for a second as I try to regulate my breathing. It barely works, but it's enough to allow me to think rationally.

From how I see it, I have two options.

1. Wait for the police to arrive.

2. Find a way to get out of his room.

In reality, I only have one option, and the moment I find the solution, I don't hesitate to run out on his roof, all the way to mine, until I rush out of my room. When I take the stairs to my house, I see Nanna from the corner of my eye, but I don't stop until I'm out.

Ares's door is open, and I have to walk further to see anything else since it's still so dark outside.

"Is everything okay?" I hear a familiar voice I can't distinguish now.

No, I want to say, yet no words make it out of my mouth.

Something's wrong. Very, very wrong. I can feel it in the depth of my bones in a way that hurts as if they'll break open at any second.

I look toward where the voice came from, and even if I don't see who talked, I lay eyes on Tamara running in the opposite direction like the worst things are chasing after her. I swallow the urge to go after her and step on Ares's front porch.

The moment I catch sight of him, I land in a pile at his feet, where he's stretched out on the floor, unconscious. His eyes are closed, blood covering the left part of his head where his ear is cut.

My heart stops beating in my chest when I shake him gently and get nothing in return.

"Ares," I sob, blinking away the tears so I can see him in case he wakes up.

I don't know what injuries he has besides the one on his head, and I'm afraid to check if he's still breathing.

My palm strokes his cheek as I place my forehead onto his. "I need you to wake up," I whisper, squeezing my eyes closed as tears fall down my cheeks. "Please, please, please."

I tug at his shirt, gripping it in a fist until I'm sure I'll rip it.

This can't be happening to me. I can't lose him, or I'll break into pieces before going after him. He has to be okay. We were happy half an hour ago. This didn't happen. What I'm seeing, it's not real. It's only my imagination.

But when my lips reach to kiss his warm skin, I know it's real. I straighten my back and set his shirt free, fighting the tears that shamelessly blur my vision and steal the sight of him away.

"I should've come with you," I say, regret tugging at my chest.

"Miss..." A hand caresses my shoulder, and when I look up to find who it is, the whole neighborhood is behind me, along with the woman whose palm is on me.

"I-I..." I stammer, and she gives me a small smile before I notice she's from the ambulance. "How?" I ask, knowing I only called the police, and it can't be this long since I found him.

"Your grandmother called," she says and sits to her knees along with another colleague while I scan the little crowd to find Nanna.

She's there in her pajamas, her face white as snow. She shouldn't be seeing this. It'll only increase her stress and, therefore, affect her health.

"When did you find him?" the dark-haired woman asks me.

I look at her. "I don't know." I zoom out, my hands shaking as I bring them to my mouth. "I don't know, I don't know if he's even breathing. I didn't even think about doing CPR—"

She puts a palm on my back. "Good, because he's breathing." The woman points to her male colleague, who just finished running the basic tests on him. "We're going to take him to the hospital and make sure he's alright, okay?"

I nod my head, wiping the tears off my face as I watch them take him to the ambulance. From there, I lose track of time again. The only thing I know is that August picks us up, and we're on our way to the hospital.

No one is telling us anything. It's been two hours since we arrived at the hospital, and we have no update besides the surgery they are performing on him right now. The only thing bringing me comfort is that he's breathing. He's alive, and that's all that matters.

"Look," Caroline says from her chair, a hand on her belly as she points at the TV in front of us.

I glance up and find three photos on the news. On one side, there's a photo with me and another one with Ares, and on the other side, Tamara's. I clench my fists beside my body, feeling how I'm losing control of my breathing again.

The police asked me for more information about what happened and I wanted nothing more than to catch her and see her behind bars. They sold the story quickly, and now we have to wait for them to find her. It's the hardest thing to do, but I have no other choice than to do so.

"It's my fault." I blurt out the same thing I said to the police over and over.

Caroline opens her mouth to say something, but before she can, Court and August come to me.

Court speaks first. "Blaise, you don't know her as much as I do. She's *dangerous*." He lifts my chin from the ground with a finger. "You did nothing wrong."

I shake my head, sobbing, and before I know it, August has me tucked in his arms.

"It's okay," he whispers into my hair. "Did you see how big that guy is? He's going to be fine," he jokes, and I laugh through tears, the memory of his muscles under my fingers still fresh in my mind.

CHAPTER THIRTY-NINE

ARES

My head hurts like a motherfucker, and the pain gets even worse when I squint my eyes, struggling to distinguish the blur and blinding lights I'm seeing. The room spins with me as I blink several times, my vision slowly clearing with each flutter.

I don't remember much, but the anger is still hot in my veins, and it burns me inside out. It makes no sense. I was having a great time with Blaise, and then... everything is black.

If I'm in the hospital, surrounded by family and doctors, something bad must've happened.

Blaise is the first to touch me, caressing my hand with gentle strokes, and a river of tears ready to shed is settled deep in her eyes. I want to reach out to her, but everything in me hurts, and she doesn't let me either, pushing my hand down slowly.

She pulls out our childhood game, mouthing something I don't pick up with a relieved smile on her beautiful face. As much as I appreciate her way of trying to make me feel better, a game is the last thing on my mind now.

"What happened?" I ask, my forehead hurting when I involuntary frown.

An older man dressed in his uniform steps forward. He has papers and a pen in his hands, probably ready to examine me now that I'm awake. He doesn't get the chance to because a high-pitched sound rings in my ears, and I look at everyone, wondering if they hear it too. No one seems disturbed. They watch with smiles on their faces.

The ringing only amplifies, and I check if I still have my hearing aids. They're still there.

It makes no sense.

I touch my temples to ease some of the pain, but it's worse when a powerful sting hits. My head hangs low between my shoulders, dizziness taking over me as the sound rings louder, taking me to the point where I need to cover my ears in desperation. It's like I'm blocking the ringing from coming out.

My teeth grind, and when I think I can't take it anymore, tears gathering in the corner of my eyes, it stops. Careful not to do anything abrupt, I raise my head, afraid that any move will bring it back.

Caroline's face is red, her hand on her stomach as

she strokes Dad on the back while he tells me something I can't hear. I want to tell him it's not funny, but when I glance back at the doctor who's trying to talk to me, I freeze.

"Get out," I say, surprising everyone. The only thing I feel is a strong vibration through my body, so I must've said it loud. No one moves. "I need to be alone for a bit. Please go."

Because I feel tears fighting to escape, I close my eyes and throw my head back onto the pillow with a twitch of my jaw. I don't know if the rest are leaving, but when I feel Blaise's hand slipping from my own, I grip it tighter.

"Not you."

More vibration sneaks into my body, and I know it's not from me, which means the rest are talking. They grow quieter and quieter, and it's only when they stop that I open my eyes and face Blaise.

I let her see me the same way she lets me see her: face red from how much she's been crying, throat dry because of the unspoken words, and the buzzy feeling of denial.

My hand stretches, and I caress her tears away, but they only keep coming with no intention of stopping. Knowing her seeing me in this state only makes it worse, I open my arm enough to give her space to lie next to me.

"Come here," I say, my chest aching at the loss of my own voice.

She climbs next to me without a second thought, sneaking her head between my head and my shoulder as her arms scoop around me. I place a palm in her hair, stroking it.

Years ago, they warned Dad and Tamara about this. I remember clearly how they told them the tiniest hit could take away my hearing—

My breathing stops.

Tamara.

The memories flood over me, from the moments of heaven I was having with Blaise to when Tamara told me I was not their son right before losing consciousness when I was trying to get away from her.

I should've fucking let you rot in that orphanage.

All these years, I asked myself what could I've possibly done wrong to have my own mother hate me the way she does. Why was she treating me that way? Why did she love her other son and not me? Was I so hard to love?

Those questions seemed childish, and I put them somewhere in the back of my head, but now it all makes sense.

She regretted taking me every second of her life.

Maybe a decade ago, I would've been devastated, but now I'm relieved I'm not hers. Even after she put me in the hospital, it would've been a bit harder to drag her to trial and all that if she were my mother. Now, she doesn't have any hold on me.

She took everything from me—my childhood, my dad, my naivety, my innocence—and now, she got her dirty hands on the last thing I was so grateful to have. She stole the only thought that was keeping me going in the morning, no matter how annoying it was to put on those hearing aids or not to be able to have a conversation in public. When I was in bed, I appreciated even the questions I got every day about my hearing devices because it meant I was still hearing.

It was enough I was scared to wake up one day and have no hearing since that was always an option the doctors warned me about, and to lose it because of her... It wasn't part of my life's course, and that's what angers me the most.

She took it away from me. She had no right.

I look down at Blaise's body on mine and I don't know what to do. I can't even talk to her about it so I can get out of my head for a bit. Everything is so fucking quiet that it's deafening.

And I can't help but feel lonely, thinking this is how it's going to be for the rest of my life.

CHAPTER FORTY

BLAISE

I wake up with tears dried on my cheeks, safely tucked between his arms as my head rests on his chest. The events of the past twenty-four hours swim roughly through my mind, along with the guilt tugging at my heart.

It was my fault. I should've never let him leave on his own. If I had been there with him, he'd still have his hearing.

My chest constricts, and because I sense tears coming, I look up at him to make sure he's still sleeping before sneaking out of his hospital room to the bathroom.

A fight shaped into a traumatic moment shook me to my core. He was never in danger of dying, but I felt like his life was slowly slipping right next to me, and I couldn't do anything to help him. I was seven again, waiting for the same news I got about my parents to be delivered again.

Some would call me dramatic. Still, when you see your loved one in that state, you can't stop your mind from creating scenarios.

And I fight between my guilt and my hate for Tamara. I don't know which one is stronger because she did this, but I let it go. I wasn't there to prevent this from happening.

My phone buzzes in my pants, demanding my eyes to do something else except cry and focus on the message I got. It's an email from the publishing house, and I don't think twice before opening it, needing to hear just a positive thing today so I can be there for Ares the way he deserves.

There's nothing positive in this email—it's a paragraph written to let me know they can't collaborate with me anymore since I was on TV in a bad position. They are sending me their blessings and a lot of apologies, and I don't even know if I should be shocked or not.

I guess I never entirely realized I'm finally publishing a book because it doesn't hurt at all. I don't even care.

What I care about is Ares's health and getting through this.

After I splash my face with cold water, I get out of the bathroom. Caroline is waiting for me outside, a sad smile on her lips.

"You okay?" she asks.

"I'm more worried about him than I am about me."

She nods her head. "I won't make this suggestion to him because I don't want to overstep, but I'll make it to you. I told you about my life back in Texas, right?" I agree with a bob of my head, and she continues. "I'd love to help him with sign language when he's ready."

I give her a soft smile, touched by her kindness and also the way she respects everyone's boundaries. She's so damn nice.

Because I can't help it, I drag her in a hug, careful not to destroy the little one in her bump. Caroline sighs in my arms, patting me on the back.

"Thank you," I whisper, feeling like she's given me the greatest help when she just offered her help. Yet that's more than enough.

"I'm gonna take a shower," Ares says a bit too loudly the moment we get home, pointing his hand at the stairs.

I nod and want to tell him that I'll follow him soon enough, but I stop myself from doing it. He walks the stairs, and after the door of his room closes, I burst into tears once again, seeing August through them coming to hug me.

He keeps me in his arms while I cry for Ares, the boy who stole my first kiss and the man who stole my heart.

"He's strong enough to handle this," August says, stroking my hair in slow moves.

I agree with him with a bob of my head, knowing that's true.

It's beyond me how two people can be this connected. His pain strikes through me as if it were my own, blinding me to the point where I realize there's nothing in this world that could break us apart. Nothing. He'll be forever mine, and I hope I'll be forever his because, in this moment, I know he was never a childhood fluke. I love this man. I've loved him since I was fifteen and I'll love him for the rest of my life.

That thought makes me even more desperate to do the right thing for him, but I don't know what that is.

"I want to make it better for him," I cry, hating how helpless I feel.

"Shh." He shushes me and takes me by my shoulders, forcing me to look at him. "He's not alone. We'll figure out a way, okay? Together." He gets a nod for me without even trying. "Now go and just be there for him. I'll let Dad and Caroline know we made it safely back home."

"Tell them to give him a few days." I sniffle and wipe my cheeks once again.

"Will do."

I reluctantly walk the stairs, trying to come up with a way to make him feel better. To help him get through this.

"Just be there for him. It will be enough," August calls after me from downstairs, and I look down at him as he shifts his weight from one leg to the other, hands in his jeans pockets.

I nod. "Can you go check up on Nanna for me?"

"Sure," he says, giving me a weak smile.

I wipe my sweaty hands on my jeans before entering Ares's room.

When I walk into his room, he's sitting at his desk with round glasses on his nose. I want to argue with him about getting back to work this soon, but I don't know how to do it without hurting his feelings about the way our conversations are going to go from now on. Plus, on our way home, he made it very clear he's taking tomorrow's shift at Westnook. I was ready to have an argument and convince him that he doesn't have to before he closed his eyes, snatching the chance from me.

After all, work might be what he needs, and I'm not going to stand in his way if that's what he wants. Still, the second I feel him slipping away, I'm forcing him to take a break.

He gives me a tight smile, and I return it, taking a seat on his bed and fishing my phone out. I decide to work on my novel, even though it won't get released with a publisher anymore—something Ares doesn't know yet, and he won't find out soon, either. He'd only feel guilty for something he had no control over.

It's hard as hell to concentrate. My mind hates that I

have to lie all over again—it's not lying, it's hiding—and instead of writing, I research how to support someone who's gone deaf. A product pops up, and I don't even give it a second thought before ordering it. It might not make things better, but it will definitely make things easier.

I click on the next website. A new window pops open on my screen, and I scroll through comforting hobbies for people hard of hearing or for those who can't hear at all. Most of them are sports, but when I see writing in capital letters, I know this would be good for him.

Once I lock my phone, I sit up and place a hand on his shoulder as gently as I can. He stops typing and slowly turns to look at me.

"I have an idea," I say, mouthing it slowly enough for him to catch it.

He lifts a brow, and I sit on his legs, circling his neck with one of my hands, breathing him in. "Have you ever thought about writing before?" I ask when I'm sure his eyes are on my lips.

Ares frowns, and I repeat, this time slower. He squints his eyes and shakes his head, unsure. I stand up, take his hand in mine, grab his laptop, and drag him to the bed. He awkwardly sits on the bed while I climb in. Once I'm settled against the pillows, I open my notes on my phone and motion for him to do the same. He eyes me skeptically but does as I say.

After he's done, he lifts his eyebrows, waiting for my guidance.

"Write," I mouth, and I don't give him a chance to argue. I just start typing on my phone.

For a few minutes, I can feel him staring at me, watching every touch of my fingers on the keyboard. Soon after, he follows. From time to time, I glance his way, and I can see his speed increasing. I focus on my new story that I know nothing about, except it started with a bloody incident. No dead people, though. Ares'd laugh his ass off.

Time passes, and quickly enough, the room darkens in the night. I don't get up to turn on the lights. The laptop is bright enough for now.

When my inspiration comes to an end, I put my phone aside and watch him. He would be such a great writer. I just know it. He's helped me with a lot of ideas, he worked on phrases that needed touch-ups, he turned my book into something I'm proud of, and I don't see why he wouldn't do the same with his work. After all, everything he does in his free time is related to books.

A little frown grazes over his forehead as he writes, and the moment couldn't be described even if I knew all the words in the world. He's so in his... element. This is so *him*.

"What?" he asks, a tiny smile tugging at his lips. He doesn't move his eyes from the screen.

I shrug, and his smile grows after he taps that last

key. He closes the docs bar, then looks at me. "Thank you."

My heart squeezes. I brush him off with a *pfft*, like it's not a big deal. And it's not. But him thanking me means I helped.,

"Come here." He lowers his voice.

He doesn't have to ask me twice.

I switch the lights on so he can see my lips and get closer to him, resting my head on his chest. His fingers dig into my hair, slowly stroking it. I sigh, relaxing in his arms. But it's not enough. I flip on my stomach and place my head on his, getting a better view of him. His hand finds my hair once again as I run my fingers all over his chest, lips, nose, and hair, taking in every detail of him.

The words are right on my tongue, but I stop myself. I don't want him to think it's out of pity. Because it's not. I love him. I love the way he touches me, the possessive way he looks at me, the way he takes care of me, how he smiles in my presence, when we read together, and when we simply exist around each other.

"Good night?" I ask mostly as a joke.

He smiles, peering at my lips. "Better."

Meaning not a good night, but I'll take "better" for now. As long as each day I get a "better" from him, it means we're adapting. Someday, he'll say "a good day," and that's when I'll know we got through this.

I nod, glancing up at him. His curly hair falls on his

forehead, meeting the spot between his fluffy eyebrows. Dark eyes stare back at me as I take in his full lips.

"Am I ever going to deserve you?" he whispers so low, I almost miss it.

My eyes close with an inhale. When I open them again, I have to stop myself from kissing him. Everything he says, everything he does just adds more to my love for him.

"You do." I match his tone, carefully rounding each word. "You always did," I admit, knowing no one could be as worthy of love as Ares is.

He sadly shakes his head. "I'm going to hold you back," he says, brushing my cheek. Instantly, I disagree. "I'll be a burden for you."

I stop him with a hand over his mouth, shaking my head uncontrollably. "No."

He nods his head under my grip, and I place another hand over his head, making sure he can't move anymore. He can't disagree with me on this. Not when it's about me. I decide if he's a burden or not. And he'll never be. No matter if he has one leg, no matter if he can't see, eat. I'll always be there to carry him, guide him, and feed him.

"Let me be the one to decide that." I say each word calmly, staring into his eyes as I do. "You'll never be a burden." When he frowns, I repeat, setting him free but placing my palms on each side of his face. "You will *never* be a burden."

"Maybe not now." He fakes a smile.

"Never," I counter, and he doesn't argue back.

Ares thinks for a little, all the time touching different places on my body. My cheek, my nose, my neck, my arm.

"It's too quiet," he says, and that sends daggers to my soul. I try to hold my reaction in, to not think about what it must feel like to be in his position.

I don't know how to reply to that. I don't know how to give him a different perspective on this. There's no way to describe losing your hearing.

"You know the worst thing about this?" he calmly asks. My attention on him is enough to make him continue. "It's not about the music or the conversations around me. It's about you. I'll never hear your voice again. I'll live my entire life with a memory of it, a sound made up in my head. I'm going to forget your beautiful laugh." He wipes my tears with his thumb. "And that's a fucking curse."

My heart shatters in a million pieces right there on his chest.

CHAPTER FORTY-ONE

ARES

A tap on my shoulder whips me out of the novel I'm working on—all I've been doing in the past week, thanks to Blaise.

I turn around and find her behind me, with a tiny box between her fingers. It's covered in a bright red bow —classic Blaise.

She nudges it toward me, and I lift a brow, making her roll her eyes. She grabs ahold of my hand, twisting it upward and placing the square on top. She sits down on my bed, her braids bouncing in the process.

I eye her for a while before deciding to finally untie the knot. As soon as the spiral falls on the floor, the box of a smartwatch comes into view.

"Blaise," I say.

She got me a fucking watch. She shouldn't spend my money on me. *For me.*

With slow movements, I roll the box between my fingers. I stare at the floor, not really knowing what to say. Out of all the words in the world, there's nothing I can use.

Blaise takes the watch and puts it on my desk, then sits on my lap, circling her arm around my neck. Her tiny hand scoops my chin up and forces me to meet her gaze. A beautiful smile plays on her lips, warm eyes caressing my face.

"It's just a gift." I watch her mouth move. "It'll make your life easier."

"It's expensive," I counter and try to look away, but she keeps me still.

"You would've done the same thing in my position," she whispers, brushing my hair with her fingers.

My jaw clenches.

Of course, I'd fucking do the same. She's worth every penny, every second, every breath. No gift in the world would meet her real value. No matter how expensive, no matter how luxurious. Blaise is priceless.

"Yes. I would've."

She leans down and presses her lips on my cheek. "Now open it," she mouths, the biggest smile on Earth spreading across her face.

I've been mulling over this decision since a few days back when Blaise told me Caroline offered to help. And I finally decided to give her a chance, which brings me here, knocking on her door even though everything I want is to head back home. But the door opens before I have time to, and Caroline's shy smile invites me in.

"Thank you," I say, then take my coat and put it on the hanger.

She's nervous. I don't like it. She wipes her palms on her pants all the way to the living room, turning from time to time to give me a tug of her lips.

I clear my throat. "Is Dad here?"

Caroline shakes her head and sits in a chair that's placed in front of a tiny couch, her back to a fireplace. I choose the sofa, knowing this way I can easily see her face in case she decides to talk and I have to read her mouth. But I have a feeling she won't.

"So?" I look around. "How are we going to do this?"

The question somehow brings her some confidence because she straightens her back and motions her hand in a salute. I lift a brow.

"Does that mean 'yes, sir'?" I ask jokingly, relaxing in my seat.

Caroline laughs.

I know the salute is usually performed to show respect in the military, but I also know it means "hello" in sign language—I googled it before coming here.

"How do you sign…" I think about the word I use

the most, but it doesn't seem that fitting right now, so I ask about my second most used word. "Shit?"

With a smile on her face, she shows me, the corner of her lips only rising with each attempt of mine to mirror her movements. My left hand is clenched into a fist, and my thumb practically penetrates the hole. It's safe to say that I'm *really* mimicking shit. Or, more accurately, the process.

We both burst out laughing when I sign "hi shit," the first two words I learned in sign language.

CHAPTER FORTY-TWO

ARES

Blaise puts the movie we were watching on pause, lifts her head from my lap, and snatches the phone from my brother's hands. He hasn't even spared a glance at the TV, but who am I to tell him to stop using it.

She gapes at the screen, then back at my brother as a smile grows on her lips. Her hand stretches in front of my face, and August tries to fight her, but I take it, reading the last message he sent to a girl named Francesca.

I want to see you tonight.

"Did she leave you on read?" I ask after swiping to see the time he sent the message.

He sits up and takes it back.

"But I want to see what she says," I joke, smacking him on the head when he sits back next to me.

August raises his middle finger and types something, not looking at me.

Blaise jumps on my lap, and we both watch him as he has a conversation we're so curious about. I look at her and brush a finger over the soft skin of her neck. She shivers, then leans down and takes his phone again.

She turns it to me, and three bubbles appear on the screen. She wiggles happily in my arms, waiting for Francesca's reply. *I'd like that*, she says, and the next second, Blaise is on her feet, grinning like a child.

At this point, August doesn't even bother to get his phone back. He just relaxes on the couch, hugging his chest. I bump his shoulder, smiling.

"Do you need my books now?" I cock a brow. "For research purposes?"

He rolls his eyes, but a smile stretches on his face. I grab his shoulder and ruffle his hair, messing it up before he breaks free and flips me off.

I open my mouth to give him more shit about it, but my watch vibrates on my wrist. My eyes zero in on it, not recognizing the number. There might be a chance this is a call from the police station, so I sit up, walk to the kitchen, and pick it up, grateful for the captions option on my watch.

"Hello, is this Ares Hart?" The words appear on my screen.

"Yes. Who's calling?" I ask, leaning on the kitchen counter.

"I'm Officer Smith." My back straightens at the information, and I suck in a breath before reading what he has to say next. "We're calling to let you know that we've located and arrested your mother, Tamara Marie Johnson, in connection with the incident involving you. She's currently in custody."

For the first time in weeks, I breathe in relief. Her arrest means my brother and Blaise are fully safe from everything she might think about doing to get her revenge, and that takes a shit ton of weight off my chest.

"We understand this might be a difficult situation for you—" I look up from my watch, sensing Blaise approaching.

She gets closer to me and places a comforting hand on my shoulder, stroking it gently before giving me a curious glance. "Is it really done?" she mouths, and I immediately nod, taking her waist in my arm.

I look back at my watch, reading all the information Officer Smith provided me with. He's letting me know Tamara is about to face around five years of prison, though it could be significantly more after the trial.

After a few minutes that the officer uses to explain the process to me, we eventually end the phone call.

Blaise circles her arms around me, tightening her hold with each passing second. I inhale her scent and squeeze her into a hug.

She's the reason everything I've been through for the past month has been easier to get through. She helped me see from another perspective, be grateful for what I have, and there's no way I could ever give her back what she gave to me. But even if it means I have to offer her the world to repay her unconditional support, I'd give her the universe.

August appears from around the corner, his eyebrows rising in question.

"It's over," I tell him and notice the drop in his shoulders.

He's been doing great lately—exactly why I didn't say anything about me being adopted, and I never will. My love for both of them will never change, no matter the circumstances. The last thing we need is to have another reason to be stressed after we finally got our closure. Plus, telling them or searching for my parents would be a waste of time, and it would make no difference anyway.

I have my family right here.

"Good day?"

I flip onto my side, facing her profile. She's beautiful as always. Sad, but still beautiful. Her long lashes fall against her red cheeks every time she blinks as her lips keep twitching in thought. She moves to her side as well, staring into my eyes. Into my soul.

The constant annoying buzz is still in my ears,

The constant annoying buzz is still in my ears, taking away one of the best things life can give. Nothing will be the same without the low murmurs in the library, the sound of the waves crashing into the coast, and laughter. Especially *her*s.

If I knew this was going to happen... If I knew I was going to lose my hearing, I would've never stopped making her laugh. I would have spent day and night telling her jokes like a damn comedian.

Slowly, I give her a smile. "Better."

Blaise nods, swallowing hard as her gaze moves to my lips. "Do you want to read?" she asks.

She's become an expert in moving her lips as slowly as possible, making sure I understand everything she says.

"Sure."

We sit up, resting our backs on the headboard as she scoops up a book. It's the second book in the duet I told her to read a while ago.

She puts her head on my chest and places the book on my stomach. I keep one corner, and she keeps the other.

Before starting, she looks at me and smiles like she just remembered something. "Let's switch places," she suggests, already climbing off me.

I don't argue. I do as she says, no questions asked. We sit in the same position but switch places.

Blaise lifts my right hand. I look up at her, not

knowing what to expect. I watch her putting it on her neck and forcing me to lower my head in the middle of her chest.

My eyes are pinned on the first page of the book, and tears sting in them as soon as she starts talking. I can feel the vibration of every word escaping her mouth. It shudders all over my body.

I fucking hate how weak I am lately. But I remember it's only in her presence.

This moment means more to me than anything she could possibly give me. It gives me life. Hope. Purpose. It's almost as if I can hear her talking, and this is the closest I've ever felt to normalcy lately. No signing session with Caroline makes me feel this way.

Right now, Blaise takes the pieces of my shattered heart in her palms, and when they open, she gives it back in perfect condition.

I let go of my corner of the book, letting it fall on her stomach. I gaze up at her, not caring if every wall of mine is crashing under her eyes.

My hand cups her cheek. Her eyes widen, and her mouth parts.

"I love you," I say.

And I don't know how it sounds, if my voice is raspy or if it's cracking. I don't even care. What I know is that I love her.

I love Blaise North.

She's the one who, for the past weeks, took care of

me without making me feel disabled. She's the one who made me feel at home. Only her. She washed me, my tears too, made sure I ate, and made sure I knew I had someone next to me every time I needed a shoulder to lean on.

"W-what?"

I can see the hesitation in the way her lips part, and I lean close, brushing my nose to hers.

I take her hand and put it over my heart. "I love you, Blaise North. I love how clumsy you are, I love how fast you talk when you're excited, and I love how good you are. I also love how you fight for your dreams and the ones you love. I love everything about you and I can't handle another minute without knowing you're mine." She opens her mouth to talk, but I continue, not ready to know she may not love me yet. "You asked me to kiss you only when I have feelings. Blaise, they were there the whole time. I didn't want to give you the future my parents had; I wanted to make sure you get what you deserve."

She swallows, and my heart skips a beat as I try to focus on what I'm going to say.

"I told myself that I wouldn't enter a relationship until I know the person I want to spend the rest of my life with." I stop only to wipe a tear from under her eye. "And *you* are that person for me."

Blaise stays silent, and I involuntarily release a shaky breath. Fuck that, I've never been this nervous before. I knew I wanted to say this to her, but I wasn't sure when.

My fingers brush over her skin as I pray to get a reply from her. If she doesn't love me, it's okay. Some people fall faster, and some slower. It doesn't matter. If she has the tiniest feelings for me, those can develop.

Blaise's hand lifts and finds my messy hair. She strokes it and smiles, another tear escaping.

"I love you," she says so simply, it makes my heart pound ten times faster, so much that I can feel it in my ears. "I've been trying to figure out a way to tell you." She laughs, and I laugh, lowering my head to her chest, relief washing over me.

"Fuck," I whisper. "What I would give to hear you saying that." I shake my head and clench my jaw, hating that I'm missing the most monumental moment of my life.

I fucking love this girl, and she loves me too.

But I won't ever be able to hear her say the words.

Never.

And that cuts right through me.

A gentle grip tightens in my hair, and my head cooperates, rising enough to see her. Her features have softened, and so does my heart. Blaise takes my hand again, puts it on her neck, and then sits up enough to reach to my ear.

She says the words again slowly, taking her time. Her

breath falls over my ear, and her lips move across it, her throat vibrating under my touch.

Blaise retakes her place and brings me closer with her fingers on my chin. She whispers something against my lips, and it doesn't take me long to figure out what she said.

I can't resist the urge to pull her close. I hold her face in my hands and kiss her, starting soft but quickly deepening the kiss. She responds eagerly, wrapping her arms around my neck.

And it feels like it's not enough. It feels like all the time we didn't kiss was wasted, and I try, I try, I *try* to get back all the moments lost. I kiss her like we have to recover every kiss missed. I kiss her hungrily, not caring about holding it in anymore.

She's mine.

Electricity shoots through me as I feel her body against mine. Our mouths explore each other, and the taste of her is intoxicating. Time seems to stand still as we get lost in the kiss, our bodies fitting together perfectly.

We finally pull away, both of us left breathless. I look into her eyes and can tell she feels it, too. We share a smile, unable to put into words what just happened. All I know is that I never want to let go of this feeling, of her.

We both sink into the bed, relief taking over us. In one quick moment, our clothes are on the floor, and I'm buried deep inside her. Inside her heart. Inside her mind. Exactly how she's in mine.

She feels so good. She feels like the girl I want to marry, the wife I want to have my kids with, and the woman I want to grow old next to.

She feels like coming home.

CHAPTER FORTY-THREE

BLAISE

Life got a bit easier after we confessed how we felt about each other. It's like every heavy breath turns into a lighter exhale than before, and every step forward seems closer to success than the awful end we thought was coming.

Ares is good. I'd like to say he's doing amazing, but he's not. While he's a lot better, I can tell he's hurting. Whenever he laughs, he does it silently, and when I do, he looks away like he can't stand seeing me laugh and not hearing it.

It's killing me that I can't do anything to help him. I'd give my life if it meant taking the pain away from him. Then I remember I should be grateful that Caroline exists. She's been so supportive, and unlike me, she knows what to do for Ares.

Ares clears his throat, interrupting my thoughts. I

look up at him, catching sight of the curly hair lying on his forehead as his face mirrors the busy day we just had at work.

"What do you want to eat? I'll order us some take-out," he asks, speaking loudly.

I give him a soft smile and try to think about something I could mouth so he'd pick up easily. It doesn't take me long to find the right thing.

"Pasta," I mouth, and he nods, scooping up his phone from his jeans.

He taps a few times on his screen and locks it before sitting down next to me. "Should be here in thirty minutes."

I take his hand in mine, caressing it with my finger. Because I can't help it, I kiss his lips. Not being able to do this for so long has turned me into a desperate woman who'd never refuse a kiss. Not even when I'm a bath of sweat after my run, because I'm never keeping myself away from his kisses again—they are just that good.

Ares murmurs something and buries his fingers in my hair, making my toes curl up under my socks. He catches my lip between his teeth, and I squirm in my seat, ready to take the tempting place on his lap.

But he breaks away. "Unless you want August to find you naked on my couch when he comes home, we should go upstairs."

Smiling at the sound of his voice, I place my forehead on his as I nod. Truth be told, I completely forgot he even has a brother. I'm not sure if I should be ashamed, but when we're together, I don't really think. I just... act.

"*After* he gets home." He catches my chin between his fingers at the sight of lust in my eyes.

It's hard to let go of my horny ass side when he's a walking hotness. Or when he dips a finger between my breasts. Or when he brushes his lips over mine. He should know by now that I have little to no control when it comes to him.

"Have you heard from Coral's Publishing House lately?"

That is definitely a turn-off.

I drop back in my seat, and I think I don't do it in a very subtle way because his brows immediately furrow. A part of me hoped he'd forget about it, and mostly because if I told him the truth, he'd hate himself for it.

My mouth opens when I realize it's been a few moments since I became frozen, and he's getting more confused with each second passing.

"Tell me." I don't know what about the way he says it is so arousing to me, but my insides quiver at the sound of his voice.

His dark eyes wash over me in the softest way, almost as if he knows what I'm about to say. And maybe that's why I don't say it.

"No." I shake my head.

He squints at me. "Why?"

I raise my shoulders in a shrug, and it doesn't take me long to realize how badly I'm lying. Well, I knew all along, but I thought I'd gotten better at it.

"Why?" Ares asks again, this time with a graver tone.

A smile forces its way to my mouth. "No reason."

By the look on his face, what I want to be a smile looks far away from it. Ares's eyes zero in on me, searching through me for the truth I don't want to give him but that I know he'll eventually get because I'm so bad at lying. That or he'll figure it out himself.

He's silent for too long, only watching me as he keeps twitching his eyes constantly, and I want him as far away as possible from whatever he's thinking.

"They didn't want to work with me anymore," I tell him, and his brows furrow in confusion. I repeat it for him slowly. "They didn't want to work with me anymore."

"Why?" he demands, fully focused on my lips in the wait for my reply.

"No reason."

"You said that already. Try again."

I don't need to look at his face to know he has an idea about why they don't want to work with me anymore or that he won't back down until I tell him. I know it's not fair to keep this away from him, but I also don't want to ruin the great progress he's made. The progress *we* have made.

Our relationship is in a really good place apart from the struggles he's facing every day and even so, we know how to get past them. When the worst nights hit, we still find peace now that Tamara is locked up. It's the relief that keeps him going so strongly, and it's making me so proud.

That's why telling him about the publishing house is so scary to me. For the past week, we've been in our bubble—with ups and downs, sure—and it's as safe as it could be.

"They saw us on the news," I say slowly, wanting him to understand the first time I say it because I don't want to repeat it.

Ares blinks twice, not a muscle twitching on his face. I'm surprised not to see him furious. Not at me, of course. He'd never be mad at me for something like this. But at himself. At the publishing house.

"And how do you feel about it?" His voice comes out soft, and quiet, and it catches me off guard that this is the first thing he has to say.

I smile, picking one of his curls from his forehead. "I don't care."

He shakes his head at me. "You don't have to lie to me, Moon. I know how badly you wanted to publish this book." He caresses my cheek in a slow move, and I want to sink into his touch, to forget about this trivial thing.

"I still do," I admit, and his eyes close as if I just hit him.

Ares curses under his breath, and I cup his face, forcing him to look at me. He does, sadness waving through the black of his eyes.

"I will."

He squints at me but stays quiet.

"And I know that now isn't the right time." Even with me saying it slowly, he can't understand what I'm saying.

I take my phone out and text him instead.

ME

> Now is not the time and I'm glad they closed the contract. I want to write more books before publishing and I also realized I don't need a publishing house to follow my dreams.

"What do you mean?" he asks, watching me closely.

ME

> I mean I'd like to open a self-publishing company one day. Preferably with you.

Ares is silent for a few moments, and now that I've said this to him, I know it's something I'd love more than anything to do. With him by my side, everything is possible.

Not being able to restrain myself, I drag him into a kiss. He meets my tongue halfway, swiping his along mine before sucking it into his mouth like a hungry animal. His palm sneaks its way to my neck, tightening lightly to get me closer to him, and it still feels like miles away.

I have no doubt we're seconds away from ripping our clothes off when the door squeaks open.

We break apart, and his dangerous eyes gleam at me. I smile at him.

"You and me, okay?" I ask.

He nods. "I love you, Moon." That's the only thing he can say before his brother storms into the living room, screaming at the top of his lungs.

"I got in!" He delivers the news about college in uncontrollable excitement.

CHAPTER FORTY-FOUR

ARES

Two months later

Time around Blaise flies by as swiftly as a shooting star across the night sky. Every moment with her feels fleeting, passing in the blink of an eye. Around her, a lifetime is nothing more than a second. It's like yesterday we were just kids playing in the mud, and now... she's finally mine.

She makes me treasure each second like it's the last, and it's hard not to realize how much time I've lost. That thought makes me spend the nights watching her instead of sleeping, and I can't stop. I always tell myself I'll stay two more minutes, but I end up wide awake with the sun streaking through the curtains.

Losing my hearing made me realize nothing is forever. I'll do whatever I can to make her happier because if she has a constant smile on her face when she's around me, I don't need anything else.

A warm hand brings me back to reality in Blaise's room. I look up at her. She steps in between my knees, her eyes capturing mine. My hands graze her waist covered in a tight, sinful red dress, making their way to her ass. I squeeze it firmly, and there's a depth in her smile that has been missing for too long.

We've finally pushed through everything.

"How do I look?" she mouths as her high blonde ponytail falls on her shoulder.

I gently drag her on my legs, then sneak a hand under her ear. I lean down and kiss her freshly lined lips.

Fuck. She looks so good in red.

She parts her mouth open and lets me in. I take her tongue in my mouth and suck it, greedy for her. I feel the vibration as Blaise lets out a slow moan, bringing my dick to life in my pants, and I can't help but tug her ponytail a little, only to feel her smile stretching on my lips.

With regrets, I lean back, knowing she needs to hear what she looks like to me.

"Like everything I've ever dreamed of," I murmur, placing a kiss on top of her left breast. "Like the moon in a dark sky." She arches her back under my touch, then buries her hand in my hair. "Like the love of my life."

Her chest vibrates, and I look up at her to meet her love-drunk eyes.

"I love you," she tells me, her gaze turning watery.

"I love you, Moon." I kiss her forehead and feel her sigh in relief under it.

I scoop her up, and she can't hold her giggle as I take her downstairs.

She pats me on the chest when we get to the end of the stairs. "My purse," she mouths.

"You don't need it." I don't wait for her reply. I continue walking and stop in front of the living room, where Catherine is watching a show.

She eventually figured it out and told us to stop sneaking from one house to another and made a joke about how she doesn't want me to risk falling on the roof. We wanted to tell her anyway, but we were waiting for the right time to come.

Blaise tells her something, and she looks at us, then sits up, an enormous smile taking over her features. She grabs my cheeks and kisses each of them, then does the same to Blaise. I raise my lips into a smile and lean down to kiss her forehead before we walk out in the hallway.

We get out with her still in my arms.

"Take the key from my front pocket," I tell her.

She stuffs her hand in my pocket and pinches the tip of my cock as a joke. I bite back a groan as she tries to hide her grin behind her shoulder, finally taking out what I asked for. She unlocks the car and flashes me an innocent smile.

Thank God she's not as innocent as she makes it seem.

I shake my head and lower the two of us so I can open the door. I place her on the seat, put her seatbelt on, and before turning on my feet, I pinch her peeking-through nipple. When she opens her mouth to say something, I shut the door in her face, letting out a chuckle.

And it feels good to laugh. The winter wind blows gentler around me, the sun strikes harder, and... I just realized I'm turning into a sentimental prick.

As soon as I get in the driver's side, Blaise tries to attack my nipple, but I stop her in time, holding her wrist hostage. She fake pouts, brows snapping together as her eyes peer out from under them. I lean over and kiss those pouty lips. It's my way of saying we're even and that for now, if she doesn't want us to go back upstairs, we should stop pinching each other.

We leave, and the whole drive to the restaurant, I keep my hand on the skin under her dress. I don't move it because fuck, if I do that, I'll undress her in the parking lot. While that might be tempting as hell, this is the first time I've been out of the house besides West-nook since I lost my hearing.

It's not because I care about what others think. I'd wipe my ass with their opinions if anything. From their end, it might look like we're completely normal. They wouldn't guess I'm reading her lips. Or that I've learned not to talk as loud as I did at first. But what I know is that this is how we're going to be.

And I guess that's fine.

We park in front of the restaurant, and I get out first to open the door for her. She analyzes my black outfit with lustful eyes before finally stepping out of the vehicle. Blaise has told me a thousand times that she adores how I look in this shirt, and it would be a lie to say that's not the reason I put it on in the first place.

She puts a hand on my chest, then lifts on her tiptoes to give me a kiss. When she wants to break it, I put my palm on her neck and request one more. She drops back on her feet as her face splits into a smile.

"You look handsome." Her head tilts to the side.

I want to tell her I'm nothing compared to her, but when Blaise analyzes me with that gaze of adoration, I keep my mouth shut and savor this moment as if it's the last.

That's how life's been for me lately—living every second like the next doesn't exist.

My fingers gently graze her cheek, and in that touch, I convey everything my heart wants to say. No words could capture the depth of what I feel right now, but my eyes tell her the story as her reflection gleams in them.

The only thing I feel is *her*.

With our hands tangled, we enter the restaurant, and the hostess guides us to our booth. Private, small, cozy. Exactly what I wanted. We thank her when she brings us the menus, and then Blaise puts it over her nose. I can see her eyes smiling from here.

"What?" I put mine down, smiling.

She shrugs, and I give her a look. And because that's how easily Blaise gives in, she puts it on the table, then grabs my palms into hers.

"Tell me your favorite word." Her excitement is so fucking adorable that I don't question the reason, I just tell her.

"Moon."

A blush takes over her cheeks as she takes her hands back and places them on her lap. She sighs, the corners of her mouth still lifted as high as possible. Once she evens her breathing, she raises her hands and does something I don't see coming.

Blaise signs the word "moon," and I don't recognize it the first time. It might be because I certainly didn't expect her to use sign language.

Caroline and I have gotten closer over the last few months, and apparently, she's also helped Blaise learn how to sign.

It's strange how fast my heart starts beating, fighting to get closer to her and the sounds of her own heartbeats. My hand grabs her neck, stroking her hair, and I put my forehead on hers, breathing her in. Blaise moves her palm into my hair, playing with it.

God, this woman.

I want to do something. Say something. But it's just... too much.

Blaise hooks her finger under my chin and lifts it, forcing my eyes to meet hers. She gives me a weak smile, her features softening.

"Good night?" she signs, and for the first time in months, I feel like I can give her more than "better."

My lips break into a low smile as I trace the outline of her lips with the tip of my finger, then sign, "Best."

We end up ordering only something to drink, then hurrying in the back of my car like two horny teenagers.

I close the door after me and thank God I have the darkest shade of black on my windows because I'm so desperate for her in this moment. It's a lie—I'm desperate for her every moment of the day, and I'd have her whenever she'd let me.

Blaise drops on her back, arching it as she strips down from her dress. She signs, "Stop looking at me like that and fuck me."

I didn't even realize I was eye-fucking her, and maybe it's because I got so used to doing it all the time that now it seems normal to do it, no matter where we are.

"Did Caroline teach you how to sign that?" I raise a brow, smirking from ear to ear as I imagine how that would go.

She blushes, hiding her chin in the crook of her

neck, a shy smile stretching on her lips. "No, I searched it on Google."

I laugh and lean down to kiss her forehead before unbuckling my belt. "Remind me to thank the founders later."

The drive back home was supposed to help me calm down a little, but it only increased my need for her, knowing she was still wet under her panties.

Every dark thought of mine—almost—dies when we see everyone in Catherine's kitchen. A cake is on the table, and I look at Blaise, who's next to me. I raise my brows in question, and she shrugs, acting like she has no idea, which I know is a lie.

I know Caroline and Blaise are behind this.

When I look back at the table to ask Dad about it, everyone raises their hands and signs, "Happy Birthday" to me, big smiles accompanying the movement.

My chest tightens at the image in front of me. Dad has his arm on Caroline's chair. She's holding Iris, and next to them are August and Catherine. And on the other side are Rhodes and Selah.

Once I swallow the lump in my throat, I shake hands with everyone and thank them for surprising me today. Rhodes slaps me on my shoulder and points his brows towards the bulge in my pants with a laugh, but I ignore him with an innocent chuckle before sitting down.

"How was dinner?" Caroline signs and winks at Blaise, who's blushing next to me.

"It was nice," she signs back with a smile, throwing a shy glance at me.

I nod and put my hand on her knee, squeezing it under the table. She's making it very hard for me to hold back from touching her. She did all this. For me.

My gaze slowly wanders over everyone at the table.

Caroline and Dad are happy. Iris is finally here, and I can see the worry already settling in Court's brain. Something tells me he's going to do great with her, though. When he looks at Caroline, it's different from the way he looked at Tamara.

Catherine feels a lot better. She started cooking again and put some color on her cheeks. Her mouth moves almost perfectly, and her eyes rarely flutter. Looking now at her, I notice something: she's happier than ever.

August met a girl. She's making him work for it, but I've never seen the sparkle in his eyes that he got in the past few weeks. He's spending most of his time out, and it does him good to finally stop burying himself in drawing.

All the phones buzz on the table, and everyone takes them in their hands. I frown, trying to understand what's happening. Blaise must notice my hesitancy because she takes my device from the table and hands it to me as my watch vibrates on my wrist. I unlock it and see a notification in a group chat with all of them, which was most likely created now.

> **BLAISE**
> Are we going to open the gifts
> or not?
>
> **CATHERINE**
> *confetti emoji* *heart emoji* gift
> emoji*

I peek at them at the end of the table and try to hold in a laugh. She has no clue how to use it. It buzzes again on my wrist, and I look down. The messages appear one after the other.

> **CAROLINE**
> Yes, pleaseeeeee
>
> **RHODES**
> if there's any competition, I'm
> definitely winning
>
> **SELAH**
> It's NOT a competition and my gift is
> better
>
> **COURT**
> How about just opening them?

AUGUST

Dad, you missed the whole point of
this group chat

ME

I vote baby Iris

A grin breaks on my face as I wipe the corner of my mouth. Everyone starts laughing, and Blaise takes me by the shoulders. She hugs me and kisses me quickly after she places her lips on my ear, whispering the words that become my favorite in the world. I don't need to hear them because I know the only moment she says something in my ear, it's when she tells me those words.

I love you.

She returns to her seat, and my eyes never leave hers as I grab her hand. I tap three times and when the recognition sparkles in her eyes, I know she understands that it's me saying I love you.

EPILOGUE

BLAISE

3 years later

"Benji," I say in a serious tone after he keeps throwing blocks on the floor. He doesn't look at me as he picks another one up, then launches it as far as he can. "Benji, can you come here?"

He grunts like a little dinosaur—as his father likes to call him—and stomps his foot twice before hugging his chest and bringing his bottom lip forward. Benji walks to me, pouting all the way to the couch.

When he reaches me, I circle an arm around his waist and scoop him up, inhaling the scent I'm obsessed with even when he drives me crazy. Benji giggles when I kiss his neck and tickle his belly, wiggling in my arms like I'm torturing him.

Angry steps hit the ceiling, and Benji gasps, looking

above him with scared eyes. I keep him tighter in my embrace, sheltering his head with my hand as if the house could fall on him.

"Who dares to wake me up from my afternoon nap?" the monster I sent a text to a few moments ago shouts in a deep voice as he walks down the stairs.

Benji lets out a scream and jumps from my lap. He runs on his little legs, hiding under the table.

Ares stops in the living room, sniffing his nose to find the dinosaur by his smell. He gives me a wink as a smirk stretches on his face. "Where's the dinosaur, princess?"

I touch my heart, shaking my head, before signing, "I'll never tell you."

"You will, or else—"

Before his dad has time to say anything else, Benji sits up and crashes into Ares's leg. My husband falls on the floor, pleading for mercy with pained sounds. Our son grins in victory, and when he's not paying attention, Ares grabs him in his arm, squeezing his chest. Ares kisses his cheeks until he can't breathe because of the adorable giggles escaping him.

I join them on the floor, kissing both of my boys. We play a little more, happy to spend every little moment with Benji. He's growing so fast that I sometimes think tomorrow is the day I have to pack his bags and see him leaving for college—a thought I can't bear for now. He's still a little boy, and I'm glad to have a few more years before he'll be too ashamed to let his mom shower him in kisses.

The doorbell rings, and I grab Benji's cheek between my fingers.

"Guess who's here?" I ask, raising my brow at him, knowing August must've dropped Nanna off before going to class.

He sits up on his feet, a smile as big as him stretching on his face. "Nanna!" Benji shouts, then runs to the door.

Ares stands up, offering me his hand. He pulls me up, and I throw my arms over his shoulders, then place my lips onto his. His palms find my waist, pushing me into him as my core clenches with need. He murmurs something, then grabs a handful of my ass.

"I love you," he tells me when we break apart.

"I love you," I mouth, staring at his beautiful dark eyes. "Come on." I drag him by his hand, and he comes willingly.

With Benji demanding so much attention, we barely get time alone anymore, and if we want to leave, we have to do it without him noticing. It's easier if we distract him with Nanna's arrival since he's so obsessed with her that he won't notice our absence.

Once I grab the book I published not too long ago from our library and my bag, we walk out through our back door.

Shortly after Ares told me he loved me, he asked me

to marry him on the rooftop of my Nanna's house, and I think that's the night I ended up pregnant with Benji. We decided to move, and the beach seemed like the best place—still close enough to Nanna but quiet and full of memories.

Our feet get buried in the sand as we walk, and even if it's hard to ignore his curious gaze, I keep quiet until I find the perfect place to stop. Ares lowers on his knees at the same time I do, squinting his eyes my way.

"I love you," I sign to him.

His brows furrow. "You're being weird, Moon... Is this your shitty way to say you want a divorce?" he jokes, pinching my cheek. "Because I'm not letting you. You're mine as long as the Moon rises in the sky every night."

My eyes catch him as I place a palm on his face, caressing his skin with my fingers. I quiver under his hungry stare, but I smile.

This is not the time for beach sex.

Since we're living on the beach and because it's the only place we have some privacy thanks to our little one, beach sex is our go-to. It's more uncomfortable than they let it show in the movies, but it does the job, and at some point, we don't even feel the pain anymore.

We tend to get lost in each other pretty easily.

With my other arm, I hand him the book. Ares takes it, ready to ask me what it is until he sees the first page. He gapes at me, then turns his eyes back at the book, flipping through the pages as he finds the words I high-lighted for him.

"You're going... to... be... a... dad... again?" he asks, tears glistening in his eyes.

"Go on," I sign to him.

He swallows, shock etched on his features, but continues and reaches to the scrapped part of the book where I cut a hole and placed the pregnancy test and the ultrasound in it. My husband's hands shake, and before I know it, he has me at his chest.

Seeing him getting emotional never gets old. It reminds me of the time I told him I was pregnant with Benji. It wasn't nearly a very sweet announcement since I was so scared of the thought of building a family and his reaction too. Despite my overthinking ass, Ares was happier than ever.

"Do you know what it is?" he asks with his chin propped on the top of my head. I shake my head in his arms. "But if you had to guess?"

I remove myself from his embrace, then sign to him, "A girl."

"A girl." Ares smiles. "Our little Luna." The name we picked out before we knew Benji would be a boy. "Are you sure it's not my birthday? Because you just gave me the best present," he tells me, his voice cracking. "I fucking love you, Moon."

Struggling to hold back tears, I sign, "Take a walk with me." And he does. We walk away, and I grab a bottle from my purse, Ares eyeing me curiously the entire time. He has never been with me to the beach for my yearly tradition. That was a moment for me and my parents only, but I want him with me today.

He lets me take the ultrasound from his hands, then watches how I stuff it into the bottle. I grab the cork from my bag, closing it.

Ares doesn't say anything when I grab his hand in mine and walk closer to the water. He stays still as a statue, not knowing how to react.

"I want to tell them too."

He smiles. "And do you want me to do it with you?"

"Yes," I sign.

We hold the bottle together and send it to the sea, and we watch it crash into the calm waves, spending a few minutes in silence to appreciate the beauty of this moment.

Having him by my side is a true blessing, a precious gift I cherish daily. We often take for granted what can be gone in a heartbeat, so I never let a moment pass without treasuring it. He is my constant source of support and strength, and I am grateful for every day I can call him mine. He's—

"If I fuck you right now, do you think we'll have twins?"

Acknowledgments

When I published *Indigo Eyes*, I told myself I was going to publish three books a year. Well, here I am, eleven months later, releasing only one book after my debut novel.

At first, I was devastated at the thought of pushing my release, but thanks to Hailey Dickert, I made the right decision and delayed *Safety Measures* by six months. It's the best decision I could've made, and it's mainly the reason this book got where it is today. Thanks to the extra time, I got the chance to work my ass off until I was proud enough to not change everything over again.

Hope you guys loved it as much as I loved writing it —not editing though, because editing has been a cascade of tears for me—and even if you didn't, it's completely fine. We all have different tastes, and that's what makes us so unique.

My boyfriend – Thank you for supporting me through all of my breakdowns and patting me on my back to sober up or stopping me when I didn't realize I should take a break. You are everything to me, and you've been a light in my life since you stepped into it, along with your mother, who I love unconditionally. I love you, and prepare for me to ignore everything you say when I'm writing.

Gheeti – I'm so grateful to have you in my life, and it's been so amazing to have you with me through the process of writing this book. Our FaceTime chats were a lifesaver. Love you so much, and I'm so excited for *Tainted Ties* to release. So proud of you!

Jaclin – Celebrating over one year of our friendship? Yessiir. Thank you for being always by my side and for sending me ranch—the best American thing ever—and for making me laugh every day.

Hailey – Thank you for your unconditional support and for showing me the right path when I was blindfolded by other factors. I'll always be grateful for you!

Alli – Thank you for being my editor and keeping up with my stubborn ass. You made *Safety Measures* what it is today, and I'm never going to stop saying this. Your patience and observant nature helped make this learning process much easier for both of us. I can't find the right words to thank you properly because you deserve much more than two words, but THANK YOU!

Anca – Like usual, you were one of the first people to read *Safety Measures*. Thank you for always supporting me, my birthday twin. Hopefully, I'll have you by my side as an author one day. I believe in you!

To my booksta/booktok besties – You guys are the reason I'm here today. If it weren't for you, I wouldn't be a full-time author doing exactly what I've dreamed about since I was a baby. Thank you all for always believing in me and supporting me. You are everything to me!

Ankita – Thank you, thank you for always being brutally honest with me. You helped me make this book better, and I can never thank you enough. I LOVE YOU!

Ellen – Thank you for being by my side and for your cute little voice messages. I love you from the bottom of my heart! You know how much you matter to me.

K — thank you for being my editor and helping me polish this book. I couldn't do it without you, and I'm forever grateful. I love you so much!

Salma — thank you for proofreading and making sure I publish the best version of this book. I love you!

Meg Jones — an amazing author who came up with an amazing idea of creating a dicktionary for readers, thank you for letting me include your idea in my book! You are the best and I'm so glad Hailey Dickert told me about you!

About the Author

Maeve Hazel is a nineteen years old author who published her first book at eighteen. Indigo Eyes was a great success and now she's a full-time author, spending most of the time writing or editing at her desk. She lives with her boyfriend and their two cats, Mia & Kit.

Also by Maeve Hazel

Indigo Eyes - A Fake Dating Romance

They say that love is predestined.

It could be true for all I know.

However, there's a tiny difference in how I see it. Love is meant to heal, not to be. Something ethereal is the root of this. You can't touch it, smell it or see it. You can only feel it.

You don't need time to love the right person. Once you see it, your heart simply does it, gradually developing until your brain is able to process the emotion. No matter how hard you love or how slowly you realize it, it's still there.

Could you imagine? We're filled with something that we are completely unaware of.

That's what Elias Madden did to me. He slowly stepped on a tough road toward my soul, buried himself there, and sent signals to my brain which I ignored for a long time.

Read now on Amazon or Barnes & Noble!

If you want to know more about Maeve's next project, follow her on her Instagram (@maevehazelauthor) TikTok (@maevehazelauthor) and Goodreads

Pre-Order Maeve's Next Novel Now!

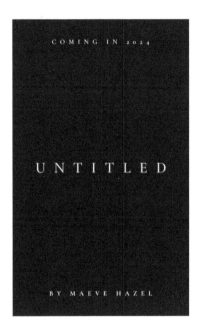

Printed in the USA
CPSIA information can be obtained
at www.ICGtesting.com
LVHW091635021123
762913LV00006B/111